T0196016

A COLD BREW KILLING

The All-Day Breakfast Café Series by Lena Gregory

Scone Cold Killer

Murder Made to Order

A Cold Brew Killing

A COLD BREW KILLING

An All-Day Breakfast Café Mystery

Lena Gregory

LYRICAL UNDERGROUND
Kensington Publishing Corp.
www.kensingtonbooks.com

Lyrical Press books are published by
Kensington Publishing Corp. 119 West 40th Street New York, NY 10018

All Kensington titles, imprints, and distributed lines are available at special quantity discounts for bulk purchases for sales promotion, premiums, fund-raising, and educational or institutional use.

To the extent that the image or images on the cover of this book depict a person or persons, such person or persons are merely models, and are not intended to portray any character or characters featured in the book.

Special book excerpts or customized printings can also be created to fit specific needs. For details, write or phone the office of the Kensington Special Sales Manager:
Kensington Publishing Corp.
119 West 40th Street
New York, NY 10018
Attn. Special Sales Department. Phone: 1-800-221-2647.

Kensington and the K logo Reg. U.S. Pat. & TM Off.
LYRICAL PRESS Reg. U.S. Pat. & TM Off.
Lyrical Press and the L logo are trademarks of Kensington Publishing Corp.

First Electronic Edition: November 2018
eISBN-13: 978-1-5161-0464-2
eISBN-10: 1-5161-0464-1

First Print Edition: November 2018
ISBN-13: 978-1-5161-0467-3
ISBN-10: 1-5161-0467-6

Printed in the United States of America

Logan, your energy and imagination inspire me. I love you with all of my heart!

Chapter 1

"Oh, please, gag me." Savannah Mills slid the tip of one long, lime-green nail beneath the tab of a diet soda can and popped it open. With one eye on the TV, she poured it into a glass over ice. "That man has no more business being mayor than I do."

Gia Morelli finished wiping down the counter from the breakfast rush, tossed the rag into a bin beneath the counter, and turned toward the muted TV. "What did Ron Parker ever do to you, and why do you insist on drinking soda from a can when there's a perfectly good fountain right behind you?"

Savannah kept her gaze on the TV and waved Gia off. "I like it better from the can, more bubbly. And Ron never did anything to me. It's the way he presents himself, all squeaky clean and snooty. In the meantime, that man is as phony as a three-dollar bill."

Earl Dennison, the elderly gentleman who'd been the All-Day Breakfast Café's first customer and still hung around regularly, reached over the counter, grabbed the TV remote, and turned up the volume. Then he sat back down on his usual stool and dug into his massive breakfast. "What makes you say that?"

"Just look at him, that slick grin plastered on his face everywhere he goes." She lifted a brow toward Earl and wagged a finger at the TV. "I don't care what anyone says; no one is that happy all the time."

Though Gia could see Savannah's point—Ron Parker stood behind a podium, his smile so big he had to speak through clenched teeth—she didn't need the two of them arguing over politics. The few customers who still lingered over breakfast or coffee didn't seem to be bothered by the conversation, but still… "Knock it off, you two, or I'll ban all talk of politics in the café until after the election is over."

Earl held up his hands, still clutching his fork. "Hey, not our fault there's nothing else on the TV but election coverage."

"Yeah, well, I don't want anyone getting riled up in here." Gia fiddled with the valve on the new Cold Brew Coffeemaker sitting on the counter behind the register.

"True enough. People do tend to get worked up over politics," Earl agreed.

Gia accidentally nudged the valve handle, just a little, and coffee poured out onto the floor. She flipped it back into place and grabbed a handful of paper towels. "Shoot!"

Earl cleared his throat—to cover his laughter, no doubt. "Granted, I don't know much about making cold coffee, but isn't that thing a little big?"

"Ya think?" Savannah snickered. "How much does it hold, anyway?"

Gia's cheeks heated. She mopped up the spill and tossed the paper towels into the garbage pail, then mumbled, "Fifty gallons."

Earl laughed out loud. "What on earth are you going to do with fifty gallons of cold coffee?"

"Hey, in my defense, I got a good deal on the machine. Besides, Trevor split the cost with me, and every day when it's ready, I'm going to send half down to the ice cream parlor for him." Gia wet a wad of paper towels and bent to clean the stickiness off the floor.

The front door opened.

"Well, I'll be doggoned," Savannah said, amusement clear in her voice. "Speak of the devil."

Gia looked up at the back of Savannah's head. "Who is it? Trevor?"

Savannah shot a grin over her shoulder at Gia. "Nope."

With most of the stickiness cleaned up enough for the moment—she'd give it a good mopping later—Gia stood and stared straight into Ron Parker's trademark smile.

"Good morning, good morning." He approached the counter, his hand held out. "Ron Parker. Nice to meet you."

Gia shook his hand. "Gia Morelli. It's a pleasure to meet you."

The leggy blonde standing next to him, wearing a mini skirt and a halter top, held out a pamphlet, a hundred-watt smile deepening her dimples.

Ron took the pamphlet and handed it to Gia. "I'm just making the rounds, visiting all of the establishments along Main Street, hoping to share my message."

Gia took the proffered pamphlet and glanced at Ron's smiling face on the front cover before dropping it onto the counter. Savannah was right; he'd do better to drop the fake grin. "Thank you. I'll be sure to read through it later."

"Of course." Ron looked around the café. "I have to admit, I expected you'd be busier."

Gia bristled. Business had improved quite a bit in the past few months. Unfortunately, not as much as she'd hoped. "You probably should have come earlier, when the breakfast crowd was still here. You could hang around for a little while if you want, maybe have something to eat and catch the lunch rush. Can I offer you a cold brew coffee?"

His smile diminished, just a little, but Gia still caught the change.

"No, thanks. Can't stand the stuff. I wouldn't mind a black coffee and a blueberry muffin, though. To go." He gestured toward his assistant, and for a minute Gia thought he was going to ask her what she wanted. "Get that for me, will ya, hon?"

Savannah swiveled on the stool, until her back faced Ron, then pursed her lips and stared pointedly at Gia.

Gia had known Savannah long enough to spot an *I told you so* look, even in her peripheral vision. She ignored her and turned to pour his coffee.

By the time she got his order ready and rang it up, Ron had already swept through the room, shaking hands and making promises, and was ready to leave. He held both hands out in front of him, his forefingers and thumbs extended like pistols. "It was a pleasure to meet y'all. I sure hope I can count on your votes."

Thankfully, Savannah waited for him to leave before she started in. "I hate to say I told you so—"

"You don't have to. It was written all over your face," Gia said.

"The way he treats his poor assistant is awful. And what's with that outfit she had on? You'd think she'd dress more professionally if she's going to campaign with him. He'd do better to leave her back at the office. People might take him more seriously."

"Not to disagree," Earl piped in, "but some people just talk that way, especially those used to flipping orders and having them obeyed. He might not have meant any offense. And she sure is a mite easier on the eyes than the candidate."

"Hey…" Savannah pointed her almost dagger-length nail toward him. "You watch it now, buddy. You don't see Mitchell Anderson parading a woman around like some sort of prized trophy, treating her like his servant. Of course, he doesn't have to play games like that. Mitch Anderson is no slouch. If you ask me, he's sort of a hottie. And talk about squeaky clean…"

"I'm not sure he's as clean as everyone says," Earl argued. "There ain't no one don't have a skeleton or two buried somewhere."

"Yeah, well, that may be true, but that woman ain't got nothin' buried." Savannah lifted a brow toward the door, where Ron and his assistant had stopped on the sidewalk to speak to a woman pushing a baby stroller. "Look at that skirt; if it were any shorter, you'd be able to see clear to the top of the Christmas tree."

Earl winked at Savannah, then laughed and shoved a forkful of sausage into his mouth.

Savannah shot him a scowl.

Gia left them to their bickering. She'd just opened the register and started to count out the money from the breakfast crowd when the front door opened. She went to drop the bills back into their slots as she looked up, then kept them in her hand. "Oh, hey, Skyla."

"Hi, Gia, Savannah, Earl. Is Willow around? We're supposed to meet for lunch." Skyla Broussard dropped her big canvas bag onto an empty stool and slid onto the one next to it at the counter.

"Yup, she'll be right in. She just brought the garbage out." Gia squashed down the pang of guilt she felt. She'd pretty much managed to go everywhere in the café, and even out back to leave Harley's dinner, but she still parked out front on the street and had someone else take out the garbage whenever possible. And she still hated looking in the direction of the dumpster, ever since she'd found Bradley's body. "Would you like a cup of coffee while you wait? I have cold brew now."

"Just a regular coffee would be great, thanks." Skyla glanced over at Earl. "You're in late today."

"Yup." He puffed up his chest and sat a bit straighter. "Spent all night at the hospital."

"Oh, no." Skyla's hand fluttered to her chest. "Are you all right?"

"Oh, yeah, I mean no, I mean…" Earl's cheeks flushed a deep crimson. "My whole clan spent the night at the hospital awaiting the arrival of Becky Lynn, grandchild number sixteen."

"Oh, Earl, that's awesome. Congratulations."

He nodded. "Thank you. Sure did take her sweet time comin', that one did."

Skyla laughed. "That's okay. The things you appreciate most in life are those you have to wait for."

"Ain't that the truth." Earl soaked a biscuit in gravy and took a bite.

Gia finished counting the twenties and dropped them into the deposit bag, then turned to get the coffee.

Savannah beat her to it. By the time Gia turned, she already had a mug in front of Skyla and the pot held over it.

A couple approached the counter, and the man handed Gia his check and a twenty-dollar bill.

"How was your breakfast?" Gia asked as she took the check from him.

"Very good, thank you."

She held his change out to him and smiled. "I hope you'll come again."

"Thank you. I'm sure we will," the man said as he pocketed his change, then turned to go.

"Bobby, wait." The woman he was with caught his arm, staring past him at Skyla. "Skyla? Skyla Broussard, is that you?"

Skyla turned toward her with a smile, but the instant their eyes met, Skyla's face paled and the smile disappeared. "Gabriella Antonini?"

"In the flesh." Gabriella smiled at the man she was with and rubbed a hand up and down his arm, seemingly unaware of Skyla's obvious discomfort. "Well, Fischetti, now. Bobby and I have been married...well... pretty much forever."

"What are you doing here?" Skyla demanded.

"Um..." Gabriella faltered. "We just got back into town last night. We were going to look you up, but we hadn't gotten around to it yet."

"Actually, we were going to look up all of the old gang." Bobby Fischetti held Skyla's stare. "We were feeling a bit nostalgic, figured a reunion of sorts was in order."

Skyla swallowed hard and nodded. "It was good seeing you."

"Sure thing." Gabriella resumed her perky attitude as if nothing awkward had happened. "We'll let you know when we can all get together."

Skyla just nodded again and watched them go, then shifted her gaze to the TV.

Gia glanced at Savannah and drew her eyebrows together.

Savannah shrugged and shook her head.

After a moment, Skyla took a deep shuddering breath, then said, "So, what do you guys think of Ron Parker?"

"Oh, please, don't get them started." Accepting Skyla's change of subject, though curiosity was dang near driving her crazy, Gia started straightening the condiments on the counter.

With one last glance at Gia from the corner of her eye, Savannah chimed in. "Earl and I were just discussing that. Personally, I prefer Mitchell Anderson. He just seems more honest."

Skyla's eyes darkened, just for a second. If Gia hadn't been looking right at her, she'd have missed it.

Hmm...something there. Skyla was definitely not her usual self this morning, but Gia wouldn't press. There were still customers in the café, and Savannah and Earl were still at the counter with Skyla. Maybe later, if she could get her alone, she'd ask if she was okay. For now, she'd just leave her be.

Gia hadn't yet made up her mind whom to vote for, and she was actively searching for a reason to choose one candidate over the other. Each had strong points, and she hadn't yet come across any major weaknesses for either candidate, but there was still time. Ron's visit definitely hadn't helped his cause. If anything, he'd pushed her more toward Anderson. "You don't like Anderson?"

Skyla tilted her head as if contemplating the question. "I don't think he should be mayor."

Savannah finished pouring Skyla's coffee, then topped off everyone else's and put the pot back on the burner. "You prefer Ron Parker?"

Skyla shrugged. "He's not my favorite, and I don't think he's the best role model for young men and women, but he's better than Mitch."

"Oh, please, Mom, are you bashing Mitch Anderson again?" Willow let the door from the back room swing shut behind her and crossed the café. She laid a hand on her mother's shoulder and kissed her cheek. "Sorry I'm running a few minutes late."

Skyla patted her daughter's hand. "No worries, hon. I'm in no rush."

Gia always enjoyed the interaction between Willow and her mother. She'd never had a relationship with her own mother, but if she had, she liked to imagine it would have been like Skyla and Willow, and if she ever had a daughter of her own, she'd do anything to attain that close of a bond.

It struck Gia, as it often did when seeing Willow and Skyla side by side, how much alike they looked. They shared the same long, dark hair, the same exotic green eyes, and the same petite build, but Willow carried herself with a confidence Skyla hadn't quite mastered.

"So, what's the deal with Anderson?" Willow sat down next to her mother and took a blueberry muffin from a cake dish on the counter. "Why do you dislike him so much?"

"I don't know." Skyla stared down into her coffee cup, stirring the milk around, seemingly mesmerized by the tiny whirlpool. "I just don't care for him."

She was lying. The realization hit Gia like a ton of bricks. She'd never have expected Skyla to lie to Willow.

"Yeah, well, Ron Parker is everything you've taught me not to be." Willow broke her muffin in half. "He's phony and arrogant, and he treats everyone around him like they're his minions."

"Mmm-hmm…" Skyla dug through her bag and pulled out a few singles and held them out to Gia.

"Don't worry about it." Ignoring the money, as she always did with Skyla, Gia glanced up at the TV. A clip of Ron Parker working the crowd at last week's campaign event played in the background while a news anchor rambled on about the election.

"You didn't answer, Mom. Why do you dislike Mitch Anderson so much?"

Skyla dropped the money on the counter, as she always did after Gia refused to take it, then turned to Willow. "Do you want to sit here all day arguing politics, or do you want to eat lunch and go shopping?"

Nice dodge. Maybe Skyla should have been the politician.

"Definitely shopping." Willow took the last bite of her muffin, hopped off the stool, and rounded the counter to grab her purse. "I'll come in a little early tomorrow to help prep since it's Saturday. Thanks for giving me the afternoon off, Gia."

"No problem."

"And thanks for covering for me, Savannah."

"Anytime, kiddo. Have fun."

"Thanks." Willow smiled, waved, and held the door for her mother before bouncing through after her.

Savannah looked after them for a moment, then turned to Gia. The corners of her mouth turned up slightly, but there was no mistaking the sadness in her eyes.

Gia had no doubt Savannah's thoughts were running along the same line hers had earlier. Both of them had lost their mothers when they were young. Only difference was, Savannah grew up surrounded by family who adored her. Gia grew up alone, unless you counted the father who threw her out the day she graduated high school.

Gia waited until they were gone, then leaned close to Savannah. "Skyla seemed a little off today, don't you think?"

"Definitely, but I didn't want to push it in the middle of the café," Savannah said.

"No, me neither, but if I get a chance, I'll try to talk to her." And if the opportunity didn't present itself, Gia would make time to talk to her. Whatever may be wrong, she certainly wasn't acting like herself.

Chapter 2

Friday morning started off pretty much the same way Thursday morning had ended, with Savannah and Earl bickering over politics. When Gia couldn't listen to it any longer, she strode through the dining room, shut the TV off, and stuck the remote beneath the counter. "Enough already. I could hear you two arguing from the kitchen."

Savannah pouted.

Earl opened his mouth to protest, but Gia cut him off. "Isn't there anything else going on in this town beside the election?"

"There's a craft fair in two weeks." Savannah's perkiness returned at the mention of a fair. "It's running from Sunday to Wednesday. Want to go?"

"Sure." Gia had been wanting to attend a fair for a while, but they usually fell on weekends, her busiest time in the café. Since she was closed on Mondays, it would work out perfectly. "Can I bring Thor?"

"Of course. I bring my dogs all the time."

"All of them?" Savannah had like four or five dogs at Gia's last count.

"Not all at once, silly."

Two young women approached the counter, backpacks slung over their shoulders. They studied the chalkboard she'd written the cold brew selections on.

Yes!

Gia's resisted the urge to pump her fist. She'd been playing with different recipes, and she was dying to try some out. But, so far, the people of Boggy Creek didn't seem all that interested. She grabbed an order pad. "Hi there. What can I get for you?"

The first girl tore her gaze from the menu. "They all look so good it's hard to decide. I think I'll try the peppermint mocha."

"And I'll take one with vanilla and low-fat milk," her friend chimed in.

"Coming right up. Would you like it to stay or to go?" She crossed her fingers beneath the pad, hoping they'd stay so she could see their reactions.

"Do you mind if we take a table in the corner and study for a while?"

"Not at all. I'll bring your coffees when they're ready."

"Great, thanks. Could we get a couple of muffins as well, please? One chocolate and one banana?"

"You've got it."

While the two went to sit, Gia set to work. She poured two cups of coffee and added vanilla syrup and low-fat milk to the first.

"You know," Earl said, watching her like a hawk. "I'll never understand all these newfangled contraptions. I don't get what you needed the big machine for. Why can't you just pour regular coffee over ice or stick it in the fridge or something?"

Gia added chocolate syrup, a bit of cocoa, and peppermint extract to the second cup, topped it with whipped cream, then added a couple of mint leaves. "Regular coffee gets brewed with hot water. This doesn't. Instead, you soak the grounds in cold water overnight to make the coffee."

"What's the difference?"

She put the coffees on a tray along with the muffins. "It tastes better. Want to try one?"

Earl laughed. "I'll stick with the old-fashioned kind, if it's all the same to you. That thing looks more like dessert than coffee."

"You should see the s'mores one I'm playing with for Trevor."

Earl shook his head.

Gia set the drinks in front of the girls, who already had books spread open on the table.

"Thank you."

"No problem. Enjoy."

"And thank you for letting us study here."

"Anytime." Gia left them to their work. Hovering over them until they took a drink was probably unprofessional, though she had to admit, she wanted to.

Another customer approached the counter to pay his bill. Gia returned to the register and rang him up, then started an inventory of what she'd need to restock before lunch, keeping a close eye on the girls. Only one slice of meat lover's pie remained beneath the glass cover of the cake dish she kept on the counter. She'd have to get out a new one and refill a few of the muffin dishes.

Finally, the girl who was facing Gia sipped her peppermint mocha. A huge smile lit her face, and she lifted her cup toward Gia. "Mmm… delicious."

Gia nodded once in acknowledgment. Maybe they'd tell their friends and she could start bringing in a younger crowd. If the college kids came in during the slow time between breakfast and lunch, that would be perfect.

"So, about next week…" Savannah grinned as she dug through her oversized, yellow leather purse, pulled out a stack of brochures, and laid them on the counter. "Three days of uninterrupted girl time."

Gia groaned.

Savannah rolled her eyes. "I'm not taking no for an answer this time, Gia."

Savannah was not going to let up on her. She'd been insisting for months that Gia take a little down time. The fact that she was right, and Gia really could use a break, didn't matter. She didn't have time to go traipsing off to the Keys. Or the money. "I really can't afford—"

"It's my treat. Think of it as a belated welcome to Florida present." Savannah sipped her coffee, then tapped the stack of brochures. "The one on top is an adorable little bed-and-breakfast, right near the water."

"Savannah—"

"And look at that pool." Ignoring Gia's protests, she spread the brochure open on the counter and pointed out a beautiful, huge, kidney-shaped pool surrounded by palm trees. Several people lounged on rafts in the water with drinks in cup holders by their hands, seemingly without a care in the world. The sky was bluer than any Gia had ever seen, not a cloud anywhere.

Gia could almost feel the heat of the sun pouring down on them, cocooning them in warmth. "How can I leave now, when I'm just introducing the new cold brew menu?"

"Nice try, but you've already trained Willow on how to make the specials."

A row of drinks in coconut and pineapple shells, with fancy little umbrellas sticking out of them, were lined up across a tiki bar in the far corner, along with several trays piled high with appetizers.

Gia couldn't deny the small surge of desire. After everything she'd been through over the past several years, losing herself for a few days with nothing to do but lounge around the pool or on the beach with her best friend did appeal. Three days of nothing but rest, relaxation, warm sun, good food and drinks… "Okay."

"Besides, Cole already said he'd work the grill for you," Savannah nudged.

"Okay."

"And you know you can trust him and Willow to...hey...wait." Savannah's already big blue eyes widened. "Did you just say yes?"

Gia grinned. "Yup."

"Yes!" Savannah squealed and started shuffling through the rest of the brochures.

Earl laughed and shook his head. "You really don't know what you've gotten yourself into, do you?"

Gia looked over at him and frowned. "What do you mean?"

He gestured toward Savannah. "You'll see."

Savannah was sorting the brochures into three piles at a frantic pace. When she was done, she glanced up at Gia with a huge smile and laid her hand on one of the piles. "Okay. This stack is the stuff we definitely have to get to. This pile in the middle is the stuff I'd like to do, and this is the stuff we'll probably have to do next time."

"Uh, Savannah?"

"Unless you want to make it a week. I'm pretty sure we could get to do everything if we stayed for a week, instead of only three days." Her eyes filled with hope Gia hated to dash.

"There's no way I can leave Cole and Willow alone—"

"And me." Earl held up his fork. "I offered to pitch in and lend a hand too."

"Right." Gia scowled at him. He wasn't helping matters.

Earl grinned as he returned his attention to his plate and shoved in a forkful of home fries. Where in the world he put all of that food was beyond Gia.

"And Earl," she conceded. "There's no way I can leave the three of them alone through the weekend rush."

"You're right." Savannah tapped a nail against her cheek. "Okay, we'll do four days. You're closed Mondays anyway, so you'll only actually be taking three days off if we come back Thursday night. Or maybe even Friday morning..."

"You're pushing it now, Savannah."

She laughed. "I know. I just figured I'd see what I could get away with. Four days it is, then. I'll call and make the reservations."

Gia spun the brochure from the top of the must-do pile toward her. A creepy looking lighthouse stood in the distance surrounded by dark clouds. A far cry from the gorgeous blue sky that had half convinced her to go in the first place. "What is this?"

"Oh, that's the haunted lighthouse tour." Savannah took out her phone and looked at the front of the bed-and-breakfast brochure where a phone number was printed in big, bold letters. She shoved the rest of the stack toward

Gia. "And there's scuba diving, exploring shipwrecks, paddleboarding through mangroves, seeing the manatees. There's even an old fort you can only get to by seaplane."

"Seaplane? Uh…"

"Told you so." Earl winked at her.

"Savannah, I don't know—"

She held up a finger toward Gia and shifted the phone closer to her mouth. "Yes, hi. I'd like to make a reservation."

"Ah, jeez."

The front door opened, and Gia plastered on a smile, ready to greet whatever customer had interrupted her talking herself out of going.

Trevor Barnes, owner of Storm Scoopers, the ice cream parlor down the road, stumbled through the doorway, his usually tan face deathly pale, his eyes wide and unfocused.

"Trevor?" Gia started around the counter. "Are you okay?"

Earl looked over his shoulder, then spun his stool toward Trevor.

Trevor stopped and stared at them. "I think he's dead."

"Who?" Gia asked.

"I'll call back," Savannah said into the phone, then hung up. "Who's dead, Trevor?"

"He's in the freezer." Trevor's eyes rolled back in his head and he crumpled straight down.

Gia and Savannah lunged toward him, but they were too far away.

Earl lurched to his feet and caught one shoulder just in time to keep Trevor's head from smacking against the floor.

Chapter 3

"Help me lay him down." Earl guided Trevor's head gently to the floor and rolled him onto his back.

Gia straightened his arms and legs. "Trevor?"

Earl tapped his cheek. "Trevor."

"Should I call an ambulance?" Savannah stood over them, wringing her phone between her hands.

"Does anyone know what he was talking about?" Gia thought he was saying something about a body in the freezer, but that couldn't possibly be right.

"I think he said someone was dead in the freezer." Savannah chewed on her lower lip.

"Trevor, come on, man. Wake up now." Earl tapped Trevor's cheek a little harder.

"I think we'd better call an ambulance and probably the police." Savannah still made no move to place the call, simply twirled the phone around and around.

"Go get a cold rag." Gia pulled her phone from her pocket. "I'll call."

Savannah nodded and ran toward the back room as the front door opened.

Gia jumped to her feet and held out a hand to keep whomever it was from tripping over Trevor.

Cole Barrister, her good friend and sometimes cook, stopped just short of plowing into her. "Gia, what's—"

"Watch your step." She gestured toward Trevor and Earl on the floor just inside the doorway.

"What happened?" Cole stepped over Trevor, then squatted at his side. "Trevor?"

Trevor groaned.

"I need an ambulance," Gia said into the phone and rattled off the address. "A man just fainted in my café."

The 911 operator gathered the necessary information, then Gia hung up, despite the woman's efforts to keep her on the line.

Cole and Earl were still bent over Trevor. At least now he was sitting up, though his head still lolled a little as if he wasn't quite together yet. Regardless, he was in no condition to answer questions. He'd obviously seen something traumatic in his freezer, but who's to say it was a dead body. Maybe someone was alive in there, just unconscious, and needed help.

"Stay with him." Gia bolted out the door and ran down the sidewalk, glancing over her shoulder every few seconds for oncoming cars, then crossed Main Street as soon as there was a break in traffic.

Storm Scoopers' front door was shut, the Closed sign visible through the glass.

Gia pressed her face against the door, cupping her hands around her eyes to reduce the glare. It didn't help. The inside of the shop remained dark. She pulled the door handle, and the door swung easily open. Obviously, in the state he was in, Trevor hadn't bothered to stop and lock it. She poked her head inside. "Hello?"

Silence greeted her.

"Hello?" she tried again as she entered the shop and looked around for something to prop the door open with. Holding the door open, she grabbed a stool from the counter along the front window and wedged it between the door and the frame.

Then she started across the shop toward the big walk-in freezer in the back room.

A soft click startled her and she jumped and whirled back toward the entrance. The keys hung from the lock, swinging gently back and forth, clicking softly against the door. She blew out a breath and continued across the shop. She shoved the door to the back room open and poked her head through. "Hello? Is anyone here?"

The still silence hanging over the shop gave her pause, fear creeping in to intrude on the sense of urgency that had overcome her in the café. She stared at the closed freezer door for a moment before wiping her sweaty hand on her jeans, then grabbed the handle. Holding her breath, she yanked the door open.

The empty freezer stared back at her.

A nervous laugh burst out. Had she really expected to find a body in Trevor's freezer? Obviously, whoever Trevor had seen was gone now.

A prank, maybe? Or maybe someone had gotten trapped in the freezer somehow, then bolted when Trevor had opened the door? As terrified as Trevor was when he ran into the café, it wasn't a far stretch to imagine him seeing someone and being so frightened he turned and fled before realizing the someone in question was still alive.

A large hand landed on Gia's shoulder.

She screamed and lurched into the freezer as she whirled toward her assailant.

"Sorry!" Cole held his hands up and took a step back. "I didn't mean to startle you."

"Jeez, Cole." Gia pressed a hand against her chest, her heart dancing wildly beneath her palm. "You scared me half to death. What are you doing here?"

"You took off before anyone realized what you were doing. I wasn't about to let you walk in here alone. What if an attacker was still hanging around?"

"I didn't think of that." She probably should have. She'd been so worried someone might need help, she hadn't stopped to think about anything else. She laid a hand on Cole's arm and squeezed. "Well, thank you for coming to my rescue, but it seems Trevor was mistaken."

"No body?"

"Nah, nothing at all." She stepped aside so Cole could see into the freezer. Commercial-sized tubs of ice cream and Italian ice lined the shelves. Boxes of frozen waffles were stacked on a shelf to her left.

Hmm…maybe she could talk Trevor into using her homemade waffles for his ice cream sandwiches. They'd taste much better, and it might even help her get a few new customers. She'd have to remember to ask him about it.

She picked up one of the boxes and turned it over, looking for a price. Waffles weren't that expensive to make. She was pretty sure she could probably match, if not beat, what he was paying for the frozen ones. When she didn't find a price sticker, she shoved the box back into place. The cold finally registered, and she shivered and turned back to Cole. "Is Trevor doing any better?"

He nodded. "Yeah, though he swears there was a body here."

"I don't see anything out of the ordinary." She scanned the freezer once more, then turned to leave. Her gaze fell on something in the far corner behind the rows of ice cream, a few tubs of which lay scattered on their sides on the floor. She squinted and moved closer.

An arm stuck out from behind the shelves, its fingers frozen closed in a fist.

"Oh, no." Gia squeezed her eyes closed, then opened them again, but the arm remained where it was, a wide gold watch encircling its wrist.

"What's wrong?" Cole's gaze followed hers to the corner. "Ah, man."

Gia started toward the corner, but Cole held out a hand to stop her.

He crossed the freezer, squatted down beside the arm, and closed his fingers over the wrist, then rubbed his free hand over his face. "Why don't you go back and see how Trevor's doing and wait for the police? I'll stay here."

"Is he…?"

Cole shoved to his feet, his knees cracking loudly. "Yeah."

"You're sure?"

"Positive."

Gia backed away. "Can you tell who it is?"

"No. Not without moving anything. There's an apron over his head and chest, and I don't want to disturb any more than we already have."

Gia pulled her phone out of her pocket and dialed her sort-of-boyfriend Detective Hunter Quinn's number.

Hunt answered on the first ring. "Yeah, I already heard," he said before she could get a word out. "Where are you?"

"Storm Scoopers, but I'm going to head back to the café. Cole will wait here with the…uh—"

"Just don't touch anything. I'm on my way."

Gia bristled. "Oh, please. You think I don't know better than to touch anything?"

Silence hummed over the line.

Okay, in all fairness, though she might know better, that hadn't always stopped her from getting involved in things better left alone. She sighed. "Fine. I won't touch anything. I'm going to see how Trevor's holding up."

"I'll see you there." He disconnected before she could say anything else.

"He on his way?" Cole asked as soon as she stuffed her phone back into her pocket.

"Yes, but if it's okay, I'd like a chance to talk to Trevor before they take him to the hospital." *If I can make it back to the café before Detective Tall, Dark, and Snippy gets there.*

"Yes, of course. Go ahead."

Gia turned toward the front door. "You're sure you're okay here?"

"I'll be fine." He walked her to the front of the shop, then stepped outside onto the sidewalk and rubbed the back of his neck. "Better to wait out here."

Gia nodded and hurried back down the block.

A police cruiser and an ambulance already sat in front of the café, lights flashing. A small crowd had gathered on the sidewalk. For a second, Gia hoped Savannah's fiancé, Officer Leo Dumont, would be the first officer to arrive. Then she remembered he'd been promoted to detective when Hunt had been assigned as temporary Captain, until Captain Hayes could return or be replaced.

Gia's heart ached for Trevor. He was a good guy, sensitive and caring. Something like this would hit him hard. She also grieved for whomever had been left in Trevor's freezer. Though it didn't seem likely whoever it was had ended up there by accident, she held onto the hope that he had. It was better than the alternative. Who knew? Maybe he accidentally got locked in the freezer and froze to death. Was that even possible?

She strode through the front door someone had left propped open and stopped short.

Trevor sat at the table nearest the door, elbows propped on the table, head resting in his hands.

Two police officers stood behind him, and an EMT bent over a blood pressure cuff on Trevor's arm, whispering in his ear.

Trevor shook his head, then straightened his arm and tried to pull away. "I told you, I'm fine."

"Well, you can't be too careful." The petite woman clutched his arm tighter between her elbow and her side and continued taking his vitals as if he'd never protested, apparently used to treating reluctant patients.

Savannah grabbed Gia's arm and pulled her to the far side of the door where Earl stood waiting. "Well?"

Gia looked back and forth between them and nodded.

Savannah's breath whooshed out. "Ah, jeez."

"Yeah," Gia agreed.

"What happened?" Willow rushed to Gia's side. "I was in the stock room when he came in."

With a quick glance at Trevor, Skyla followed right behind Willow. "I was at the salad bar down the street when I saw the police car and ambulance pull up. What happened? Is Trevor all right?"

Gia closed her eyes, blocking out the chaos for a brief moment, then opened them again and faced Skyla and Willow. "He found a body in his freezer."

"A body?" Skyla paled and pressed a hand against her chest.

Gia held her gaze and nodded.

"Oh, no," Skyla said. "Do you know who it was?"

"I didn't go all the way in. Cole came in behind me and felt for a pulse, but it was too late. He's still there, waiting for the police."

Earl crowded against Gia's other side. "When Trevor first woke up, he started rambling something about Ron Parker."

Skyla gasped. "You think it's Ron Parker?"

Earl shook his head. "No idea. He wasn't makin' much sense. I don't know if he was saying it was Ron in the freezer, or if he was just babbling something about him."

Gia recalled the gold watch and dark hair on what she could see of the arm. Try as she might, she couldn't recall if Ron had been wearing a gold watch when he'd come in the day before. "From the little I saw, I think it was a man, but I couldn't say who."

"I don't need to go to the hospital. I'm fine." Trevor slid his chair back away from the EMT and shoved himself to his feet.

Apparently giving up on getting Trevor to cooperate, the EMT went and spoke quietly to one of the police officers.

"Excuse me." Gia started toward Trevor, but she needn't have bothered excusing herself as Savannah, Earl, Skyla, and Willow stayed glued to her side. When Gia reached him, she laid a tentative hand on his arm. "Are you okay, Trevor?"

He stared at the floor and shook his head. "I don't know."

Gia's heart ached for him.

"Willow, could you get Trevor some water, please?" Skyla asked.

"Of course." She headed toward the small refrigerator behind the counter for a bottle of water.

Skyla watched her for a moment, then moved to his other side and gripped his wrist. "Trevor, Earl said you were rambling about Ron Parker when you came to. Does he have anything to do with this?"

Trevor looked around, then pitched his voice low and leaned closer to Skyla.

Savannah, Gia, and Earl leaned in too.

Trevor met Skyla's gaze. "I only lifted the apron for a second, but it looked an awful lot like Ron Parker."

Skyla slapped a shaky hand over her mouth, then leaned even closer and whispered, "Are you sure?"

"No, I'm not sure," Trevor snapped. "Why do you think I said it looked like Ron?"

"Trevor!" Shocked at his tone, Gia jerked back.

"No, it's okay." Skyla also backed away from their small circle.

Sirens blared, coming closer.

Skyla looked over her shoulder toward the front door. "I have to go. I'm sorry."

"Here you go, Trevor." Willow held the bottle of water out to him, then glanced at her mother, who'd paled even more since finding out it might be Ron. She frowned. "Are you all right, Mom?"

"I'm fine, but we have to go now." She made a beeline for the door.

Willow looked at Gia and raised a brow.

Gia simply shook her head. She had no idea why Skyla was acting so strange.

Savannah laid a hand on Willow's arm. "Go ahead, Willow. Your mom seems like she needs you. This week's been kind of slow at the office, and I'm going to hang around here, anyway."

"Thanks, Savannah. I'll see you guys tomorrow. I hope you feel better, Trevor." Willow waved as she followed her mother.

"Thank you, Willow," Trevor called after her, then uncapped the bottle and took a tentative sip. He pressed a hand against his stomach, put the cap back on the bottle, and set it down on the table.

Gia racked her brain, but she hadn't paid much attention to what Ron was wearing when he'd come into the café the day before. "Do any of you remember if Ron was wearing a gold watch when he was in yesterday morning?"

Savannah caught her lip between her teeth and scowled. After a moment, she shook her head. "I can't swear he wasn't, but I just don't know."

Not wanting to have to explain herself, Gia dropped the subject. "Do you know what that was about, Trevor? Does Skyla know Ron Parker?"

Trevor's gaze shifted a little too quickly away from Gia. "I have no idea."

Chapter 4

Acting Captain Hunter Quinn strode through the door with newly promoted Detective Leo Dumont on his heels.

Leo dropped a quick kiss on Savannah's head on his way by.

Hunt nodded toward Gia. "Could you guys give us a few minutes, please?"

"Of course." She led Earl and Savannah toward the back of the café, then rounded the counter while Savannah and Earl each took a seat on stools at the far end. When Hunt didn't protest, she figured it was far enough.

As he approached Trevor, he gestured to the two officers still standing behind him.

The officers walked out without saying anything.

"What was that all about?" Savannah whispered.

Gia shrugged. "No idea."

Hunt turned a chair around, then straddled it and rested his hands on the back and faced Trevor. "You all right?"

Trevor nodded. "I'm fine."

"Want to tell me what happened?"

Leo took out his notepad and pen and took a seat at the table on the other side of Trevor.

Trevor spared him a quick glance before turning his attention back to Hunt. He leaned back, spread his hands wide, and shook his head again. "I have no idea. I opened the shop this morning, and everything seemed fine. Then, when I went into the freezer…"

Hunt waited a minute, but when Trevor made no attempt to continue, he shifted to rest his forearms on the chair back. "Why don't you start from the beginning and just walk me through your morning routine."

Trevor nodded, his gaze riveted on the floor. "I went in—"

"The front or the back?" Hunt asked.

"The front."

"Was the door locked?"

"Yes."

"Do you usually use the front door in the morning?"

"Yes, okay?" he snapped.

Hunt nodded to Leo, who wrote something down in his notepad.

Gia tore her attention from them for a moment to glance back and forth between Earl and Savannah. They both shook their heads but remained silent. None of them wanted to chance missing what was going on.

"Okay, then what did you do?" Hunt continued.

Trevor's shoulders slumped. "I don't know. I...uh...I guess I did what I always do. I was running late, so I ran in. I locked the door behind me, turned on the lights, looked around to see if anything got left undone last night. I checked the cases and made a list of flavors I had to restock."

"Do you always restock in the morning?"

When Trevor spoke, his tone held none of the tension it had a moment before. "Not always. Sometimes I do it at night after we close or while we're still open even, if we're not too crowded, but the high school musical was last night, so we were swamped all night, and then we had a big clean up, so I just left restocking for this morning."

Hunt nodded.

"Anyway, when I went into the freezer, I started collecting the flavors I'd need. When I rounded the back shelf, I...I..." He started to hyperventilate.

"Relax, Trevor. Do you want me to call the EMT back in?"

He shook his head, but continued to suck in deep gulps of air.

"Gia?" Hunt called.

Startled, Gia did her best to appear as if she wasn't staring right at them hanging on every word.

Hunt just rolled his eyes. What could she say? He knew her too well.

"Could you bring Trevor a glass of water, please?"

"That's his on the table." Gia gestured toward the water bottle Trevor had set down earlier.

"Thanks." He uncapped the bottle and held it out to Trevor.

Trevor sucked down half the bottle, then handed it back to Hunt and wiped his mouth with the back of his hand. "I still can't even believe it's real. It was him, right? Ron Parker?"

Hunt nodded. "You knew him?"

"Not really."

Hunt frowned and looked over at Leo.

Leo shook his head, barely noticeable, just a slightest twitch, the sort of subtle communication people who'd been friends for a long time could get away with.

Hunt's eyebrows drew together as he turned his attention back to Trevor. "If I remember correctly, you two used to hang out together, back in the day."

Trevor shrugged. "That was a lifetime ago."

Hunt's posture stiffened. "I thought you guys used to be pretty tight?"

"Look." Trevor glared at Hunt. "It was a long time ago. I haven't even spoken two words to the man in almost nineteen years."

Hunt laced his fingers together, letting his hands hang casually over the back of the chair, but his back remained rigid. He waited.

Trevor grabbed the water bottle Hunt had put back on the table and rolled it against his forehead, then lowered it without taking a drink, still clutching it tightly as if needing to hold onto something. "Look, man, I'm tired. It's been a long day."

Gia's gaze shot to the clock hanging above the cutout. Not even eleven o'clock in the morning. In all fairness, he probably didn't even realize less than an hour had passed since he'd walked into work and found a dead man in his shop. Even if they hadn't spoken in years, it was still someone he'd obviously known and been friends with at some point in his life. Odd that he'd remember it had been nineteen years, though. Why not just say almost twenty or a long time? Almost nineteen years. As if he knew exactly when they'd last spoken.

"I'm sorry, there's nothing more I can tell you," Trevor said.

"You said you haven't spoken two words to Mr. Parker in almost nineteen years. What about when you ran into him on the street? Or when he came into the shop? Did you two say hello, how are you, catch up on old times?"

Trevor tightened his fist, crushing the water bottle, then slammed the bottle onto the table. "I already told you, I haven't spoken to him since before we graduated high school. He didn't come into my shop. Ever."

"Well, he obviously came in last night."

"No." Trevor lurched to his feet, knocking the chair over behind him. "That's just it. He didn't come in. Didn't you hear me? He never came in. He wouldn't have come in. Someone had to have put him there after... Well, after."

Hunt took his time standing and righting Trevor's overturned chair before standing toe to toe with him. "Why didn't he ever come in, Trevor? Did you two have some kind of a falling out?"

Trevor's eyes widened, and he took a step back. "I'm done answering questions."

"You can answer my questions here or at the station, but you are not done answering questions."

Trevor's jaw clenched, and he lifted his chin. "Then I'll answer them at the station. With my lawyer present."

Hunt stared at him for a moment, his expression too neutral for Gia to read, then nodded, took Trevor's arm, and gestured toward the door.

Trevor yanked his arm from Hunt's grasp, whirled around, and stormed out with Hunt and Leo right behind him.

Gia started after them.

Earl put a hand up to stop her and shook his head.

"But—"

"Let it go," Savannah said.

"Now's not the time," Earl whispered.

She watched them get into Hunt's jeep and pull away. "What do you think that was all about?"

Savannah shook her head. "I have no idea, but that sure was a side of Trevor I've never seen before."

"Yeah, no kidding." Gia could barely believe the man who'd just stormed out was the same affable, easygoing friend she'd become so fond of. When they'd first met outside her café, he'd almost fallen over himself he was so clumsy. Adorable, really. Then she'd gotten to know him better. While he could trip over his own feet trying to walk, he was as graceful as could be while paddleboarding and kayaking. He'd introduced her to a whole side of Florida she never would have experienced otherwise, showed her the most beautiful lakes and forests, always gentle and kind to both her and any wildlife they encountered. The man didn't have a mean bone in his body. "I wonder what got into him."

Earl returned to his usual seat. "Cut him a little slack, you two. Trevor's a delicate soul, and walking in and finding someone who used to be a friend, even if it was a lifetime ago, couldn't have been easy for him. People react to stress and grief in different ways."

Gia nodded. Earl was right. She knew Trevor. He was kind and loving and sensitive. His outburst didn't change that. "Besides, Hunt was grilling him kind of hard."

"What do you mean hard?" Savannah stood. "There was a dead body in his freezer, and he was hostile while Hunt was trying to ask him questions."

"Hostile?" Gia couldn't believe what she was hearing. How could Savannah possibly think Trevor had been hostile? "If Hunt hadn't kept pushing him, maybe he wouldn't have blown up."

"If Trevor had just answered the stupid questions, maybe Hunt wouldn't have had to push him," Savannah huffed. "What would you have had him do, Gia? Ask Trevor politely if he killed Ron Parker and dumped him in his freezer? Then accept his word that he didn't just because he said so?"

Gia squirmed. When she put it like that…

"If I remember correctly, you were once on the receiving end of one of Hunt's interrogations, and you didn't blow up like that."

"I—"

"No, I'm not done. Hunt may question him hard, but just like with you, he'll do right by him, and he can't do that by going easy. Y'all weren't here when the first two officers arrived on the scene, and Hunt radioed them to leave Trevor alone, to be sure he received medical attention but not to question him until Hunt got there."

"I didn't—"

Earl held up his hands. "All right, ladies, that's enough. Hunt will do the right thing by Trevor. Gia knows that, Savannah. Everyone's a little stressed right now, but bickering won't help anyone."

Gia nodded. "You're right, Earl. I'm sorry, Savannah. I didn't mean to imply Hunt did anything wrong. I'm just worried about Trevor."

"No, I'm sorry. I just…I can't believe Trevor would do anything like that…" Savannah looked down and took a shaky breath. "But what if he did?"

"What are you talking about?" How could she even suggest something like that? "You know Trevor. How could you think for even one minute he could have killed someone?"

She lifted her gaze and stared into Gia's eyes. "I don't *think* he killed someone, Gia, but what if he did? You hang out with Trevor all the time. Off in the woods, kayaking by yourselves. Think about that."

Gia had been spending a lot of time with Trevor lately, especially since Hunt had taken over as captain, often spending her day off each week kayaking on the lake in the woods. In a very remote area. "He didn't kill anyone. Trust me, Trevor is no killer."

Savannah simply nodded and let it go. If Gia knew her at all, which she did, she knew she'd bring it back up again later, but for now, at least, she was willing to drop it.

"Thank you for worrying about me." Gia hugged her. "And I'm sorry for saying that about Hunt. You're right—when I was in trouble, Hunt did everything he could to help me, and I have no doubt he'll do the same for Trevor."

"Yes, he will." Savannah massaged her temples for a minute, then looked up at Gia. "So, are we still going to the Keys? I have to call back and finish making the reservation."

Gia thought about it for a minute. There really was no reason she couldn't still get away. They weren't supposed to leave until Monday morning. Surely, Hunt would have cleared Trevor by then. She smiled. "Sure thing."

Savannah smiled back, and that easily, the tension between them evaporated. Savannah returned to the stack of brochures and pulled out her phone.

Gia returned to Earl. "Thanks, Earl."

"Anytime," he said with a wink.

"Do you think I should go down to the station?"

"For what?" Earl wrapped a hand around his coffee mug and started to lift it.

"Hang on, Earl. That's probably ice cold, and we've already established you have no interest in cold coffee." Gia stuck his mug in a bin under the counter, poured him a fresh one, and set it on the counter in front of him. "I don't know. Maybe it would be helpful to know someone's there for him."

"For what it's worth, I think you should leave him alone for a little while. When Hunt's done questioning him, he'll either give him a ride home, or Trevor will call someone he trusts for a ride."

"I guess you're right. It just doesn't feel right to sit here and do nothing."

Savannah came up behind Gia and rubbed a hand up and down her arm. Apparently, all was forgiven.

"He's right, Gia. There isn't much you can do right now. After Hunt's done, we can go pick him up if you want, see if he needs someone to talk to."

She nodded, but it still didn't feel right to go on with her day as if nothing had happened. The sudden realization that she hadn't had a customer since Trevor came in hit her, and she glanced out the window at the small crowd gathered outside and the two police officers blocking the door. "Maybe I should go see how Cole's making out."

"They'll never let you in." Savannah finished tying an apron around her waist and started clearing the table Skyla's old friend had been sitting at, the friend she'd acted totally weird about running into.

Come to think of it, Skyla had been acting strange all morning. "What do you think is up with Skyla?"

Savannah dumped the dirty dishes into the bin with Earl's mug. "No idea, but did you see her expression when she realized it might be Ron Parker?"

"Poor girl was shaking like a leaf," Earl said.

"And earlier, when that couple came in, the instant she laid eyes on the woman she looked like she'd seen a ghost." Gia had wondered even then what was up with her.

Savannah leaned against the counter. "You know how weird it can be sometimes when someone from your past pops up unexpectedly."

A vision of Bradley flashed before Gia, and she gasped.

Savannah's eyes widened, and she reached for Gia. "Oh, Gia, I'm sorry. I didn't mean—"

"No, it's okay." Gia waved her off. "Really. I'm fine. But you're right. Even under the most normal of circumstances, running into someone from your past can be awkward."

The sound of voices cut off any further contemplation as the Bailey twins walked through the front door. Apparently, Gia was once again open for business.

Savannah grabbed a couple of menus and started around the counter to greet the women.

Estelle and Esmeralda had been customers since Gia had first opened, when they'd come in amid rumors and controversy to judge her for themselves. As much as she liked the two elderly women, the last thing Gia needed this morning was their gossip. On the other hand, who knew how long they'd been lingering outside with the rest of the crowd? Maybe they'd heard something about what was going on at Storm Scoopers. "I'll get it, Savannah."

Savannah handed Gia the menus, grabbed another stack, and went to greet the group of customers coming in behind them. Since Cole hadn't returned yet, it looked like Gia would be heading back to the kitchen. She plastered on what she hoped would pass for a genuine smile. "Good morning, ladies."

Esmeralda greeted her with a warm smile.

"Gia, how are you?" Estelle gave Gia a quick hug, then stepped back and patted her blue up-do. Not a single hair out of place, as usual.

"I'm doing well, thank you." She led them toward a table in the middle of the room, where she knew they liked to sit so they could hear everything going on around them. "Have you ladies been waiting long?"

"Oh, no, dear, not at all," Estelle assured her.

"Did the hold-up have anything to do with the body they found at Storm Scoopers?" Just like Esmeralda, straight to the point.

Gia wasn't about to get into a discussion about Trevor being questioned by the police. These two would have him tried and convicted by noon. As much as she'd come to like the Bailey sisters, they tended to jump to conclusions. And when you spent as much time gossiping as they did, that could be downright dangerous. She dodged the question with one of her own. "Do they know who it is yet?"

Esmeralda and Estelle shared a knowing look.

Esmeralda looked around then leaned closer to Gia. "Rumor has it, it's Ron Parker."

She stepped back and watched for Gia's reaction.

Gia feigned surprise. "Seriously?"

"That's what they're saying."

"Not surprising, really." Esmeralda settled in her seat and opened her menu.

"No," Estelle agreed as she sat. "When he was a kid, that boy was always as sneaky as a fox in a henhouse."

"Yup. Always up to no good, that one was."

"Never did figure he'd amount to much."

"To be honest, I was more surprised to see him running for a respectable position such as mayor than I was to hear he was murdered." Esmeralda turned over her coffee cup for Savannah to fill.

Savannah filled her cup, then her sister's, then moved off to see to the next table.

"If anything, I'd have expected him to back Mitch Anderson," Estelle said.

Esmeralda was nodding before her sister even finished. "Two of a kind, those two. Thick as thieves when they were kids."

Estelle sighed. "Like everything else, alliances change over time."

"You're so right, Estelle. This used to be such a peaceful little town, and now a prominent citizen has been murdered."

Estelle's mind obviously changed as much as everything else, since Ron Parker had gone from a sneak to a prominent citizen in a matter of seconds.

"They're sure he was murdered?" Though Gia knew that already, it still felt strange to have it confirmed. As if it were any less real if it hadn't yet hit the Boggy Creek gossip mill.

"So I've heard," Esmeralda confirmed.

"How?" Gia would only have another second or two before Savannah would start putting orders up.

"Haven't heard yet. But he obviously managed to get on someone's bad side."

Esmeralda snorted. "If that ain't the understatement of the year."

With the crowd in the café growing, and Cole still unaccounted for, Gia excused herself and headed for the kitchen.

Chapter 5

Three order slips already hung above the grill. With her mind racing, Gia pulled on a pair of disposable vinyl gloves and started the first order.

She scrambled a bowl of eggs, tossed in some pre-cooked crumbled sausage, diced green peppers, onions, and tomatoes and poured the mixture onto the grill, then laid three homemade tortillas on the grill to warm.

She couldn't get Ron Parker out of her mind. Could whatever had happened to him have had something to do with the campaign? His visit to the café had been somewhat annoying, but even if he'd annoyed everyone along Main Street, she couldn't see that as a motive for murder.

Her thoughts shifted to Mitch Anderson. With Ron Parker out of the picture, Mitch would have an easy time getting in, since he'd be running unopposed.

Earl, who'd been around Boggy Creek forever, had suggested something about Anderson having skeletons buried in his closet. And Skyla had agreed he shouldn't be mayor.

If the majority of Boggy Creek's citizens felt that way, then how had he ever become a candidate?

Of course, Savannah had also been born and raised in Boggy Creek, and she planned to vote for him. But in her case, it seemed more because she didn't trust Ron Parker than any great love for Mitch Anderson.

And what was the deal with Ron Parker and Mitch Anderson being friends? Why would Ron have run against a friend? Wouldn't they have shared the same views? Of course, people changed over time.

Gia sprinkled grated cheddar cheese onto the egg mixture, then laid the warm tortillas on plates, filled them with the eggs, rolled them, ladled some homemade salsa over the top, and added a generous helping of her new Southwestern home fries.

She made them similar to her regular home fries, with onions and crumbled bacon, but added diced tomatoes and jalapenos instead of green peppers. They were a little spicy for her taste, and she'd only been serving them for a week, but so far, people seemed to like them.

She stuck the plates onto the cutout counter between the kitchen and the dining room. A quick peek into the packed dining room told her she'd better get her head in the game.

Savannah rushed in and stuck two orders up over the grill. "I swear half the town is in there."

"They must have all rushed in the minute the police moved away." Gia checked the orders and started pulling out what she'd need.

"On the bright side, none of them seem to be in much of a hurry. Most of them are lingering over coffee and gossip. Sorry to say, it's more for the gossip," Savannah said before she hurried out.

Remembering what Willow had once told her about becoming a gossip hot spot, meaning she'd finally gained acceptance in the community, Gia smiled to herself. She tried to settle into the routine of working the grill and tried to keep her mind from wandering toward Trevor or Ron Parker. Though used to the speed at which she had to work, she still had to concentrate if she was going to get the orders right.

She cracked four eggs onto the grill, put several pieces of precooked bacon beside them, then dropped two slices of rye bread into the toaster and cut a bagel and dropped that into the next toaster in line. She grabbed two plates and added a heaping pile of home fries to each and set them on the counter beside the grill, then flipped the eggs and added a slice of American cheese to one. She scanned the line of order tickets, pulled out the pancake batter, and ladled six puddles onto the grill.

When the toast popped, she stuck a piece on one of the plates and stacked the egg with the cheese and four slices of bacon on top, topped it with salt, pepper, and the other piece of toast, then did the same with the bagel, remembering at the last minute to add ketchup, and shoved the plates onto the cutout.

She flipped the pancakes, stuck a few sausage links on the grill, and started scrambling eggs.

"How's it going?" Cole headed straight for the sink to wash his hands.

"Was it really Ron Parker?" Gia blurted. She stacked the pancakes onto two plates and set them beneath the warmer.

He nodded, then finished washing his hands, dried them, and pulled on gloves. "I heard one of the police officers say it was him."

"Do they know what happened to him?"

"Nah, not that I heard, anyway."

She poured the scrambled eggs onto the grill and added sausage to the plates, then slid over to give Cole room to work beside her. "Well, what are they saying?"

Cole scanned the tickets and started cutting the pieces of breakfast pie they'd need. "Not much, from what I could hear. But what I did hear doesn't bode well for Trevor."

Gia faltered, almost dropping the spatula full of eggs she was flipping. Cole steadied her arm. "Easy, there."

"What do you mean it doesn't bode well for him? You can't honestly believe he killed the man."

"Of course I don't think he killed him, but according to the detective I overheard… Not Hunt," he clarified.

Gia nodded for him to continue, impatient with how little information he was giving her.

"Trevor and Ron Parker had history. Apparently, the two of them didn't get along."

"When Hunt was questioning Trevor, Trevor sort of admitted as much. He said Parker never came into Storm Scoopers."

"Why not?"

Gia was already shaking her head. "He didn't say, but he did say Parker would never have come in on his own, that someone must have put him there."

Cole pulled down two tickets and moved the plates to the cutout for Savannah to pick up. "Did Trevor say what happened between them?"

"Nope." Gia moved through the routine of cooking automatically, working in sync with Cole, never getting in each other's way. "And when Hunt pushed him, he clammed up and asked for a lawyer."

Cole's eyebrows shot up. "You don't say."

"I don't know what got into him."

"Well, you can't really blame him for being on edge, all things considered."

"True."

Silence fell between them as they banged out one order after another, barely keeping up with the rush. Gia took four plates to the cutout and chanced a quick peek into the dining room. Almost every table was full, along with most of the stools at the counter. Seemed a mayoral candidate being found dead in a local ice cream parlor had brought flocks of people to Main Street. She glanced over her shoulder at the grill. Still too many orders for her to leave Cole alone, though she would have liked a chance to get out there and see what people were saying.

"So, if Trevor isn't responsible, which he isn't," Gia said, "then who do you think is?"

"Hmm…"

"I mean, it doesn't seem random, right?"

"I wouldn't think so. Especially, since the body was left in Trevor's shop," Cole agreed.

"Exactly. So it has to be someone with a grudge against Trevor."

"And Ron."

Gia couldn't imagine anyone harboring that sort of animosity toward Trevor. He was too laid-back, too kind, too naïve to have made such a violent enemy. "Can you think of anyone who had something against both of them?"

Cole thought for a minute. "I can't even think of one person who doesn't like Trevor."

"No, me neither. Granted, I haven't been here that long, but everyone really seems to like him."

"They do. Even the high school kids think highly of him, since he lets them hang out in his shop as long as they don't get too rowdy."

"Only two orders left." Cole scraped the oil off the grill into the small pan at the front. "Why don't you take a break, and I'll finish these up. Then I'm going to head out."

"Sure, that'd be great, Cole, thank you." Gia stripped off her gloves, threw them in the trash, and washed and dried her hands. Confident Cole would get the orders out with no trouble, Gia headed for the dining room.

Some of the tables had emptied, though a small handful of people still lingered, talking quietly amongst themselves. Gia headed behind the counter.

Savannah slid a bin of dirty dishes onto a shelf underneath the counter.

"Did you sell any cold brews?"

Savannah held up two fingers.

Not really the news Gia had been hoping for, but probably for the best since Savannah wasn't trained to make them yet and Gia had been swamped at the grill.

"And they just had milk in them, so it was easy enough for me to do."

"I was hoping with how busy we were, more would sell."

Lena Gregory

"Don't worry. Cold brew coffee is the thing right now. Most people coming in this morning weren't looking to try something new. They were looking for information."

"True," Gia conceded.

Savannah leaned back against the counter and huffed. "Willow sure did pick the right day to leave early."

Though she didn't exactly choose to leave. With a couple of people still sitting close enough to overhear, it wasn't the time to get into whatever was going on with Skyla. "No kidding. I don't think we've ever been that packed."

"No way. For a little while, not long mind you, but we actually had a short line of people waiting for tables."

"Seriously?"

"Yup." She grinned.

"Wow. Nice." Then, remembering the reason for the crowd, Gia sobered and lowered her voice. "Too bad someone had to be killed for me to be so busy."

"Don't worry, Gia. You'll get there. It just takes time. And just think… A good portion of the people who came in today were from town and will probably return."

"I hope so. My breakfast and lunch crowds are usually pretty good, but I'm not doing as well as I'd hoped with the dinner hour."

"At least you're making a profit now."

"That's true. I was worried about that for a while."

"I know, but look at you now." Savannah's grin was contagious.

"I'm not sure why I'm having such a hard time building a dinner crowd. I was hoping the addition of the cold brew coffee would help with that. Kind of dessert-like, you know?"

Cole grabbed a coffee mug, filled it, went around the counter and took a seat on a stool. "Why don't we look at the menu again, see what we can do to make breakfast for dinner even more appealing?"

"I did, and I came up with the Southwestern menu, but it's not really taking off like I'd hoped."

"You have to give it time, let people get to know about it."

"Told you so." Savannah punched her arm. She gestured toward the register. "You go ahead and ring them up, and I'll clear the table."

"Thanks, Savannah, and you're right, Cole. Let me know when you have time, and we'll see what we can come up with."

"You bet, but off the top of my head, I can tell you I make a mean steak and eggs."

"Mmm… That sounds delicious. Okay, that works. Now I'm in the mood for steak and eggs." She laughed as she went to ring up the two women waiting at the register.

When she returned, Cole was jotting something on a napkin.

"What's that?" Gia tilted her head to see what he was doing.

"Here you go." He turned the napkin toward her and stuck the pen back into the pocket of his Hawaiian print shirt. "Steak and eggs."

She read over the list he'd started.

"There are so many different ways to make steak and eggs. You can use different cuts, you can do omelets, you can add vegetables or biscuits and gravy."

"I love it. Thanks, Cole. This is a great idea."

"You can even use your home fries scrambled together with a few eggs as a side dish."

Gia yanked the pen from his pocket, grabbed an order pad, and copied his list, then added the scrambled eggs with home fries. "I'll put together a list of ingredients and order what we need, and I'll add it to the menu as a special next week."

"What's that you're adding to the menu?" Savannah shoved the tub full of dirty dishes beneath the counter.

"Steak and…uh…" A commotion on the sidewalk in front of the café caught Gia's attention, and she leaned around Savannah to see if she could tell what was happening.

Savannah turned and looked over her shoulder out the front window.

"What's going on?" Cole frowned and followed their gazes toward the sound of raised voices outside.

"Was there an accident?" Savannah asked.

Gia strode toward the front door with Savannah and Cole on her heels.

The three customers who still remained in the café looked up briefly but then returned to their food and coffee.

Gia opened the front door and stepped out.

A woman she'd never seen before had a firm grip on another woman's arm. "Don't play stupid."

"I don't know what you're talking about." The second woman kept her voice low, her gaze darting around the street.

Though she looked vaguely familiar, Gia couldn't place her.

She tried to pull away. "Stop it, Allison."

Allison yanked her closer but made no attempt to lower her voice. If anything, she yelled louder. "You know exactly what I'm talking about, Gabriella!"

Gabriella? Why do I know that name? Gia mused.

"Knock it off." Gabriella finally yanked her arm free. "You're going to get us both in trouble."

"Trouble? Really? How much trouble did he get in?"

Gabriella looked around, her gaze falling on Gia for an instant, then took off—not quite running, but close.

"You think Skyla doesn't know, but she does. Even back then she knew you wanted him," Allison yelled after her.

Skyla. That's where she knew the name from. Gabriella was the woman who'd made Skyla so uncomfortable the day before.

Allison watched Gabriella run across the street and disappear down a side road, then mumbled, "Coward," and whirled around in a huff. Her gaze locked with Gia's. "What are you looking at?"

Gia gasped and stepped back.

"Here's an idea, why don't you go inside and mind your own business?" She stormed off, muttering to herself, and headed down the street toward Storm Scoopers.

The police barricade still remained. Police cars blocked the far end of the street, crime scene tape was strung around the front of the building, and reporters had started to gather out front. Of course, the death—probably murder—of a mayoral candidate would be big news.

Allison slipped into the crowd.

Gia turned to go back inside. "Why do I have the sneaking suspicion that conversation had something to do with what happened to Ron Parker?"

"I don't know." Cole stepped aside to let her pass through the doorway and glanced down the road. "But I think you should probably heed her advice."

Chapter 6

Gia set a paper bag with a bacon, egg, and cheese sandwich and home fries on the table she'd set up outside the back door of the café. She added a large sweet tea, then hurried back inside, pulled the door shut, and locked it.

Ever since she'd found Harley hanging out of her dumpster searching for newspapers, putting out his dinner was the last thing she did every night before locking up and going home. Since the homeless man who'd become a friend refused to enter a building, she had no choice but to leave his food on the table out back. Hopefully, Harley would eat before everything got cold.

She took her time walking through the café, double-checking that everything was turned off and locked. Although she took pride in all that she'd accomplished over the past months, she couldn't help worrying about keeping the café open when she couldn't seem to maintain a steady stream of customers. She had regulars who came in often, and Earl who came in every day, but she had to do something to bring in more business. She added "look into more advertising" to her mental to-do list.

Once she locked the front door, she strolled down Main Street toward Storm Scoopers. Though there was still a small police presence, including the crime scene van parked directly out front, most of the crowd had already dispersed. A small group of what she assumed were reporters still dawdled next to a news van, but other than that, not much was happening.

A quick scan of the surrounding area didn't turn up either of the women who'd argued outside the café. She'd have to remember to ask Skyla what the deal with Gabriella was, since Allison had mentioned her directly.

She still hadn't heard a word from Trevor. Or Hunt, for that matter. And his jeep was nowhere in sight. She continued past Storm Scoopers to the doggie day care center to pick up Thor.

Often, while she was walking to the day care center, Trevor would spot her out the window and run to catch up, usually tripping over something on his way.

She smiled at the thought. Trevor could trip standing still, and yet when it came to outdoor activities, like paddleboarding and kayaking, he was as graceful as some of the wildlife he was always pointing out. No way could he be a killer. It just wasn't possible that sweet, charming, clumsy man could ever hurt a fly.

She wiped a tear from her cheek and glanced back at Storm Scoopers. It felt weird for it to be closed at this time of day. It just wasn't right. She turned and pulled open the day care center door.

"Hi, Gia." Zoe, who ran the day care center, stood behind the desk, flipping through paperwork.

"Was he good today?" Gia always asked, though the answer was always the same.

"Of course. Thor is a big teddy bear," she answered, without her usual enthusiasm.

"Is everything okay?"

Zoe shook her head and looked up from the book on her desk. "I'm not sure. You're friends with Trevor Barnes, right?"

"Yes."

Zoe already knew that because they often came in together to pick up Thor and Brandy, Trevor's German shepherd.

"Why? Is something wrong?"

"I don't know." She caught her bottom lip between her teeth while she checked something on the computer behind the counter, then looked up at Gia. "I know there was a lot of commotion at Storm Scoopers today, but no one who's come in seems to know much. Have you heard anything?"

Gia shrugged, unsure how much she could, or should, share. "I know someone was found dead this morning. Rumor has it, it was Ron Parker."

She figured that much was safe since she'd heard people discussing it in the café.

"Do you know where Trevor is?" Zoe asked.

She hesitated. She wasn't about to admit he'd been taken to the station for questioning. She'd never known Zoe to be much of a gossip, but something like that could ruin the man's reputation if it started spreading. "No, I don't."

Technically, not a lie, since she had no idea if he was still there or not. "Did you need him for something?"

"He dropped Brandy off last night for an overnight visit and never came to pick her up."

Gia sucked in a breath. Trevor hadn't mentioned having plans last night, not that he always told her when he was going out, but he usually did. "I'm sure he was busy with everything going on today."

"Yes, but I've called both numbers he listed on the paperwork, numerous times, and he never answers, and now there's no room in his voicemail to even leave another message."

"Is there a problem with Brandy? I could take her home with me if you can't keep her."

"Oh, no, not at all. She's a sweetheart. And I wouldn't be able to release her to anyone but Trevor without his permission, anyway." Red patches flared on her cheeks. "I was just worried."

Realization dawned. Zoe didn't want to get rid of Brandy. She wanted to know Trevor was okay. Gia smiled. "Why don't you give me your cell number, and I'll call and let you know if I hear from him?"

Her shoulders slumped a bit as some of the tension left her. "That would be great, thank you."

"No problem. I'm sure he's fine, just busy."

"I'm sure you're right." Zoe jotted her number on a card and handed it to Gia. "Thank you, again, Gia. I really appreciate it. And don't worry about Brandy. I'll take good care of her until he can come get her."

"I know you will, and I'm sure Trevor knows that and appreciates it too." Actually, if she knew Trevor half as well as she thought she did, the first thing he'd do once he was released would be stop and pick up Brandy. "Would you mind calling me if Trevor comes in to pick up Brandy?"

"Of course, I will."

"Thanks." Gia stuffed the card into her purse while Zoe ran in back to get Thor.

As soon as Thor trotted through the door and spotted her, he strained against the leash.

Zoe laughed and released the leash. "He's getting strong."

Thor lunged.

"Easy, Thor." Gia bent to hug him and pet his long, black fur. She couldn't believe how big he'd gotten. Though she knew Bernese mountain dogs were a large breed, she hadn't expected him to grow so fast. She slid her fingers into the white fur on his chest, and his eyes rolled back.

Thor's entire body vibrated.

"Did you have a good day?"

His whole back end wagged wildly, so she took that as a yes.

She stood and waved to Zoe. "Thanks, Zoe. Have a good night."

"You too, and don't forget to call if you hear from Trevor, no matter how late it is."

"I'll call the minute I hear from him. I promise." She made sure she had a tight grip on Thor's leash, then opened the door. Not that Thor had ever taken off on her after that one incident with the squirrel, but you could never be too careful. And if he took off on Main Street, he could get hit by a car.

Once she reached the sidewalk, she stood looking at Storm Scoopers. The late afternoon sun still blazed warm enough to feel good, and she tilted her face toward it for a moment, then looked down at Thor. "So, now what, boy?"

She pulled her cell phone out of her purse and dialed Savannah's number.

Savannah answered on the first ring. "No, I haven't heard from Hunt or Leo."

"Me neither. What do you think that means?"

Savannah sighed. "I think it means they are detectives, and they just got a tough case with an important public figure as a murder victim, and they are probably busy trying to figure out who killed him."

"Ha, ha, smart aleck."

"I'm just as worried as you are, Gia, but there's nothing we can do until we hear from someone."

"I guess you're right, but it feels weird to go home and go about my routine under the circumstances."

"Don't go about your routine. Go home and pack."

"Pack?"

"Yes, pack. For our trip to the Keys on Monday?"

"Oh, right. With everything going on, I forgot about that."

"Gia." Savannah's tone held a note of warning. "Don't you dare use this as an excuse to back out of going. There's nothing you can do here anyway."

"I know. You're right. It's just…"

"Just nothing. Go pack, and I'll talk to you later." She disconnected.

Gia stared at the phone for a minute, willing it to ring. When it didn't, she shoved it into the back pocket of her jeans and started back down the street toward the café. When she passed Storm Scoopers, she scanned the area. Though a few familiar faces remained, the women from earlier hadn't returned. The closed sign still hung in the window.

Gia reached her car, parked on the street in front of the café rather than in the back parking lot, and settled Thor in the back seat. She dialed Willow's number before shifting into gear, pulling out, and heading toward home.

The phone rang four times before Willow finally answered with a quiet, "Hey, Gia, hang on."

Footsteps followed by the sound of a door squeaking open, then closed, came over the line, before Willow returned. "What's going on? Have you heard from Trevor?"

"No, I haven't heard anything." Gia didn't know how much to say to Willow about Skyla. Until this morning, she'd have sworn Willow and Skyla shared everything. But after Skyla had seemed so secretive earlier, she wasn't sure. "How's your mom doing? She seemed shaken."

"That's why I came outside to talk. She's in her room, been in there since we got home before. She said she had a headache and went to lie down, but when I tried to check on her, the bedroom door was locked. When I knocked, she didn't answer, but I could have sworn I heard her crying."

Something was going on with Skyla, but how could she help if she couldn't figure out what it was? There had to be a way to get information without saying too much. The first time she'd noticed Skyla acting out of character had been when the woman had recognized her in the café. "Is your mom friends with a woman named Gabriella Fischetti?"

"Not that I know of. Why?"

Gia racked her brain. Although she was pretty sure the woman had mentioned her maiden name, she couldn't remember what it was. "She was in the café earlier, and it seemed she and Skyla knew each other."

"My mom is very outgoing and does a lot of volunteer work in the community, so she knows a lot of people."

Unless she could think of Gabriella's maiden name, that was a dead end. But she'd also acted strange about Mitch Anderson. Gia switched tactics. "When Savannah and Earl were discussing the candidates this morning, Skyla said she was voting for Ron Parker, and you seemed surprised."

"Not really surprised, because I knew she planned to vote for him. I just don't understand why."

"Don't you like Parker?"

Willow paused as if thinking.

Gia waited her out. As she drove out of town, the scenery changed drastically. She left behind the small bungalows lining the streets of Boggy Creek and passed acre after acre of primitive-looking forest, trees soaring into the sky, blocking the sun as it sank lower toward the horizon.

"It's not so much that I dislike him, more that I don't believe he has a strong sense of anything other than himself. I think Ron Parker looks at everything in terms of how it will affect him or what he has to gain from it."

"Why does your mom feel differently?"

"I don't think she does. It seems she's voting for him more to keep Mitch Anderson out than to get Ron Parker in."

"Does your mom know Mitch Anderson?"

"Not that I know of."

Gia fell quiet. She couldn't think of any more questions.

"Have you heard anything about Mr. Barnes?" Willow asked.

"No. Nothing." And it was driving her crazy. "I'm sure everyone's busy with everything that's going on."

"I'm sure. I just wondered if he was feeling better."

"I'll let you know if I hear anything."

"Okay, thanks. I'm gonna run, though. I think I hear Mom up and around."

"I'll talk to you tomorrow. Tell your mom I hope she feels better."

"I sure will, thanks."

Gia disconnected and stuffed the phone into her bag on the passenger seat. She hit the turn signal and turned into her development. "Hungry, Thor?"

Thor barked once. He was always hungry.

Gia pulled up to the house, took a minute to go through her usual precautions—firm grip on Thor's leash, house key at the ready, bear spray close at hand—and made her nightly dash to the front door. Sooner or later she'd probably get used to living in the forest, but for now it made her feel safer to go through her routine.

Once inside, she locked the door and fed Thor. She checked the yard for anything dangerous before letting him out in the pen to do his business. While she waited on the deck, she dialed Trevor's number. No answer, voicemail full, blah, blah, blah... She disconnected and stuffed the phone into the back pocket of her jeans.

"Come on, Thor."

He trotted to her, and she led him into the house. A quick rummage through the refrigerator came up with leftover barbeque from Xavier's, which she arranged on a plate and stuck in the microwave.

She briefly considered calling Hunt, but dismissed the idea just as quickly. If he had time to talk, he'd already have called. She thought of trying Trevor again while she waited, but what use was it? She'd only have the same results she'd had the last hundred or so times she'd called.

If there was nothing she could do to help Trevor, maybe she could figure out what was going on with Skyla, since Willow didn't seem to know anything. She took her dinner to the living room, put her laptop on the coffee table beside her barbeque, settled Thor with a bone, and flipped on the local news station. They repeated their stories every half hour, so she'd probably have to wait fifteen minutes or so before the story of Ron Parker's murder would come on. She had no doubt that would be the lead story.

She took a bite of chicken. Mmm…almost as good leftover as it was fresh. Savoring the tangy flavor, she opened her laptop and typed Gabriella Fischetti into the search engine. Several social media sites popped up. *Gabriella Antonini Fischetti.* Antonini, that was her maiden name.

Gia clicked around on Gabriella's social media for a few minutes, but there was no mention of a trip to Boggy Creek. Her "About Me" sections all listed her home as Atlanta, Georgia. She had more than five hundred friends on Facebook, and Gia clicked on the "search friends" box and typed in "Allison." *No results* popped up.

A breaking news alert pulled her attention from the computer.

A somber-looking newscaster appeared on the screen and started right into the Ron Parker story. "Mayoral Candidate Ron Parker was found dead, presumed murdered, today in a local ice cream shop. With only weeks before the election, opponent Mitch Anderson had a considerable lead over Parker and was highly favored to win the election."

With Anderson already favored to win, that pretty much let getting him in as mayor out of the equation as a motive.

The anchor paused and pressed a hand against his ear. His eyes widened. "We just received word that Trevor Barnes, owner of Storm Scoopers, the local shop where Parker was found, has been arrested and charged with second-degree murder."

Gia gasped, which caused the potato she was chewing to lodge down her throat. She choked it down as she fumbled her phone from her pocket with tears running down her cheeks.

Savannah picked up on the first ring. "I was just about to call you."

"Did you see the news?" Gia wheezed. "What is going on? Trevor was arrested?"

"I don't know. I'm trying to reach Leo, but he's still not answering."

"No, Hunt's not either." Gia rubbed the ache in her chest—whether it was brought on by the thought of Trevor being arrested or the piece of potato she'd sucked down, she had no clue.

"I tried to reach Hunt too. His voicemail box is full." The all-too-familiar sound of Savannah's rhythmic nail-tapping came over the line. "Gia, you know Hunt wouldn't have arrested Trevor without good reason, right?"

She squeezed her eyes closed. As much as she hated to admit it, even to herself, Hunt wouldn't arrest anyone without good reason. She swiped her tears as she strode down the hallway to her bedroom and grabbed a tissue from the box on the nightstand.

"Gia?"

She sniffed. "Yeah, I'm here."

"Do you want me to come over?"

Did she? She didn't really know what she wanted. Trevor was a good friend, a friend she'd come to trust, which didn't come easy to her. Hunt was more than a friend, though not as much as she'd like since fate seemed to keep them both too busy to pursue anything serious.

"There's Hunt," Savannah said in her ear, reminding her she was still hanging on the phone.

"Where?"

"On the TV."

Gia ran back to the living room just in time to see the tail end of a clip of Hunt escorting Trevor down a hallway, Trevor's hands cuffed behind his back. Lights flashed as photographers and reporters jostled for better positions from which to catch Hunt's attention amid demands for answers.

Chapter 7

"Gia?" Frustration tinged Earl's voice.

"Sorry, what did you say, Earl?" She pulled her attention from the TV over the counter, where they kept replaying the same clip of Trevor being escorted into the station, long enough to check if he needed more coffee. His cup was still almost full. "I just can't believe they arrested him. I kept thinking it was a mistake and they'd run a story this morning correcting it, you know?"

"Yeah. But I'll say the same thing I said the past ten times we discussed it this morning. You can't make a determination one way or the other until after you hear his side of the story."

"I guess. In my head, I know you're right, but it's so hard to believe." She'd lain awake most of the night watching the news, hoping for any new information.

"It'll work out. Now, while you were zoning out over there, I asked if you were planning on opening anytime today."

She glanced at the clock above the cutout to the kitchen. "Yikes, I should have opened five minutes ago."

"That's what I was trying to tell you."

She hurried around the counter and unlocked the door. Only a few customers stood waiting outside. She ushered them in, seated everyone, and handed out menus, then returned to the counter for a coffee pot. "Thanks, Earl. I lost track of time. Willow is usually here before I open, so I don't really pay attention to the clock until after she comes in."

Earl frowned and looked over his shoulder toward the door, then back at the clock. "You're right, she should have been in by now."

"Luckily, it's Saturday, so I have Cole here to cook, but I wonder if Skyla is okay. Willow said she had a headache last night." Gia rushed to fill coffee cups, then grabbed an order pad and started taking orders.

She burst through the door to the kitchen and tacked the line of order slips above the grill for Cole. "Have you heard from Willow?"

"No, not a word." Cole read the first ticket and started cracking eggs into a bowl to scramble. "Why? Isn't she here?"

"No, and she hasn't called."

"That's unusual, isn't it?"

"Very." Gia hurried back out front.

A group of six customers stood waiting by the door chatting. She tried to catch snippets of the conversation, but it sounded like they were discussing a business meeting and made no mention of Trevor or Ron Parker that she heard.

She took a quick detour behind the counter, topped off Earl's coffee cup, and held her cell phone out to him. "Could you do me a favor and try to reach Willow, please?"

Willow almost never missed a day of work, despite the college courses she took at night and online. Even during exams, she hadn't missed a single shift, often bringing a stack of books with her and studying when they weren't busy. And if she did have to miss, she always called. Always.

"Of course." He took the phone. "If I don't get her, should I try Skyla?"

"Don't call Skyla yet. Give it a little while longer, and see if Willow's just running late. I don't want to worry her if nothing is wrong." Gia counted out six menus and approached her new group. "Good morning. Follow me, please."

The four men and two women followed her to a large table by the window. They all thanked her and opened their menus right away.

Leaving them to figure out what they wanted, she went once again to get the coffee pot. Years of working with people had taught her to read them fairly well. This group, all dressed in business attire, while friendly, did not want to chat. They wanted to eat and be on their way.

Obviously, she'd have to wait for the rumor mill to get up and running to get any information on Trevor, since Hunt had never bothered to return any of her calls. He knew better than to call while she was working, since she rarely had time to stop and chat on the phone. That meant the earliest she'd hear from him would be tonight after she closed.

She poured coffee, took orders, and ran back to the kitchen to give them to Cole.

"Any word on Willow?" Cole asked as she rushed past.

"Not yet." She ran back toward the door just as the bell rang, signaling a new customer.

"Let me know, will ya?" Cole called after her.

"Will do." She let the door to the dining room fall shut behind her and grabbed the plates Cole had left on the cut-out counter. As she set them on the table, she scanned the room to see if everyone seemed to have everything they needed.

One gentleman's coffee cup was more than half empty, so she grabbed the pot and headed over to refill.

"Excuse me." A woman across the room held up her hand for the check.

Two more customers came in, joining the line of three who were already waiting for seats.

Having spent so much time on the grill since she opened, Gia had forgotten the hectic pace of taking order and serving customers. Though she occasionally pitched in to help Willow, she'd never run a busy shift on her own.

Willow did it every day, and she did an amazing job, but it might be time for Gia to consider hiring another waitress. If she hired someone part-time, only to help Willow out during the busier shifts, she might be able to swing the extra paycheck, especially since tips would factor into the hourly rate.

She grabbed a stack of menus and started seating the customers waiting on line. Though she caught bits and pieces of conversations—can't believe that nice man is a killer. Did you hear about Trevor Barnes? Who'd have guessed he was a killer all along? Poor Ron Parker. I feel so bad for his family. Wonder what they'll do about the election now. Looks like Mitch Anderson is a shoo-in—she garnered no new information. It seemed even the Boggy Creek rumor mill had no more dirt than she did.

The last woman on line seemed to be alone.

Gia smiled at her. "Good morning. Will anyone else be joining you?"

"Um, no, just me. A seat at the counter would be fine, thank you." The petite, soft-spoken woman turned and scanned the street outside the window before following Gia. "Your café is lovely."

"Thank you. Have you been here before?"

"No, this is my first time. I own a flower shop on the other side of town and don't get down here often." She held out a hand. "I'm Donna Mae."

"It's nice to meet you. I'm Gia." Gia shook her hand. "Can I get you some coffee? Maybe a cold brew?"

"Coffee would be great, please."

Gia turned over a coffee cup and filled it. "I know what you mean about not getting out. Since I opened the café, I haven't had a chance to do much else either. It feels like I'm always working."

"Don't I know that feeling." Her smile held a rare warmth that made Gia take an instant liking to her.

"Do you know what you'd like, or would you like a few minutes to look at the menu?"

"You don't happen to have oatmeal, do you?"

"I do, and if you'd like I can add fresh blueberries."

"That sounds wonderful." She rubbed her hands together as if cold, then wrapped them around her coffee cup. "I hadn't planned on eating, just having coffee, but it smells so good in here."

"Thank you." Since she was there all day long, Gia didn't always notice the smell unless she went out to run errands and came back in while Cole was cooking. But she did do her best to maintain a cozy atmosphere that encouraged people to relax, enjoy a meal, and linger over coffee. Hopefully, she'd succeeded.

As much as she would have enjoyed talking more, she was falling behind, and once that happened, she'd be hard-pressed to catch up.

She took a quick detour past Earl. "Anything?"

He held her gaze, the concern evident in his expression. "No. Do you know where she lives? I'll take a ride and see if anything's wrong at the house."

"Yeah, I can—"

"Excuse me, miss?" a man called loudly from across the room. Apparently, she'd ignored him for too long.

"In the file cabinet in my office," she told Earl.

He nodded, and she took off toward the man who'd yelled. "I'm sorry, sir. What can I help you with?"

"Got any ketchup?" He held up a ketchup bottle and shook it back and forth. "This one's empty."

"Of course; I'm sorry." She ran into the stock room and grabbed a new bottle. Willow restocked the dining room before her shift each morning, and Gia had never given it a second thought, assuming it would be done, as it always was. But since Willow hadn't shown up that morning...

After she dropped off the ketchup, she continued running around greeting people, taking orders, and manning the register. Earl had disappeared, so she hoped to have news on Willow soon.

By the time things started to slow down, she was exhausted, her feet and back were killing her, and Earl still hadn't returned with any news of

Willow. With a quick check to make sure everyone was comfortable, Gia checked her phone for messages. Nothing.

She stuffed the phone back into her pocket and looked up, surprised to realize Donna Mae was still seated at the counter, her brilliant green eyes red-rimmed and puffy as if she'd been crying or was exhausted. Gia could relate. "How was your oatmeal?"

"Oh, it was delicious, thank you."

"Can I get you anything else? More coffee, a muffin, maybe? I made a fresh batch of banana ones this morning." At three a.m., when she'd given up on getting any kind of sleep and gotten out of bed.

"Thank you, but I couldn't eat another bite. I'm hoping you can help me, though. I've been waiting for you to get a free minute." Donna Mae smiled. "Apparently that doesn't happen very often."

Gia laughed. "It's not usually this bad, but my waitress didn't make it in this morning."

"Oh, I'm sorry."

"Me too." She grinned. "Anyway, before it gets busy again, what can I help you with?"

Donna Mae twisted on her stool and looked around the café. Then, seemingly satisfied no one was listening, she leaned closer to Gia across the counter. "I was wondering if you'd seen Harley Anderson?"

"Harley? The man who hangs around town?" She didn't know his last name, but Harley wasn't that common of a name, so she figured chances were good Gia's Harley and the Harley this woman was looking for were one and the same.

"Yes, I need to find him."

Because she always came in the front door, Gia hadn't noticed if last night's dinner was still on the table out back. "Oh, no, is he missing again?"

Her eyes widened. "Again? Harley was missing?"

"Well, I guess, technically, he wasn't missing. He just wasn't here, and no one knew where he was. Then, one day, he just showed back up as if nothing was wrong. I guess maybe it wasn't." Gia had been worried sick, especially when the town had been hit by a tornado, and Harley was still unaccounted for. "Do you mind if I ask why you're looking for him?"

"I'm sorry, but it's personal." She shifted her cascade of curly blond hair behind her back, then sat and put her purse on the stool beside her, dug out a business card, and handed it to Gia. "But if you see him, would you mind giving him this and telling him I'm looking for him?"

"No, of course not."

"Thank you, again. It was nice meeting you."

"Nice meeting you too. I hope you'll come again."

"I will, for sure." She left money on top of the check on the counter and left.

Gia looked down at the black business card she held. *Donna Mae Parker* was printed in gold script beneath *Boggy Creek Florist.* Her business and cell phone numbers were listed in the bottom corner. She turned the card over, but the back was blank. She stuck it in the register with a mental note to check if Harley had eaten his dinner last night and include Donna Mae's business card with a note that she was looking for him in the bag with tonight's dinner.

First Willow, then Harley. What was going on?

Chapter 8

Once Gia closed the café for the night and picked up Thor, she drove past Willow's house. Even though there was no car in the driveway, she pulled in and ran up to the front porch of the small bungalow. She rang the bell and waited. When no one answered, she knocked on the door and called out to Willow and Skyla. Still nothing.

Just like Earl had said when he returned to the café earlier. No one was home. And when she'd tried both of their numbers, neither of them had answered.

Gia cupped her hands against the window and peered through the sheer curtain.

Nothing moved inside.

Frustrated, she dropped her arms to her sides and looked out over the neighborhood, composed of small cottages, mostly built in the fifties and sixties, that lined the narrow streets. Lawns were neatly trimmed, lights had started to come on in a few downstairs windows, and the scent of barbeque filled the evening air. A comfortable place to call home.

Gia sighed and returned to the car. If she didn't hear from either of them by tomorrow, she'd have to look at Willow's employment papers and see if she'd listed anyone other than her mother as an emergency contact.

"Looks like no one's home, Thor."

He barked twice in response, or maybe because a cat sauntered along the front of the garage door. Hmm… She hadn't checked the garage. "I'll be right back, Thor."

She jumped out and jogged to the side window, then tried to peer into the garage. Blinds blocked her view, and no matter how hard she tried, she couldn't maneuver herself into a position that allowed her to see beneath them or between the slats. So much for that idea.

She returned to the car and slammed the door. "Come on, Thor, let's go home."

With one last glance around the property, Gia shifted into gear and pulled out. She tried Willow's number again, but it went straight to voicemail. Skyla's did the same.

She threw the phone onto the passenger seat and settled in for the twenty-minute drive home. There was no sense even trying Hunt, since she already knew he wouldn't answer. Calling Trevor was a waste of time. Savannah would have called if she'd heard anything. So that left going home, heating up the breakfast pie she'd taken with her for dinner, and...

She had no clue what to do. The waiting was driving her crazy, and it had only been one day. What if she didn't hear from anyone for days?

She turned on the radio, flipped through the stations, and settled on one playing soft rock. Leaving the more crowded area of Boggy Creek behind, she started up the road that cut straight through the forest toward Rolling Pines. Thick forest crowded both sides of the road, giant pine trees soaring into the sky. Bushes and some sort of palm leaf-looking shrubs battled for space beneath the trees, and green murky water came right up to the top of the ditch running along the side of the road in several spots.

The encroaching forest had intimidated Gia when she'd first moved to Boggy Creek, had made her feel small and vulnerable, as if it could swallow her whole. Over the past few months, that had changed. She'd come to love the feeling of losing herself in the serenity of the forest.

Thanks to Trevor.

Though he'd tried to get her to share his enthusiasm for many of the outdoor activities he enjoyed so much, he'd never been able to accomplish that until he took her kayaking. The peace she felt while gliding over the lake through the mangroves and palm trees was like nothing she'd ever known. Of course, that peace only came while she was in the kayak and only when Trevor was with her. She'd never venture into the forest alone.

How could the man who'd become such a good friend have ended up arrested for murder? There had to be a mistake.

Movement in the distance caught her attention. Gia flipped off the radio and sat up straighter, squinting to bring the dark figure moving along the side of the road into focus. She tensed as the stories Trevor had shared with her about the skunk ape flooded her mind. The skunk ape was a Big Foot-like creature that was said to roam Florida's forests.

As she got closer, she recognized the dark, hunched figured shambling along the shoulder. She passed, then pulled over to the side of the road and got out, not wanting the woman to think a stranger had stopped.

Thor whimpered and wiggled around in the back seat.

"Stay, Thor. I'll be right back." Gia waved as she walked toward the woman. "Hi, Cybil."

Cybil Devane shifted the hood of her long cloak farther back, her long salt-and-pepper hair spilling over her shoulder. "Gia. How are you, dear?"

"I'm doing well." She stopped and looked around the deserted stretch of road. "What are you doing out here?"

"Walking." Cybil laughed, her piercing blue eyes bright with humor. Cybil had lived her whole life traipsing through the Florida wilderness, and she probably couldn't understand Gia's trepidation any more than Gia could understand her comfort in the isolated surroundings.

"Do you live out here?"

"Close enough," Cybil said.

"It's good to see you again. I wasn't sure I would."

"I told you last time we met, we'd happen upon each other again."

Gia grinned. Last time Gia had run into Cybil had been on her first kayaking trip with Trevor. "Yes, you did. You also said maybe next time we'd chat for a while."

"And so we shall." Cybil shifted her long walking stick to the other hand, then took Gia's hand in hers and squeezed. "You seem troubled, my dear. Is everything okay?"

Gia lowered her gaze and started to pull her hand away.

Cybil held on tight, with a surprisingly strong grip. "I see you on the lake with your friend sometimes, and you've seemed at peace lately. What's changed?"

"Trevor, the man I go kayaking with, is in trouble, and I'm not sure how to help him."

"Are you sure he needs help?"

Of course he did; he'd been arrested for murder. "I'm sure he needs help. I'm just not sure I'm the person he needs it from."

"Sometimes there's nothing to do but be there and lend support."

Gia only nodded. What could she say? Cybil was right. Unfortunately, at the moment, she couldn't even get in touch with Trevor to let him know she believed in him. "Where are you headed?"

"Nowhere in particular."

Somehow Gia didn't quite believe that. While Cybil swore she wasn't psychic, had even laughed at the prospect, Gia had her suspicions. It seemed awfully coincidental that she always showed up right when Gia needed guidance.

"I brought home a breakfast pie from the cafe to have for dinner." Of course, she'd left it in a bag in the car with Thor, whose face was plastered in the back window at the moment. If she was lucky, which she doubted today, maybe he hadn't already eaten it. "I was just headed home to make a cup of tea and have dinner. Would you like to join me?"

Cybil studied her.

"I'll drive you home after."

"I'd love to join you." Cybil started toward the car with Gia at her side, resuming the same steady pace she always seemed to move at. "And there's no reason to drive me home afterward."

The sun sat just on the edge of the horizon, painting the sky with streaks of pink and blue. "It'll be dark soon."

"I can walk in the dark just as easily as I can walk in the light."

Gia had already found Cybil hiking in the forest twice, and both times she was alone. "Don't you ever worry about walking everywhere alone?"

"Nope. Been hiking these forests my whole life, and I'll never give up the peace it brings me."

Gia could certainly understand that. She'd felt it every time she went kayaking, as if all of her troubles slipped away. But that was in a kayak, and with a companion, not running around in the forest, by herself, at night. She wasn't about to argue with Cybil, but she had no intention of letting her walk home alone in the dark either.

Cybil just shook her head and laughed, as if she'd read her mind.

Gia walked her to the passenger side and opened the door for Cybil. Thankfully, the bag was still intact. Apparently, Thor had been more interested in what Gia was doing than food.

She grabbed her cell phone off the seat and handed the pie to Cybil to hold in her lap.

Thor poked his head between the seats and nudged Cybil's shoulder.

"Hello there, boy." She petted his head, then fished a treat out of her pocket and handed it to him.

Gia lifted a brow at her.

"What?" she asked, her face a mask of innocence.

"Do you always carry dog treats in your pocket?"

"Always. You never know what you might run into in the forest."

Gia put the walking stick in the trunk, then got in and resumed her trip home. "Do you live nearby?"

"About a twenty-minute walk, not far at all."

"Is there anyone at home you'd like to call?" Gia held out her cell phone. "I don't want anyone to get worried if they're expecting you."

Cybil sighed. "There's no one. Hasn't been since my Duke passed on more than ten years ago now. He used to walk these woods with me all the time. Every night after dinner, we'd head out to hike. On the weekends, we'd pack a picnic lunch and take it with us, then lose ourselves in the forest for the entire day, as if we were the only people in the world. When I walk now, even after all these years, I can still feel the warmth of his hand wrapped around mine."

"I'm sorry."

Cybil lifted her hand and studied it, then closed it into a fist and laid it on the seat. "His hand was so big it used to swallow mine up. He always made me feel safe. Still does."

"How long were you married?"

"Forty-three years."

"Forty-three years? You don't look old enough to have been married that long."

A grin shot across her face. "We married a lot younger back in those days."

Gia laughed. She really liked Cybil, had since the first time she'd met her. Whether or not the woman actually had any sort of sixth sense, she didn't know. But either way, she had no doubt they were meant to meet. It was rare for Gia to meet someone and feel an instant bond with them. The last person that had happened with was Savannah. "Do you have any children?"

"Nah, it was just Duke and me. There was a time when I wanted children, wanted the joy of a big family, children and grandchildren home for the holidays, but it wasn't meant to be for us. And we were okay with that, but now… Well, now I do get a little lonely at times."

Gia's heart ached for her. She resisted the urge to reach out and take her hand. Cybil's tone had been one of sadness tinged with resignation, but she'd accepted her life and been happy. She wouldn't want sympathy.

"We always had dogs, though. Big dogs, like your boy here. And they'd walk with us in the evenings, never on the weekends, that was our special time together, but most evenings, and I got to keeping treats in my pocket." She offered Gia a sly smile.

"Do you have a dog now?"

"No, the last of them left me a few years ago, and I never got another."

"Why not?"

"I'm not getting any younger, dear, and who would take care of him if something happened to me?"

The thought of leaving Thor alone brought a lump to her throat, and she choked it down. If anything ever happened to her, Savannah or her brother, Joey, would surely take care of Thor. Or maybe Hunt would. Though she knew that with absolute certainty, she made a mental note to ask. You never could be too careful. "Would you like a dog?"

"Of course. I love dogs, but I won't be irresponsible."

"I'll tell you what—why don't we go to the shelter, and you can pick out a dog you like, and if anything happens to you, I'll take care of him. I promise."

Her eyes went wide. "You'd do that?"

"Yes. When Savannah first suggested getting a dog, the whole concept was completely foreign to me, but since I got him… I can't imagine living my life without him."

"You are a truly kind woman, Gia. Your friend is lucky to have you."

Her cheeks heated. "When would you like to go?"

She sat up straighter. "No time like the present."

"You want to go now?"

Cybil shrugged. "Why not? Debby at the shelter has been after me to take home a pup for years. We used to get all of our pups from her mom when she ran the shelter before she passed. Unless you don't have time now?"

To be honest, she had nothing to do, and she'd enjoy looking at the puppies. She had a feeling it wouldn't be quite as overwhelming now as it had the first time. "I'd love to go. Do you think they're still open?"

"I'll give Debby a call and tell her we're coming." Cybil dug beneath her cloak and pulled out a cell phone.

"You have a cell phone?"

"Of course I do, dear. What do you think I go hiking all over with no way to get help if I need it? It even has GPS, in case I get lost. If I can get service, that is."

Her image of Cybil obviously had nothing to do with reality. For some reason, Gia imagined her living in an overgrown, ramshackle cabin in the middle of the forest surrounded by wildlife and gardens with none of the modern conveniences people had come to depend on. "Don't even tell me you live in a condo complex."

"No. But I do have a beautiful house on the edge of the forest. It even has a big screen TV and an elaborate computer system."

"Seriously?"

"My Duke was a very successful computer programmer."

Gia just shook her head, her lesson about jumping to conclusions based on appearances learned.

A niggle of guilt crept in. Hadn't that been what she'd done to Hunt? Condemned him for arresting Trevor without any idea what the reality of the situation might be. She barely kept a groan from escaping as she turned onto the narrow dirt road that led to the shelter.

Chapter 9

The minute she opened the car door, Thor made a beeline for Debby, who stood waiting on the front porch of the shelter.

Debby dropped to one knee and threw her arms around his neck. When he snuggled against her, she straightened and petted his side with both hands. "Look at you. You got so big already, fella."

"He did, didn't he?"

Debby stood and shook Gia's hand. "I don't know, looks like it might be time for a little brother or sister."

"Bite your tongue. I love Thor, but I'm not ready to get another one yet."

"Yet." Debby grinned. "We're making progress."

Gia laughed. The fact she'd even consider another dog still came as a bit of a surprise. "Anyway, for now, I'm just along for the ride."

Debby turned and greeted Cybil. "I'm so happy you finally decided to come in."

"Me too."

She ushered them inside. The local news played on a small TV on the waiting room's far wall. Debby muted a story about the art and craft fair coming up the following week. "Sorry, I was waiting for the story about Ron Parker to come back on. Not that I haven't seen it a hundred times already, but I just can't wrap my head around the fact he's dead. Murdered, no less."

"Did you know Ron?"

"Come sit." She gestured to a seating arrangement in the far corner, then took a bone from a bin on the far wall and handed it to Thor. "Would you like coffee?"

"No, thank you." Gia was already having enough trouble sleeping without adding caffeine. She took a seat on a beat-up armchair, while Cybil and

Debby sat on the love seat opposite her on the other side of a low table. Thor settled at her feet to gnaw on his bone.

It felt good to finally be off her feet after running around all day.

"As for Ron Parker…" Debby clasped her hands together, her knuckles turning white. "Yes, I knew him. He was my boyfriend, once upon a time, for about a week in the ninth grade."

"I'm sorry for your loss, dear." Cybil patted her hands.

"Thank you, but I haven't seen Ron since high school. When we started dating, he seemed like a nice boy, but when he was around Mitch Anderson and his groupies, he turned into a real jerk. He took me to hang out with them one time, and it was awful, so I cut my losses and moved on."

Someone else had said Ron and Mitch Anderson were friends in high school as well, but Gia had listened to so much gossip about them over the past two days, she couldn't remember who'd said it. "Were Ron and Anderson close?"

"Very. That whole group was, to the exclusion of practically everyone else. The one time I was with them, not one of them even bothered to talk to me, and when I tried to talk, they ignored me. And what did Ron do? Nothing. He just laughed along with them like I wasn't even there."

If Debby had been half as friendly and talkative in high school as she was now, Gia could see how uncomfortable that would have been for her.

Debby frowned. "That's why I was so surprised to see Ron running against Mitch."

"You're not the first person to say that. Do you think they had some kind of falling out?"

Debby lifted her hands wide. "I have no idea, but I also haven't seen Ron in…well…more years than I care to admit."

Gia didn't see a way to push for more information on Ron and Mitch, so she tried a different tact. "Who else was part of that group? Do you remember?"

"Umm…let me think. I guess it was the two of them, Bobby Fischetti and Trevor Barnes. I don't remember one of the girls' names. Andrea or Abigail, something with an A. I didn't really know her. And Gabriella Antonini. She was dating Bobby Fischetti at the time. Don't know what ever happened with those two. They left town right after high school."

"Actually, they were in the café yesterday. They were talking to Skyla, said they'd gotten married right out of high school and moved to Georgia." Okay, so they hadn't exactly said they'd moved to Georgia; Gia had stalked them on Facebook, but why split hairs?

"Skyla Broussard?"

"Yes. You know her?"

"Not well, but if I remember correctly, she was part of that group too. She used to date one of the boys. Ron, I think. Or maybe it was Mitch." Debby frowned and stared off into space for a minute or two. "No, sorry. I can't remember which one. It was a long time ago. Well, not that long, but my memory is not as good as it once was."

If Skyla had dated Ron, that would explain her reaction when she found out he'd been murdered. But why wouldn't she just say she'd known him? It didn't explain her weird reaction to seeing the Fischettis, though. "Was Skyla friendly with Gabriella Antonini?"

"As far as I remember, they were all pretty tight. Like I said, they didn't really bother with anyone else."

"Did they ever fight amongst themselves?"

"I don't know. I never paid them much attention after that one night. I wasn't interested in the same things as they were. Hard to forge friendships with no common ground."

"That's true." She thought of Gabriella and Skyla. Somehow, Gia couldn't picture them as close friends, though she couldn't say why. She saw a flash of Gabriella standing on the sidewalk outside the café, held still by the other woman's firm hold on her arm. "Could the other woman you were thinking of be named Allison?"

Debby pursed her lips, but then shook her head right away. "It's possible, but I don't remember. Why?"

She couldn't see any reason not to share what had taken place on a public street. "I saw Gabriella out in front of the café today, and she was arguing with a woman named Allison. I thought maybe that was her."

"It could have been, but I'm not sure." Debby's gaze shifted to the TV.

The lead story began with the footage of Trevor being escorted into the station.

"Do you really think he could have done it?" Debby asked quietly. "I wasn't friendly with Trevor in high school, but I've seen him around since he opened the shop, and he always seemed like such a nice guy."

"He is a nice guy. There has to be some mistake." A bit of anger surged in Gia, not at Debby for asking the question everyone in Boggy Creek wanted the answer to, but at Trevor for avoiding Hunt's questions. If he had simply answered honestly, none of this would be happening. Unless, of course, he was guilty. Gia gasped. How could she have even thought such a thing?

Cybil stood. "It's getting late, and I want to have time to get my new baby home and settled tonight."

Debby jumped to her feet. "Oh, you'll be taking him home tonight?"

"Is that okay?"

"Um…" Debby headed for the counter and held the half-door open for them to precede her through to the back room. "It depends on who you pick out. Why don't you choose a pup you like, then we'll figure it out?"

When Thor stood to follow Gia, she told him to stay and petted his head. "I'll be right back, boy."

"Puppies are nice and all," Cybil said, "but I was thinking of taking something older, something not everyone would want."

A huge grin lit Debby's face. "I wish more people thought like you. Most people want a puppy, but some of these guys have been here for a long time, and they don't have much chance of finding a forever home. As much as I love all of them, they need families."

Debby led them through the puppy room and through a door on the opposite side. Several small pens lined one wall, all with half-doors that allowed you to see the dogs living in each pen. "You can look around and see if one catches your eye."

Gia walked along the corridor, peeking into each pen. Some of the dogs jumped and propped their front paws on their doors, some stayed lying where they were and simply looked up as she passed, others continued to sleep as if nothing could disturb them. "How long can they stay here?"

"As long as they live." Debby pulled a hardcover ledger out of a desk drawer. "We're a no-kill rescue and adoption organization. Our animals stay with us until they find a forever home or eventually pass on."

"Do a lot of people adopt older dogs?" Gia reached over a half-door to pet a big black dog she thought might be part German shepherd.

"Some do. Most want puppies, but some prefer an older dog."

Cybil had stopped at one of the pens and leaned over the half-door to pet one of the dogs. "Can I open the door?"

"Sure, go ahead," Debby said as she flipped through the ledger pages.

Gia started to follow, but her phone rang. She fished it out of her pocket and checked the caller ID, then excused herself and stepped out front to answer. "Hey, Savannah, what's up?"

"Where are you?"

She dropped onto the chair, and Thor propped his chin on her leg. She petted his head. "At the shelter with Cybil. Why? Is something wrong?"

"Is Thor with you?"

"Yes. Why?"

"Oh, good. I was on Facebook, and I saw a post that someone found a Bernese mountain dog roaming in your development. There's no picture yet, but the post said the dog was clean and well-groomed but didn't have any tags, and I wanted to make sure it wasn't Thor."

"Nope, Thor's right here with his head in my lap." She scratched behind his ears, and his eyes rolled back in his head. "You know who has a Bernese mountain dog, though? Nancy. She took John to the shelter to pick one out right after meeting Thor."

"Oh, that's right. I'll give her a call now."

"Wait. Have you heard from anyone?"

"Not yet. I didn't expect to hear from Hunt so soon, but I'd have expected Leo to call by now."

Gia would have expected Leo to call as well. It was rare for him to go longer than a few hours without calling to reassure Savannah all was well. "Have you tried to call him?"

"Not in the past hour or so."

Gia laughed. "Okay, okay. I get it. I'll stop asking."

"Don't worry about it. I'm as anxious as you are."

Somehow Gia doubted that. "Listen, one more thing before you call Nancy. Did you go to school with Trevor?"

"We went to the same school, but he was a few years ahead of me, around Hunt's age, I think."

"Do you remember offhand who he used to hang out with?"

"Not at all. I only vaguely remember knowing who Trevor was in high school. I didn't meet him until later, after he opened Storm Scoopers. Why?"

"I'll explain it all later, but the short version is that Trevor used to hang out with Ron Parker and Mitch Anderson, and supposedly the three of them were really close."

"Then why would Trevor kill Ron?"

Gia tempered her anger. No sense fighting with Savannah. "He *didn't* kill him."

"Oh, I know, I just meant it doesn't make sense he'd try to kill him. If he did. Which he didn't."

"And yet, Hunt arrested him."

Savannah didn't say anything. She didn't need to. They both knew he had to have just cause. "Anyway, go call Nancy. She'll be worried sick if her pup is missing. I'll catch up with you later."

Savannah disconnected.

Gia checked for missed calls, hoping she'd missed one from either Hunt or Trevor. Nothing. With a sigh, she stuffed the phone in her pocket and went to find Cybil.

She found her sitting on the floor of a pen with a medium-sized dog curled in her lap.

"Who's this?"

"This is Caesar. He's a four-year-old beagle mix, and he's coming home with me."

"He's adorable." Gia entered the pen, closed the half-door behind her, and squatted beside Cybil and her new pup.

Tears shimmered in Cybil's eyes when she looked up at Gia. "I don't know how I can ever thank you."

Warmth surged through her. "You just did."

Cybil hugged Caesar close and nuzzled her cheek against his head. "You can take him home tonight?"

"Not tonight, only because it's so late. I'll have to come back tomorrow, but this little guy is all mine." She kissed his head.

"He's adorable."

"Yes, he is."

Debby peeked into the pen. "Are you ready?"

Cybil groaned, but kissed Caesar once more, put him down, and stood.

"I'm sorry you can't take him tonight, Cybil. If I didn't have to be at my son's concert in a little while, I'd have stayed to do the paperwork, especially since you've adopted so many dogs here over the years."

"I understand. Besides, I'm going to have to dig a few things out of the shed for him and I should run to the pet supply for food and more treats."

Debby led them to the door, then said good-bye and locked up.

"Do you need a ride tomorrow?" Gia asked.

"Thank you, but I'll be fine. I appreciate you coming with me tonight, but I know you have to work in the morning, and I want to be here bright and early to pick him up."

Gia stopped with her hand on the car door handle and looked over the roof at her. "You're not going to walk here, are you?"

Cybil laughed. "Gia, I don't walk everywhere because I can't drive. I walk because I enjoy it."

"You have a car?"

"Of course, an SUV, which I enjoy taking off-road whenever I get a chance." She climbed into the car.

Cybil was so far from what Gia had imagined she had to laugh. She let Thor into the back seat then got in, started the car, and headed down the long driveway.

They drove in silence for a few minutes. If the smile playing at the edges of Cybil's mouth was any indication, she was probably lost in thoughts of her new puppy.

Meanwhile, Gia's mind ran amok with troubling thoughts of Trevor and Hunt.

"Make a right here." Cybil pointed to a narrow street lined with palm trees that met above the road and formed a beautiful archway.

"This is so pretty."

"Thank you. My house is at the end of the street."

Gia followed her directions and pulled up to a sprawling, stucco ranch house. Somehow the thought of Cybil wandering through all that empty space was sadder than the image of her living in a cozy cabin in the woods. When she'd seen her with Caesar, the realization that Cybil seemed lonely had hit her hard. "Why don't you come into the café for breakfast tomorrow morning on your way to pick up Caesar?"

Cybil took Gia's hand in her own and squeezed. "I'd like that. Do you want to know what I believe?"

"Sure."

"I believe there are a few people we meet in our lives who are meant to be a part of something special. Sometimes lasting friends, other times just part of an important event in your life. Either way, I think we recognize those people when our paths cross. When I first met you walking in the woods with Thor…"

Thor poked his head between the seats at the mention of his name.

Cybil laughed and petted him. "There was something about you that called to me. I knew you'd play a role in my life in some way."

Gia recalled their first meeting. She'd been confused—conflicted, as Cybil had phrased it—and Cybil had offered advice. She'd felt something too, a sort of connection.

Cybil held her gaze. "I'm really glad we met."

"Me too."

"I'd love to stop by the café in the morning. Thank you."

Gia took Cybil's walking stick out of the trunk, walked her to the door, and said goodnight, then headed home still thinking of Cybil. She'd seen that same loneliness in another friend's eyes too, and as much as she was hoping she and Cybil would become friends, she had to admit to herself that she had an ulterior motive for inviting her to the café early. With any luck at all, Earl and Cybil would also hit it off and become friends.

Chapter 10

Once Gia fed and walked Thor, she heated her dinner and took it to the living room with a diet soda. She set up her laptop on the coffee table beside her dinner, dropped onto the couch, and set to work. Now that she had some idea whom to look for, maybe she could make sense of what was going on. She put her cell phone right next to her computer and checked to make sure the ringer was turned on and the volume was turned up. Again.

Thor jumped onto the couch beside her, trying to wiggle his head onto her lap.

She laughed and scooted him over. "Not yet, Thor. I have to eat first."

He grudgingly settled at her side with a chew toy.

The first thing she did was look for a website with old yearbooks and school photos. She'd have to start with people she knew, then go from there.

She took a bite of breakfast pie while she waited for the site to load. She didn't often eat the meat lover's pie, loaded with bacon, sausage, ham, peppers, onions, and cheese, but she'd been in the mood for it tonight, and it definitely hit the spot.

Once the search box came up, she typed in Boggy Creek high school, then waited some more. While it took its time loading, Gia jumped up and grabbed a pad and pen from the side table drawer and made a mug of peach tea.

When she returned, she wrote "Ron Parker" in the middle of the page, then added Mitch Anderson's name below it and drew a line connecting them. She wrote "Friends?" next to the line.

When the Boggy Creek High School page came up, she typed in Ron Parker, hit Enter, then returned to her chart. She wrote "Trevor Barnes" in the upper left corner, then connected him to Ron with another line. She wrote "Friends?" next to the line, thought about adding "Killer?" then added "Suspect" instead.

What else did she know? She thought about how the three of them connected, if they even connected, while she finished her dinner. Even if Ron was friends with Mitch Anderson in high school, that didn't mean they'd stayed friends. Maybe they'd had a falling out. Or maybe they just chose different paths and fell out of touch. And even if they had stayed friends, that didn't necessarily mean they shared the same views on politics. So maybe Ron running against him had nothing at all to do with his death. Then again, maybe someone connected to Mitch Anderson wanted to make sure he won the election by eliminating the competition. Except for the fact that, by all accounts, Mitch was probably going to win anyway.

But how in the world did Trevor figure into any of it?

She tossed the pen onto the notepad and rubbed her burning eyes. Exhaustion settled as a dull throb in her temples. She pulled a blanket off the back of the couch, tucked her feet up beneath it, and settled against a throw pillow with her computer in her lap and Thor curled beside her, his head resting against her leg.

Another screen popped up, prompting her to join the site for free. Ugh… One of the downsides of living on the edge of the forest was no high-speed internet. Not bad enough her internet was slow as molasses in January—another of Savannah's favorite expressions—but now she had to waste time joining the website. She typed in her information as quickly as possible, using the email address she saved for such circumstances so as not to clutter her work email, then waited for the page to load.

A young version of the Ron Parker she recognized from the campaign trail smiled out at her from the screen, peering over the wire-rimmed glasses perched on the edge of his nose. Though his name was listed beneath his picture, nothing else had been included. No plans for the future, no senior quote, no fond memories or sports or clubs or anything, as most of the other students on the page had listed.

She typed in Mitch Anderson and sipped her tea while she waited for his picture to come up. When it did, Gia studied him. He looked the same but so much younger. Had she looked that young when she'd graduated high school? She'd felt like an adult, had become one the day she'd graduated and her father had thrown her out to fend for herself.

Mitch Anderson had worn the practiced smile of a politician even then. Beneath his picture were the words "Time to Climb."

At least she confirmed Ron and Mitch had gone to school together. She tried Trevor's name and hit Enter, then waited…and waited…and waited.

A screen popped up telling her this was the last search she could do with her free trial membership. If she wanted to search any more, she'd have to subscribe, and they would bill her credit card monthly, and blah, blah, blah. She had no intention of paying. At least, not yet. There had to be another way to find what she was looking for.

She clicked cancel, and Trevor's headshot popped up, his expression serious. Far from the fun-loving guy she'd come to know. He'd worn his hair in the exact same style in high school as he still did. The quote beneath his photo read, "'If you can imagine it, you can achieve it. If you can dream it, you can become it.' - *William Arthur Ward.*"

Gia could imagine a young Trevor Barnes, full of enthusiasm and ready to conquer the world. She wondered briefly what he'd done between high school and opening Storm Scoopers. Surely, he hadn't had the money to open the ice cream shop right out of high school. Maybe his parents had helped him. Come to think of it, she didn't even know if his parents were alive or if he spoke with them or if he even grew up with them. She didn't know if he had siblings. In all the time they'd hung out together, he'd never once mentioned his family.

Since Gia didn't have any family, she hadn't found it odd at the time, but now, in light of his current circumstances, she was beginning to wonder if he'd been purposefully evasive, avoiding talk of his past.

She shook off the suspicion starting to sneak in. She was being ridiculous. Giving up on the yearbook site, since she wasn't getting up for her credit card, or subscribing to a website she might never use again, she switched to Facebook.

She started with Trevor's name. *Yikes. Who knew the name Trevor Barnes was so popular?* She scrolled through tons of Trevor Barnes without finding her Trevor, then gave up and typed in Mitch Anderson. His name was just as popular, and she didn't find a profile for Mitch, but she did find his public page.

Though she scrolled through several months' worth of posts, Mitch didn't post any personal information. Actually, his posts were all political and routinely posted once a day and could just as easily have been posted by an assistant.

She hit pay dirt with Ron Parker. Not only did he have a profile, but he was quite active, sometimes posting several times a day. In addition to the routine "vote for me" posts, Ron also shared memes regularly, fun facts about local history, and old pictures of the area. Nothing on his profile indicated he knew he was in danger. His last post, which went up on Thursday morning, was a photograph from 1882 of what was now the park by the lake.

She searched his friends for Trevor or Mitch, but neither of them came up. The name Allison brought the same *No results* message. Since she'd already stalked Gabriella's profile, she gave up and started to close the computer, then paused and reopened it. She typed in Skyla Broussard. An image of Skyla and Willow popped up, their heads leaned close together, huge smiles on both of their faces. Skyla's profile was the same as her profile picture, happy and often involving Willow—pride at her acing her exams, an article about her doing volunteer work, even a picture of her mid eye-roll behind the counter at the café.

She had about a hundred and seventy friends, and after a quick search for the usual suspects using the search box, Gia skimmed through all of them. Though many of them were familiar from around town or the café, nothing out of the ordinary jumped out at her.

There was also no mention of going out of town or any emergency that would have kept Willow from coming to work.

She closed the lid, slid the laptop onto the coffee table, and sipped her lukewarm tea. She stared at her chart for a couple of minutes, but she couldn't make any sense of it. Finally, she added Skyla's name to the bottom right corner with a question mark after it. She had no clue how Skyla fit into the equation yet, but couldn't ignore the nagging suspicion that she did.

Giving up for the moment, she checked her phone for missed calls. Nothing. She tried Willow again for the umpteen-millionth time, again to no avail. Having exhausted all her options, she lifted her laptop lid enough to stuff the chart inside, closed the laptop, stood, and stretched.

"Come on, Thor." She yawned as she headed down the hallway toward the bedroom, then dug her suitcase out from the very back of the closet. She wanted to stay late at the café tomorrow, maybe even stay over at the apartment above it, so she'd have time to make sure everything was prepped for Monday morning. If Willow showed up, of course. Without Willow to run the dining room, Gia wasn't going anywhere.

As usual, the thought of leaving anyone else to run things brought a tidal wave of anxiety. As did the thought of leaving Thor. Even though she had no doubt Joey would take good care of him, she hadn't left him since he'd come to live with her. She petted his head where he lay sprawled on the floor next to her.

He nuzzled her for a moment, then scrambled to his feet and fled the room, the *click, click, click* of his nails against the floor following him down the hallway.

Sweat popped out on her forehead, and she wiped it with her sleeve. She'd beat herself up over going away a million times already, always with the same results. At the end of the day, she wasn't going to disappoint Savannah. *If* everything went according to plan and Willow showed up safe and sound.

She pulled a couple of sundresses out of the closet and lay them on the bed, then knelt and dug through her closet for comfy sandals. Though her idea of a vacation involved a lot of time off her feet, she had a sneaking suspicion Savannah's didn't. And if she was going to do a lot of walking, she'd need her comfy shoes. She pulled out a small stack of blankets and unearthed the beige sandals. "Ta da."

"What's that?"

Gia whirled toward the voice and screeched.

Hunt leaned against the doorjamb, arms folded across his chest, cocky grin firmly in place.

Thor stood at his side, head cocked, staring at her.

"Traitor." She pointed to Thor, then rounded on Hunt. "Remind me why I ever gave you a key."

"In case of an emergency. And so I wouldn't have to wait outside for you to come let me in."

She climbed to her feet and brushed the dust from her knees. "Yeah, well, keep sneaking up on me, and you won't have it anymore."

Hunt laughed and opened his arms.

She slid into them, pressed her ear against his chest, and wrapped her arms around his waist. "I wasn't sure when I'd hear from you again."

"Things have been crazy."

Though she waited, he offered nothing more.

She looked up at him without lifting her head from his chest. "Have you eaten?"

"Not in a while."

"I have more than three quarters of a meat lover's pie left, if you want me to heat it up and make a cup of coffee?"

"That sounds perfect."

She reluctantly straightened and headed back to the kitchen. While she started the coffee pot and stuck the pie into the oven, she bit her tongue to keep from asking about Trevor. He'd know she was going crazy wondering what was going on, so if he didn't bring it up, she figured he didn't want to discuss it. And she would respect that. For now. "Are you done working for tonight?"

He glanced at his watch. "Nah, I have to go back in a little while."

His phone rang, and he stepped out onto the back deck, taking Thor with him.

Gia heated the pie and a leftover container of home fries, made his coffee, and set everything on the table. When he still wasn't back, she peeked out the window.

Hunt held up a finger, then said something into the phone, disconnected the call, and whistled for Thor to come in. When he opened the door, Gia refrained from pouncing. She gave herself a mental pat on the back for succeeding. It wasn't easy with a million questions battering at her, begging for answers. "Is everything okay?"

"Yeah, I was waiting for that call. I'm going to have to go back."

"Will you have time to eat first, or should I put it in a container for you to take with you?"

"I have a few minutes." He sat and started eating.

Gia poured herself a cup of coffee, more for something to do than any desire to drink it, then sat across from him. When it was obvious he wasn't going to say anything to alleviate the strained silence between them, Gia blurted, "Are you going to question Trevor again?"

"He's already been released."

"Released? How? I thought you arrested him?"

Hunt finished chewing and swallowed before answering. "He was arrested, and he was arraigned, and then he posted bail and was released."

Gia waited while Hunt took another bite, then swallowed it and sipped his coffee. Now he was starting to get on her nerves. "Are you going to tell me what's going on, or do I have to sit here and play twenty questions?"

He slid his plate back. "What do you want from me, Gia? If I ask you to stay away from Trevor, are you going to listen? Seems you've been spending an awful lot of time with him lately."

The last statement sounded a bit too accusatory. "Trevor is a friend."

"Mmm...hmm..."

Gia lurched back as if he'd slapped her. "What's that supposed to mean?"

"I don't know, Gia, but I just spent the better part of twenty-four hours grilling Trevor about where he's been and who he's been spending time with lately, and your name came up repeatedly."

"We're friends, Hunt. That's it. And you already know that, because I tell you when I'm hanging out with Trevor." Gia couldn't help the hurt at his attitude. "I haven't complained once that you haven't had any time to spend with me since you took over as captain. I understood, and I've tried to be as supportive as possible. Even staying up in the middle of the night to feed you when I have to be up early the next morning for work."

Hunt raked his hands through his thick, dark hair and sighed. "Look, Gia, I'm sorry, okay? I haven't slept in more than thirty-six hours, every agency under the sun is breathing down my neck on this, and my nerves are shot. I'm not accusing you of anything, but there are things I can't tell you, and I have to ask you to keep your distance from Trevor, and I know you're going to give me a hard time about it."

She didn't say anything. What could she say? He was right. She wasn't going to stay away from Trevor without a valid reason. She was about to tell Hunt as much, when she took a good look at him.

Dark circles ringed his deep brown eyes, stress lines bracketed his mouth, and his hair was more disheveled than usual, probably from raking his hands through it as he often did when stressed.

"Hunt, I'm not trying to make things difficult for you. I understand you aren't able to tell me everything. That's the nature of your job, and I respect that. But you have to respect me too. How would you feel if I turned my back on Savannah because someone told me to, without any explanation?"

He hung his head and massaged the bridge of his nose. "You're right. I wouldn't be too happy. And one of the things I love most about you is your fierce sense of loyalty…"

Her heart skipped a beat. *Love?* Had he said *love* most? Probably just an expression.

"But I don't know what's going on with Trevor, and I'm concerned for your safety."

Gia smiled, partly over the *love most* comment but also at the thought of Trevor being in any way dangerous. "You can't possibly think Trevor would do anything to hurt me. That's man's as meek as a teddy bear."

"Or so he lets on." He gritted his teeth together as if to stem the flow of words.

The warm fuzzies she'd started to feel fled. "What's that supposed to mean?"

Jaw clenched, Hunt closed his eyes for a minute, then opened them. "Okay, I'm going to tell you something, but you have to promise me you'll keep it to yourself."

Gia nodded.

"I mean it, Gia. I'm not in the habit of keeping secrets from Savannah, but you can't even tell her. Okay?"

Though keeping secrets from Savannah didn't sit well with her, she knew Hunt would never ask unless it was absolutely necessary, so she agreed.

"This isn't the first time Trevor's been arrested."

She couldn't react in time to school her expression. Although her eyes widened, she did manage to keep her mouth shut.

"Last time, he was a juvenile, and the record was sealed. That's the phone call I was waiting for and just received. His last arrest ended with him being ordered to attend court-mandated anger management classes."

Chapter 11

Gia had tossed and turned all night, unable to sleep after Hunt had left. Despite her practically pleading, he'd clammed up and wouldn't offer another word about Trevor or his past. While she'd stopped short of agreeing to stay away from him completely, she did promise she wouldn't call him.

And it had driven her crazy all night, before she'd finally given up on getting any sleep and headed to the cafe.

Gia shook off thoughts of Trevor and Hunt and Ron Parker, who'd haunted her fitful sleep as well, and tried to focus on the task at hand. She read over the list she'd started and added "restock refrigerator" to the bottom. Most of her stock was kept in a huge walk-in refrigerated case in the back of the storage room, and she regularly refilled the smaller refrigerator in the kitchen. One thing that drove her crazy was a cluttered kitchen, especially the refrigerator. She couldn't take having to move a gazillion things around in order to find what she needed. She simply didn't have time for that, and she ran her kitchen in the most time efficient way possible. Thankfully, Cole got that.

She added "pick up supplies" to the list. Sometime during the day, she'd have to run out for a few things they were running short on. If Willow showed up for work. If not, she'd spend another day running the dining room. She glanced at the clock above the cutout and stuck the list beside the register where she'd be sure to see it a million times. Not that it would matter; she'd still probably forget something.

With one last look around that everything was ready and the coffee pots were all started, she unlocked the door and held it open.

Earl stood outside, as usual, waiting for her to let him in.

"Good morning, Earl."

"Mornin'." He tipped his fisherman's cap on his way past. "Sleep well?"

"Didn't sleep at all, actually." She followed him to his usual stool and poured coffee for both of them, then she sat on the stool next to his.

"Any word on Willow?"

Her gaze shot to the clock again. "Nothing, but she should be here anytime now."

"I'm sure she's fine." The flare of concern in his eyes belied his words.

"I keep racking my brain, trying to remember if she told me she needed off and I just forgot."

Earl gave a half-hearted shrug and sipped his coffee. "We both know that's not likely."

Gia couldn't argue. If Willow had needed off, she'd have told Gia, but she would have also told Savannah and asked her to fill in. Especially on a Sunday morning, her busiest day. "If she doesn't come in, I'll have to run the dining room again. Can you pitch in and help Cole in the kitchen if it gets busy?"

"Of course."

A knock on the front door brought a wave of relief. She looked up expecting to see Willow staring in at her, though she'd given her a key, and found Cybil waving instead. She'd forgotten she'd invited her to breakfast.

"Excuse me." Gia ran and opened the front door. Since no one else was waiting outside and she still had ten minutes before her listed opening time, she ushered Cybil inside and locked the door behind her. She left the keys hanging in the lock and offered her a seat at the counter. "I'm glad you came."

"Me too. I'm not too early, am I?"

"Not at all. Earl and I always share a cup of coffee before I open. Would you like some?"

"Sure, thank you." Cybil propped her walking stick against the wall, hung her cloak on a hook next to it, and settled onto the stool.

Gia stopped short for a second at the sight of Cybil in jeans and a long sleeve T-shirt, then recovered. Her perception of Cybil had been so far off the mark it was laughable. She introduced Cybil to Earl.

"It's a pleasure to meet you, Cybil." He held out his hand.

She captured his hand in both of hers and smiled. "Now this is a content soul."

"Why, yes I am." Earl's eyes lit up.

Gia placed Cybil's coffee in front of her and lay a menu beside the coffee. "Are you excited to pick up Caesar?"

Cybil released Earl's hand and wrapped her hands around the warm cup. "I can't wait. I was up all night getting everything ready for him. As soon as the pet supply store opens, I'll stop for what I need and go get him."

Gia's key ring jiggled in the lock as Willow unlocked the front door, yanked it open, and strode through. "I'm sorry about yesterday, Gia, I... uh..."

Gia rounded the counter and rushed toward her. "Are you okay? Did something happen?"

Willow glanced at Cybil and Earl, then apologized again and lowered her gaze, but not before Gia caught her red-rimmed, puffy eyes.

"Were you sick?"

"No, I umm... My mom needed me."

Getting the impression Willow didn't want to talk in front of anyone, Gia let it go. "I'm glad everything is okay. I was worried."

"I'm sorry to make you worry. I just couldn't get a chance to call."

"It's fine, Willow, really."

Willow nodded and set to work checking that the dining room was stocked. She grabbed an order pad and started writing down what she'd need. It wouldn't be much, since Gia had come in early enough to do it, but Willow seemed to need the routine, so Gia let her go through the motions. She watched her for a moment longer, then glanced at Earl.

He frowned and shook his head briefly.

Gia got out an order pad and pen, then forced her focus to Cybil. "Do you know what you want for breakfast?"

She grinned and gestured a thumb at Earl. "I'll have what he's having."

Gia's eyes went wide as she took in Cybil's frail build. Without the cloak, she appeared even more petite than Gia had realized. "Do you know what he eats for breakfast?"

Earl snorted.

"Oh, no offense, I'm just saying, well...uh..."

Cybil laughed. "Yes, I know what he eats. He told me, and it all sounds so delicious. Now I couldn't eat like that every day, mind you, but I am celebrating a special occasion today, what with Caesar coming home and all, so I figured why not treat myself?"

"Okay, you've got it." Gia tucked the order pad in her apron pocket. "One of everything coming right up."

Cybil and Earl laughed, then returned to their conversation as Gia headed back to start their breakfast orders. Willow would unlock the door in a few minutes, and Gia wanted to get a head start before she did.

She lined bacon and sausage on the grill, started the scrambled eggs, filled plates with home fries and grits, added a small bowl of gravy and a couple of biscuits, flipped the eggs, then loaded everything up onto the plates and put them on the cutout counter for Willow.

When she checked the dining room through the window, she spotted Willow taking an order at a table of three. All three of them already had coffee and juice, as did two other tables whose customers sat perusing the menu. Willow was definitely on her game, but a sadness still lingered in her eyes. Whatever was going on with her, Gia felt bad leaving.

Willow handed Gia the new order slip through the window, since she was standing there staring at her, then grabbed the dishes from the cutout and brought them to Earl and Cybil.

Earl and Cybil seemed to be getting along well, both smiling and laughing as they talked. Gia was glad. If nothing else, they'd both shared a meal with someone and maybe made a new friend. She hoped so. Earl had a huge family, between all of his children and grandchildren, and he seemed to have a number of friends, but he still seemed lonely at times, especially when he spoke of his late wife, Heddie.

She returned to the grill, ladled pancake batter onto hot oil, scrambled eggs, heated sausage and bacon, made toast, and fell into the routine of the busy morning rush. She placed order after order on the cutout counter for Willow as she worked her way down the line of tickets.

Willow hurried in and out too fast for Gia to ask her about what happened, but she couldn't help being worried about Skyla.

When it was almost time for the local churches to start letting out, Cole walked in. "Hey there. I see Willow's back."

"Yes." She scanned the next order and faltered. Oatmeal with blueberries. The same thing Donna Mae Parker, who'd been looking for Harley, had ordered the morning before.

"Did she say if everything was all right?" Cole asked as he washed his hands.

"She didn't really say what happened, but she did say everything was okay, so I'll have to take her word for it. For now, anyway." She made the oatmeal, added a dollop of cream and a sprinkling of blueberries, then started to put the bowl on the cutout for Willow. When she peeked through into the dining room and saw Donna Mae sitting at the counter, she changed her mind. "Hey, Cole, do you mind jumping right in?"

"Not at all." He already had gloves on and was scanning the first ticket. "Go ahead."

Leaving Cole to continue banging out orders, she changed her apron and carried the oatmeal into the dining room.

Donna Mae greeted her with a warm smile. "Good morning, Gia."

"Good morning." Gia set the bowl in front of her.

"It was so good, I couldn't resist." Donna Mae picked up her spoon and dug in. "Mmm…as good as I remember."

"Thank you. I'm glad you enjoyed it."

"One of these days you'll have to give me the recipe."

"Sure."

Donna Mae set her spoon aside on a napkin and folded her hands on the counter. "Were you able to reach Harley?"

"I put the card in his dinner bag, but I haven't looked yet to see if he took it."

She glanced over her shoulder out the window. "Would you, please?"

"I—"

"I know you're busy, and I wouldn't ask if it wasn't urgent that I reach him. Please? I don't know of anyone else he talks to regularly."

"How do you know he talks to me regularly?"

Donna Mae hesitated. "I keep an eye on Harley. Please, Gia. I have to find him."

"All right." Donna Mae's sense of urgency had started to make Gia anxious. With one quick glance around the dining room to make sure everything was under control, Gia ran to the back door, cracked it open, and peeked out. The bag she'd left for Harley the night before was gone. She returned to the dining room, uneasy, though she couldn't place why. If it was the fact that she'd left for thirty seconds, she was in for a rough four days away while everyone else ran the café.

When she returned, it didn't look as if Donna Mae had eaten even one more bite of her oatmeal, though she clung tightly to her coffee mug.

"His bag is gone, and I put your card in the bag with a note to get in touch with you, so I assume he got it."

Her smile faltered. "He hasn't called."

"I'm sorry. I don't know what else I can do. If I see him, I'll tell him to call."

She was shaking her head before Gia even finished her statement. "You don't understand. I have to get in touch with him."

As much as Gia wanted to help, she had no clue what to do. "I don't know what to tell you."

Donna Mae grabbed her wrist, looked around the crowded café, and leaned forward, pitching her voice low. "I have to find him. Now. He may be in danger."

"Danger?"

"Shh…" She leaned back on her stool. "Is there somewhere we can talk privately?"

Everything seemed to be under control in the dining room. Willow smiled as she took orders and chatted up customers, and Gia had no doubt Cole was fine. Orders continued to come out regularly.

"Sure. We can talk in my office."

"No. Not here. Believe me, you do not want to be seen talking to me right now." A tear spilled over Donna Mae's thick lower lashes and rolled down her cheek.

"Okay, wait. Umm…" Gia tried to think. Harley sometimes hung out in a clearing in the woods behind the café. "I know one place he could be. If you go out the front door and around the side of the building, there's an entrance to the upstairs apartment. Go inside and wait for me. I'll see if I can find him, then I'll meet you there."

She looked around and nodded, then took a bite of her oatmeal and waited for Gia to leave.

Gia didn't notice anyone watching either of them as she crossed the room heading toward the back, but that didn't mean anything. She poked her head into the kitchen on her way past to make sure Cole was okay. "Will you be okay for a few minutes if I run out?"

He shot her a quick thumbs-up and continued what he was doing.

She pushed out the back door and did her best to ignore the dumpster as she jogged across the lot. It wasn't only Bradley she'd found in the dumpster; Harley had been hanging out of that same dumpster the day they'd first met.

She stepped onto the grass between the trees without looking and caught a flash of something green skittering up a tree trunk at her side. Startled, she jumped back before a fairly large lizard hopped from the trunk to a bush beside the tree. One of these days she would probably get used to the wildlife in Florida, but for today, she couldn't even believe she'd almost bolted into the woods without so much as a glance at her surroundings. And her bear spray was tucked safely in her purse in the desk drawer in her office. Good place for it. Unless of course she came across a bear or any other wildlife set on eating her.

Moving more cautiously than she had been, she made her way to the clearing where a tree stump stood empty. No Harley.

The chances of him being there had been slim, but that didn't curb her disappointment. Seemed like whatever she tried to do lately wound up at a dead end. Maybe getting away for a few days was a good idea; it might give her a fresh perspective.

She emerged from the narrow strip of woods, brushed off her clothes and shook out her hair, which did nothing to relieve the sensation of things crawling on her. She shivered beneath the hot sun and strode across the parking lot toward the apartment door. She was done playing around. Time to get some answers.

She rounded the corner of the building, intent on making Donna Mae Parker tell her what was going on, and plowed straight into a man's back.

Chapter 12

Harley stumbled away from the wall he'd been leaning against, tearing his gaze away from the apartment door. "Oh, Gia. I'm sorry, I didn't know you were there."

Gia bit back an angry retort. She wasn't mad; he'd just scared the daylights out of her. "No, Harley, it's my fault. I wasn't looking where I was going. I'm sorry."

Harley smiled and smoothed a hand over his more-gray-than-blond beard. "It's okay."

"What are you doing here anyway?" Now that some of the shock of running into him had passed, she was beginning to realize something was off.

"Just watching."

A car horn beeped, and Harley whirled toward the street.

Harley didn't quite seem himself. Tremors rocked his hands, and he seemed jittery, jumping at every sound. "Watching what?"

"Watching her."

"Watching whom?" Gia reminded herself to be patient. Getting information out of Harley could be a bit like pulling teeth.

"My girlfriend."

"Your...girlfriend?" Harley had a girlfriend? Wow, the rumor mill sure had dropped the ball on that one.

"Not anymore. But once." Harley zoned out, staring off into space, a content smile softening his features. Then his expression hardened. "That was before."

"Before? Before what?"

"Before my brother…" He hesitated, his gaze somewhere far away. "He shouldn't have."

"Shouldn't have what?" Gia was more confused than she'd ever been in her life. She hadn't realized Harley had family around. "Who is your brother?"

"My brother?" Harley scratched his head through the long tangle of hair that hung limp down his back past his shoulders.

"Yes. You said you had a brother. What's his name?"

"Mitchell."

"Mitchell?" What had Donna Mae called Harley? Harley Anderson? Surely, he couldn't possibly be talking about Mitch Anderson.

"Yes. But that was a long time ago." Harley started off at his regular stilted pace, limping a little worse than usual.

Gia called after him. "Where are you going?"

He kept walking.

She tried again. "Are you okay, Harley?"

This time he stopped and turned. "I'm good."

"Why are you leaving? Didn't you get my note that Donna Mae wants to speak to you?"

Harley's eyes clouded over. "Yes."

"She's upstairs now. You know that, right?"

He nodded and turned away, then hobbled across the back parking lot and kept going without looking back.

Gia thought briefly about running up and telling Donna Mae he was there, but she stopped herself as she watched Harley limp into the patch of woods behind the parking lot. If Gia told her, she'd go running after him, and she'd most certainly catch him, so Gia would keep her mouth shut. If Harley didn't want to speak to her, whatever his reasons, she'd respect that.

But she was going to get some answers.

She whipped open the door and found Donna Mae standing in the small foyer. "Donna Mae?"

"I heard."

Gia looked over her shoulder, but Harley was no longer in sight. "I'm sorry, I tried to—"

She held up her hand. "I know. I heard."

"But you didn't come out."

"No."

"Why not? I thought you wanted to talk to him?"

Her hands trembled as she dug a crumpled tissue out of her bag. "If he was watching me, he already knows."

"Knows what?"

"That we're in danger, all of us."

"Who's in danger?"

"You seem like a really nice person, Gia, and I'm happy Harley has you for a friend." She lowered her gaze and started past her.

"I thought you said you wanted to talk privately?" No way was she walking away with no explanation. Gia grabbed her arm. "Please, tell me what's going on."

"I can't. Not here, and not now." She pulled her arm away. "I have to get my shop open. Thank you for breakfast. It was very good."

With no way to stop her—short of knocking her over, restraining her, and demanding answers—Gia watched her go. But she couldn't shake the feeling Donna Mae's odd behavior had something to do with Ron Parker's death. Especially if her suspicions were correct, and Harley's brother was actually Mitch Anderson.

Mitch Anderson, who was supposedly good friends with Ron Parker. Ron Parker, who was Mitch Anderson's opponent.

Gia gave up trying to make any sense of it for the moment, but when she got home, she'd have to remember to add Donna Mae and Harley's names to the chart she'd started. Though she had no idea how the two of them could be connected to Ron's murder.

She made a mental note to update the chart as she tried to bring it into focus in her mind. Harley Anderson. And…wait a minute…what had Donna Mae's card said? She hadn't paid close attention at the time, but if she remembered correctly, her name was Donna Mae Parker. Coincidence? While Anderson and Parker were two common enough names, what were the chances of first Harley, then Donna Mae, sharing names with two people connected to this whole mess and not being related to them? Slim to none in Gia's mind.

As she rounded the front of the café, she glanced down the street. Storm Scoopers should be open now, people sitting at the few wrought-iron table sets Trevor kept out front. Somehow, the town seemed emptier without Trevor's shop open.

After being gone longer than she should have already, she tucked the thought aside for later. She scanned the dining room as she hurried back into the café, greeting people as she moved through the room, but not stopping to chat. The room was packed, and she'd left Cole alone on the grill. A pang of guilt shot through her. Cole had agreed to pitch in and help, not run a busy lunch shift by himself.

She rushed into the kitchen, donned her apron, washed her hands, and pulled on gloves. "I'm sorry."

Cole frowned at her while flipping three eggs and didn't lose one yolk. "Sorry? For what?"

"Leaving you alone while it's so busy." She scanned the order slips tacked above the grill and counted what Cole had already started.

Cole laughed. "No worries, Gia. I told you when we first met, I sometimes miss the rush. Sometimes, mind you. I don't want to go back to doing this all day long, every day, but I'm not gonna lie—it sure is nice sometimes. Keeps the mind sharp and the fingers nimble."

"What do you need me to do?"

"Everything's set up"—he gestured toward the line of plates on the counter—"if you could just add home fries and bread to each."

She glanced at the tickets, popped four slices of whole wheat bread and two slices of rye into the toasters, then spooned out six helpings of home fries and one of grits, buttered the toast, added strawberry jelly to two slices, arranged them on the plates and held them out for Cole to add the eggs and meat, then slid them onto the cutout. She filled a bowl with gravy and put it on a plate, then added two biscuits. Cole added scrambled eggs and bacon and slid the plate onto the cutout for Willow.

The two of them worked smoothly together, each able to anticipate what the other would need. Though Gia usually worked the grill, while Cole did the extras, he seemed content, so Gia left him to it. She kept up with the breads, fruits, a couple orders of oatmeal, breakfast pies...

Her mind wandered as she worked in smooth rhythm with Cole, wondering about Harley's involvement and Donna Mae, the mysterious Allison, the Fischettis, Skyla's odd behavior of late and Trevor, whom she still hadn't heard from despite him having been released at least twenty-four hours ago.

She contemplated motives for murder. What made people kill? Jealousy. Who could have been jealous of Ron Parker? Greed. What could Ron have had that someone else could have wanted? Revenge. Had Ron done something so awful to someone it had led to his death? To keep a secret hidden.

"Gia!"

She jerked back to reality just in time to avoid burning six slices of toast. "Oh, no."

"Your mind seems a million miles away today. You all right?" Cole stacked pancakes onto a plate and slid it onto the counter for Gia.

As soon as she finished buttering the barely salvaged toast, she added a side dish of butter and a small carafe of warm syrup to the pancake plate and stuck it on the cutout. "Yeah, sorry. Just a lot on my mind."

"You know there's nothing you can do right now, right?"

She shrugged. "I just wish Trevor would call. I'm worried about him."

"Have you tried calling him?"

"Not lately." She didn't add her promise to Hunt that she wouldn't. No sense opening that particular can of worms. "But I left a million messages for him, and he hasn't returned my calls."

"I'm sure he has his reasons." He handed her another filled plate. "He'll call when he's ready."

"I guess." But Gia didn't share his certainty. And trying to figure out why he wasn't calling made her as crazy as wondering if he was okay.

"So, what did you decide about the steak and eggs? Want to give them a try as soon as you get back from your trip?"

"Trip?"

Cole just stared at her. "Seriously? Do not let Savannah hear you say that."

Ah jeez. He was right. She really had to get her head in the game. "Yes. We'll give it a try as soon as I get back. I'm excited about it. I think that's exactly what I've been looking for to bring in a busier dinner crowd."

"Get Earl to come in for dinner one night, and we'll try it out on him."

Gia laughed. "I'll see what I can do, but after the breakfast that man packs away, I can't imagine he'd be hungry for dinner."

Cole pointed with the spatula. "You could be right."

She felt bad she hadn't gotten back out to see Earl and Cybil before they'd left, though Willow had let her know Earl had picked up the bill, despite Gia's continued insistence that he didn't have to pay. And Cybil had eaten every bite. She made a mental note to call Cybil and see how picking up Caesar had gone.

Her mental to-do list was getting longer and longer. If she didn't start writing this stuff down somewhere, there was no way she'd remember to do it all. She hadn't even remembered she was supposed to go away in less than a day.

"Maybe we could ask Savannah and Leo and Hunt too. Just to make sure we get a range of opinions," Cole said.

Gia warmed to the idea. A nice night with friends over dinner. "You know what? I'll be back Friday morning; why don't we do it after I close on Saturday night? We'll invite everyone."

"Works for me."

With that decided, and the lunch rush coming to an end, Cole handed the spatula over to Gia, stripped off his apron, and washed his hands. "If you're good now, I'll go home and put together a menu and list of what we'll need."

"Perfect, thanks, Cole. For everything."

"Anytime." He winked. "And don't worry about a thing. Willow and I will keep this place running while you're gone. You just relax and have some fun."

I wish. Between leaving Thor, leaving the café, and the whole situation revolving around Ron Parker's murder, she couldn't imagine lying on a beach somewhere sunning herself would in any way relax her.

"Oh, Cole," she called after him.

"Yeah?"

"You'll remember to leave Harley's dinner out back, right?"

"Of course. Don't worry, Gia. We've got this." He waved as he walked out.

"Gia?" Willow poked her head in the door. "Do you have a minute?"

She still had to get everything prepped for the week, but it was early enough. And the worst of the day's rush should be over. "Sure."

She tugged off her apron and headed out front.

Willow stood behind the counter, two cold brew coffees in front of her.

A few customers still lingered over their lunch and coffee, but no new customers had entered.

Gia plopped onto a stool and gratefully accepted the coffee Willow offered. She sipped the cold brew. She could definitely taste chocolate, but there was something else too. Something she couldn't quite place. "Mmm...what kind is this?"

"It's something new I tried, cocoa and almond milk. Do you like it?"

"It's delicious. I'll add it to the menu."

"Awesome." A slight flare of excitement tinged her eyes but dissipated just as quickly.

Gia took another sip, then lowered her cup to the counter. "How are you doing, Willow?"

She swirled her straw, creating a small whirlpool in her coffee. "Things are weird."

"What do you mean weird?"

She shook her head and spread her hands wide. "I have no clue what's going on with my mom, but she's acting completely irrational, and I don't know what to do about it."

Gia looked over her shoulder to make sure no one was paying attention before speaking quietly. "Irrational, how?"

"Take yesterday, for instance. I'm so sorry for not showing up without calling." She seemed on the verge of tears.

"I already told you not to worry about that."

The poor girl apparently had enough on her plate without the added stress of having missed one day of work.

"I know, and thank you, but I do worry about it. My mother is the one who taught me to be so responsible, but yesterday, she wouldn't let me come in. She wouldn't even let me call you to let you know. She confiscated my phone while I was sleeping, then woke me up and told me to get dressed because we had to go out of town."

"Out of town? Where'd you go?"

"That's just it; my mom spent most of the day driving around central Florida. We drove up into the forest for a few hours, drove down the East Coast, then cut back across past the airport and the theme parks. It seemed aimless to me, like she had no clue where she was going, but she kept checking the rearview mirror as if she expected to see someone back there. I swear she spent more time looking behind her than she did where she was going. She wouldn't even stop somewhere for lunch, just grabbed something at a drive-thru and kept on driving. The only time she got out of the car was to pump gas or use the restrooms."

Gia didn't know what to say to Willow. While she was mature beyond her years, she was still only eighteen years old and obviously scared for her mother. Scared. That was it. Skyla's behavior was that of a woman who was scared, but of what? Donna Mae had said Harley was in danger. Harley was keeping an eye on Donna Mae. Could Skyla be in danger too? And Willow?

"What did your mom tell you?"

"Nothing." Willow chewed her thumbnail, her gaze darting between the few tables that were still occupied. "She wouldn't tell me anything, and when I pushed her on it, she blew up and told me she had a lot on her mind and couldn't I give her a break and do what I was told just once without asking questions."

"That doesn't sound like Skyla."

"No, it doesn't. Mom has answered every question I've ever asked since I can remember. Anything. No matter how uncomfortable, no matter how personal, no matter how…" She stiffened.

"What?"

"My father."

"Your father?"

"That's the only question my mother never answered. When I was around twelve, I asked about my father, who he was, why I didn't know him. She told me he was dead and it was too painful for her to talk about. She begged me to let it go."

"And did you?"

"Yeah." She returned to stirring her coffee. "I figured it didn't really matter, since he was gone anyway, so I dropped it. No sense upsetting her, right? I hoped she'd talk more about it when I was older."

"But she never did?"

"Nope. Not a word."

A group of five customers entered, ending the conversation as Willow went to greet them.

Gia's mind reeled. Skyla had never struck Gia as secretive, and yet, there were obviously some kind of skeletons buried in her past.

Willow hurried past to get the coffee pot.

Gia stopped her. She didn't want to overstep, but someone needed to figure out what was going on with Skyla. "Do you want me to try to talk to your mom?"

"Oh, would you?"

"Of course. I'll try to get her tonight, but if I can't, I'll talk to her as soon as I get back."

"Thank you so much, Gia. I'm worried sick, and I have no idea where to turn."

Chapter 13

Gia had tried calling Skyla several times throughout the evening with no luck. By the time she had everything prepped for the week, after picking up Thor, it had been too late to drive by Skyla's house. There was no way she could call at this time of the morning, so she'd have to call later on. It could probably wait until she got home, but Willow had been so worried.

She made one more circuit of her house to make sure she hadn't forgotten to turn anything off, dragged her bag to the foyer and left it beside the front door, then knelt down and petted Thor. "You be a good boy for Joey, you hear me?"

Thor tilted his head into her hand.

Leaving him was breaking her heart, but what choice did she have? She couldn't take him with her. The thought of rescheduling their trip popped back into her head, but she ignored it. Savannah needed this trip, and truth be told, Gia could use some time to clear her head as well.

The doorbell rang, and she blew out a breath before peeking out the window and opening the door for Joey. "Hey."

"Hey there." He bent to pet Thor. "Hey, big fella. Looks like it's just gonna be you and me for a few days."

"Thanks for picking him up, Joey. I could have dropped him off."

"I know. But it's no problem. I just finished playing my new video game, which I have no doubt I'll regret while I try to stay awake all day, and I'm getting ready to head to bed for a few hours before I drop Thor off at day care and go to work. Savannah's running a little late, though. She said to tell you she'd be here in a little while."

Gia laughed. When Savannah had said three thirty, Gia knew she wouldn't be there until at least four, maybe later. Despite wanting to get an early start, so they'd be there by lunchtime, Savannah was not a morning person.

"Thanks." She clipped Thor's leash to his collar, second-guessed her decision to leave twelve more times, then hugged him goodbye and handed the leash and Thor's bag to Joey. She watched them until they got into the car and Joey waved and pulled out of the driveway. Then she shut the door and stared around the foyer, empty but for her bags. She missed Thor already and had to resist the urge to call Joey and tell him to come back.

She needed something to occupy her mind before she followed through on the thought.

Savannah still wasn't there, so she flopped onto the couch and opened her laptop to check the weather for the week. The chart of suspects she'd started fluttered out onto the floor. She picked it up and studied it for a moment, then grabbed the pen she'd left on the coffee table and jotted Harley Anderson and Donna Mae Parker to the right bottom of the chart. She drew a line from Harley to Mitch and wrote "Brothers" on it, then drew one from Harley to Donna Mae and wrote "Couple." She considered drawing a line connecting Donna Mae to Ron, but she couldn't be sure there even was a connection between the two, though she suspected they were siblings, or perhaps cousins since they shared the same last name.

Even with the addition of those two names, staring at the chart brought no great revelation. But there was some connection. There had to be. She looked at Skyla's name on the bottom right. She needed to get in touch with her, not only because she'd promised Willow, but because she was worried about her.

Then her gaze fell on Trevor's name. What in the world did he have to do with Ron Parker's murder? Although she had no doubts at all he wasn't the killer, the fact that Ron had been killed in Trevor's shop couldn't possibly be a random coincidence. Could it?

A horn beeped out front, and Gia shut the laptop and laid the chart on top of it. She grabbed her bags, locked the door behind her, and ran to the car, careful to check for any scary critters along the way.

Savannah opened the trunk and put Gia's bags in next to hers. "Are you ready?"

"As I'll ever be." She smoothed her skirt as she climbed into the passenger seat of Savannah's blue Mustang, the leather interior cool against her bare legs.

Savannah got behind the wheel, then shot her a grin. "How many times did you think about calling to cancel?"

Gia laughed. She couldn't help it; Savannah knew her all too well. "I didn't, though. That's all that matters."

Savannah shifted into reverse and backed out of the driveway. She flipped on the radio, and soft rock filled the car.

The thick woods gave the appearance of black walls lining either side of the road, swallowing them whole.

Gia shook off her sense of claustrophobia. She hadn't had more than a few hours' sleep, and her eyes started to drift closed. As soon as they did, thoughts of Trevor flooded her open mind. "Have you talked to Hunt or Leo?"

"I saw Leo tonight. Didn't Hunt come by to say goodbye?"

"No." And Gia had been more than a little hurt. She understood there was a lot going on, but she'd hoped he'd be able to get away for a little while to come see her before she left.

"Probably just busy."

"I'm sure," Gia agreed, because what else could she say?

"Have you had the news on?"

"No." Gia rarely turned on the TV at home, usually only when Savannah or Hunt were at the house and wanted to watch a movie. Or when she was having trouble sleeping in all the quiet, which happened sometimes. Then she turned on the TV to save herself from her own thoughts. "Is something new going on?"

"Not really. Mitch Anderson issued a statement mourning Ron's loss. And someone did leak how Ron Parker was killed."

"Oh? How?"

"Rumor has it he was stabbed with an ice pick, though they were careful to remind everyone that has not been officially released or confirmed."

"Huh." An image of Trevor running into the café flashed before her. She hadn't noticed any blood on him, not that she'd been looking for it, but still. "I just can't picture Trevor stabbing anyone."

Savannah switched the radio off. "Me neither, and I'm not saying he did, but you hear people on the news all the time saying they can't believe their neighbor was a killer, he was such a nice guy…"

"But Trevor? He wouldn't hurt a fly, Savannah. You know that."

The tires hummed softly against the pavement in the early morning silence, every so often thumping over a crack.

"Yeah, I guess I do. But if he was innocent, why didn't he just answer Hunt's questions?"

And wasn't that the million-dollar question? What could have made Trevor so reluctant to talk to Hunt? "Maybe he was protecting someone."

Wasn't that another motive for murder? Could Ron have been killed—not by Trevor of course—to protect someone? But whom? And, more importantly, who would Trevor lie to protect? Could he know who the killer was?

"You think maybe he knows who the killer is and didn't say anything?" Savannah's thoughts, as usual, followed Gia's own.

"It doesn't seem likely, huh? And why? Why would he keep his mouth shut if he knew who killed Ron?" She tried to put herself in Trevor's place. Who would she lie to protect? Savannah, for sure. She'd do anything to protect Savannah, but would she cover up the fact that she'd committed a murder? Would she take the blame and allow herself to be arrested to keep her secret? She honestly didn't know. The idea of Savannah killing anyone was so far-fetched she couldn't even contemplate it as a serious scenario. "Would you lie to protect someone you love?"

Savannah remained quiet for a few minutes before answering. "I would lie to protect you, or Leo, or Hunt, or anyone in my family really, but to cover up a murder? I just don't know. I guess it would depend on the reason. But let's say you killed someone, and I felt it was justified. Why not just tell the detectives what happened?"

"That's just it; I can't think of a reason he'd stay quiet."

"Me neither."

Gia stared out the window as miles of dark wilderness passed by. "Do you know where Trevor lives?"

"No, why?"

"I thought maybe if it's not too far out of the way we could drive past."

"For what?"

She really had no good reason. "Just to see if he's home, I guess."

"Don't you know where he lives?"

"No."

"With all the time you two spend together, you've never been to his house?"

She hadn't thought about it before, and it hadn't seemed strange until he'd been accused of killing someone. "I guess we usually meet in town, either at the café or Storm Scoopers. In all fairness, he's never been to my house either...well, except to drop me off a few times."

Savannah looked at her from beneath her lashes.

"Well, he's never come in."

"Mmm...hmm."

Gia opened the search engine on her phone and typed in Trevor's name and Boggy Creek. "Maybe it's because he's a guy. I'm friends with him, but I don't invite him to the house, and I don't go to his house, you know?"

"I guess that could be why," Savannah relented. "It would probably be weird to curl up on the couch with a blanket and a bucket of popcorn to watch an old movie with Trevor."

Gia laughed, thinking of all the times she and Savannah had done just that. "Do you know where Lakeshore Cove is?"

"It's a development, right? North of town?"

"Yeah."

"I'm pretty sure I do. Show me the map."

Gia held out her phone.

Savannah waited until the road was straight for a few miles, then slowed and risked a quick glance at Gia's screen. "Yeah. I've never been up there, but I do know where it is. If I remember correctly, that's a pretty exclusive area."

"Is it?" Gia hadn't lived in Florida long enough to know much about the surrounding towns.

"As far as I know."

They drove in silence for a while, Gia contemplating how little she actually knew about Trevor. "He never talks about his past. Or anything personal really."

"Trevor?"

"Yeah."

"That's not so unusual."

"You don't think?" Gia had been friends with Savannah for years, and she'd only just recently learned the details surrounding her mother's death. "Maybe you're right."

"For instance, I don't know anything about your mother, and all I know about your father is that he threw you out. There's probably no deep dark secret there, and yet, for whatever reason, you don't talk about them."

"That's true." She didn't offer any more details. Her parents were a topic she chose not to discuss. She didn't really remember her mother, though she'd seen pictures of them together, and her mother seemed to love her very much, always smiling, always doting on her. But she'd passed away when Gia was young, leaving her at the mercy of a father who didn't want any part of her. Said he'd never wanted kids in the first place, but he'd put a roof over her head until she graduated high school, and true to his word, he'd thrown her out that very same day, and she hadn't seen him since.

"There." Savannah gestured toward a sign that said Lakeshore Cove, then hit her turn signal, despite the fact the roads were deserted at that time of the morning, and turned into the development.

"Turn right at the first corner, then loop around the lake. Trevor's is the last house on the cul-de-sac. On this map, it looks like it backs up to the lake."

"Wow. Waterfront property?" Savannah leaned forward for a better view of the neighborhood. "Exclusive may have been an understatement."

"No kidding."

Estates lined the road, most with shrub walls or concrete walls surrounding their yards. Every so often, a roof peeked over the shrubbery.

They crept through the dark neighborhood, keeping an eye on the house numbers.

According to the map on her phone, Trevor's house should be coming up. "It should be the next one."

"Over there." Savannah pointed out a driveway on the right side of the road. It curved around through a closed wrought-iron gate, then continued up to a sprawling mansion. Palm trees lined either side of the driveway, creating a canopy of palms leading to the house. She stopped in front of the gate.

Gia craned her neck but couldn't see all the way up the driveway. "Do you see his car?"

"No, but I figure it'd probably be in the garage."

"Are you sure this is the right house?" Gia double-checked the map on her phone.

"It's the address you gave me."

"Do you think he lives alone in there? Maybe he just rents an apartment in the basement or something."

Savannah laughed. "Gia, these people don't rent out their basements."

"Maybe his parents own it."

"I guess," she conceded.

Gia turned off the overhead light and opened the door.

Savannah grabbed her arm. "Where do you think you're going?"

"It couldn't hurt to have a look around."

"I don't know." Savannah caught her lower lip between her teeth and peered out the window.

"Why don't you move up past the driveway, and we'll walk around and see if we see his car by the house or if any lights are on?"

"All right, but just a quick peek, and then we're on our way. I'm not missing my vacation so you can play peeping Tom."

"Yeah, yeah. Don't worry, we'll be out of here in five minutes." Gia waited for her to pull up, then cracked the door open and started to get out.

"Wait."

"What's the matter now?"

"What about his dog?" Savannah stiffened. "I've seen that animal, and there's no way I'm getting out of this car if she's lurking around somewhere."

"Relax, Zoe was supposed to call me if he picked her up." Of course, Gia was supposed to call Zoe and let her know if she heard anything too, but there was no need to mention that.

"Make it quick." Savannah climbed out of the car with Gia and shut the door softly behind her.

They approached the wrought-iron gate and peeked through the bars. They couldn't see any more than they'd been able to see from the car.

"Do you think we should follow the wall around the back?" Gia whispered, probably needlessly since the house was like half a mile up the driveway, but it didn't feel right to talk too loudly in the dead silence. "It probably doesn't go all the way around if it's on the lake."

"Why bother with a wall if it doesn't go all the way around? Here." Savannah dropped to all fours in the dirt. "Climb on my back and peek over."

"Get up. I'm not climbing on you; I'll hurt you."

"Oh, please, Gia, I grew up surrounded by brothers and cousins. Trust me, I'm tougher than I look."

Gia grabbed her arm and yanked her up. "Still, I'm not climbing on you."

"All righty, then." Savannah brushed the dirt from her bare knees and started for the car. "Let's go."

"Here." The wall couldn't be higher than six feet tall. Gia cupped her hands and held them low. "I'll boost you up, and you tell me if you see anything."

"You can't be serious."

"Oh, come on. It'll only take a second, and then we'll go."

Savannah sighed but relented. She put one foot in Gia's clasped hands and boosted herself up until she could see over the wall.

Chapter 14

"Anything?" Gia called softly.

"It's too dark."

"Aren't there any lights on?"

"No." She glanced down at Gia. "Maybe he didn't come home."

"Hmm…"

Savannah scrambled onto the top of the wall and held her hand down to Gia. "Come on. We'll take a closer look, but then we are really out of here."

"What if we can't get back over the wall?"

"There are trees lining the inside of the wall, so it'll be easier from that side. The purpose of the wall is to keep people out, not in."

"If you say so." Gia grabbed Savannah's hand.

Using a tree branch to brace herself, Savannah helped Gia scale the wall.

"I'm not exactly dressed for breaking and entering." When Gia reached the top, she hiked her skirt up, straddled the wall and tried to see between the branches to the house while she caught her breath. "You weren't kidding. It's pitch-black and quiet as a tomb over there."

"All right, we'll run across the lawn quick and see if the garage has windows. Maybe we can just look in and see if his car's in there."

"That works." Gia turned and hung her feet over the wall, then inched her way down the other side until she was hanging with her arms fully extended before she released her hold on the wall.

Savannah swung her legs over and dropped gracefully to the ground.

"Showoff," Gia muttered.

When Savannah started moving forward between the trees, Gia started after her, then plowed full force into her back, bounced off, and caught herself against a tree trunk. "What are you doing? Why did you stop?"

"Uh, Gia," she whispered, her hands held high over her head.

Gia froze at the sense of urgency in her tone. "What's wrong?"

"Back up."

"Wh—?"

"Back up. Slowly," she bit out through clenched teeth.

Gia started to back away.

A growl brought her up short.

She shot her hands into the air, as if the dog knew what that meant. "Brandy?"

"No." Savannah's breathing had grown heavy, ragged.

"What is it?"

"Big. Really big. And not amused."

Gia took another step back, bringing another growl from the other side of the tree. "What's it doing?"

"Standing." Savannah stood frozen. "Do you have your phone?"

"I'm wearing a skirt with no pockets, where would I have my phone?"

"Reach in my back shorts pocket, get my phone, and call Trevor."

"Trevor? For what?"

"To come call his dog off."

"Uh…"

"I'm not kidding, Gia."

"The dog hasn't made any move to attack. Maybe we can just climb up the tree or climb back over the wall."

"Can you see this dog?"

"The tree's in the way."

"Take a peek." Savannah shifted to the left to give Gia a clearer view.

When Gia peeked between the tree and Savannah, and her gaze landed on the dog, the breath shot out of her lungs. "Do you see the size of that thing's head?"

Though Savannah remained silent, Gia was pretty sure she could hear her eyes rolling.

She fished the phone out of Savannah's pocket.

"Don't move." A man's voice came from across the yard, moving toward them. "As long as you don't move, he won't attack. Unless, of course, I order him to. Who are you and what are you doing here?"

The fleeting thought of saying they were reporters flickered in and out of Gia's mind. No way he'd let them climb back over the wall and disappear without checking. "Trevor? It's me. Gia."

"And Savannah! Don't let the dog bite us," Savannah blurted.

"Oh, for crying out loud, Gia. What are you doing here in the middle of the night?"

"Well, technically, it's morning."

"Gia?" His voice held a note of reprimand that in the dark, just for a minute, reminded her of Hunt.

"Oh, all right. We're on our way to the Keys for a few days, and I didn't want to leave without checking on you. I've been worried sick." She couldn't help the bit of anger that crept into her tone. "You haven't returned any of my calls."

The dog growled again, just a low growl, deep in its throat, and all the more menacing because it stood so still.

"Zeus, release," Trevor commanded.

The dog trotted to his side and stood at attention.

"Zeus? I didn't know you had another dog beside Brandy." Gia's eyes had grown more accustomed to the dark, and she could see Trevor well enough, though the big, dark-colored dog still blended with the shadows.

"Two, actually. Zeus and Ares are my guard dogs."

"Guard dogs?"

"Yes. Akitas. Trained to detain an intruder but not to attack unless ordered to."

Gia eyed the big animal. "Shh... Don't say that word out loud. It might think you're serious."

"If I wanted him to attack, I'd issue the order in Japanese. That way, there are no mistakes."

What in the world was he talking about, and who was this man? Guard dogs? Japanese? And if she wasn't mistaken, whatever he was holding in his hands was a gun. "Is that a gun?"

"Shotgun."

"Trevor?" How is it possible this was the same easygoing, affable, kind-of-goofy-in-an-adorable-sort-of-way guy she'd been hanging out with? She glanced at Savannah.

Savannah shrugged, her hands still held high.

"Put your hands down, both of you."

Gia lowered her hands and rolled the tension out of her shoulders. She hadn't even realized she was still holding them up. "Trevor, what is going on?"

He lowered the silhouette of the shotgun. "You shouldn't have come here."

"What is this place? You live here?"

He turned and glanced over his shoulder at the enormous mansion then looked back at her. "Yeah."

"With whom?"

"My dogs."

"Whose house is it?"

"Mine. Now why so many questions, Gia?"

"I…uh…" What could she say? She didn't even know who this man was. Certainly not her friend. "I'm sorry. We'll go. I was just worried."

Savannah started back toward the wall without saying anything.

Gia stared at Trevor for another minute, his big dog standing guard at his side, his shotgun cradled low, then turned and started after Savannah.

Trevor sighed. "Wait. Come on." He gestured toward the driveway. "I'll let you out the gate."

Gia looked at Savannah then started in the direction he'd indicated, one eye firmly on the dog.

Out of nowhere, Trevor laughed, and for an instant, he was the man she knew. "I have to admit, I'm kind of impressed."

"At?" Gia was in no mood for games. Her mind was reeling.

"You climbed over the wall."

She smiled; she couldn't help herself. "Savannah helped."

"I should have known."

Some of her courage returned—though, who'd have ever thought she'd need courage to speak to Trevor? "What happened, Trevor?"

"Ah, man, Gia. I didn't mean for you to get involved in any of this. Why don't you two go to the Keys, relax, and enjoy yourselves for a few days?" He reached the gate and stood face to face with her. "I'll tell you what. You get one question, and I'll answer truthfully, if you promise you'll go to the Keys and forget about this whole situation for a while."

She was more than ready for a few days to unwind, though she doubted she'd be able to forget anything. She had a sneaking suspicion this new side of Trevor would haunt her for some time. How could she have been so wrong about him?

"Did you kill him?" she blurted out before she could stop herself.

Savannah gasped.

Trevor moved closer and reached for her. He cupped her cheek in his hand. "Of course not, Gia."

Relief rushed through her, and her shoulders slumped. "I'm sorry, I—"

A loud boom tore through the night.

Pain seared Gia's arm, and she clasped her hand over it as Trevor plowed into her and Savannah, knocking them to the ground against the wall.

Savannah screamed.

Trevor slapped a hand over her mouth. "Shh…"

He scrambled into the tree line, half dragging them with him, keeping them pinned between him and the wall.

Gia lay on the ground, staring up at Trevor crouched over them, gun held at the ready.

He pressed a phone against his ear. "I'm in my front yard, and someone is shooting at us."

Shooting?

He paused a moment while a deep voice on the other end of the line said something.

Her arm stung, and she pulled her hand away covered in something dark and sticky. She sniffed her fingers, and the coppery scent hit her immediately.

"Gia and Savannah are here."

The voice on the other end of the line blew up and let loose a string of profanities Gia could hear from her spot on the ground.

For a brief moment, she was glad for the big dog standing in front of them, though she figured even he'd cower in the face of Hunt's wrath once he arrived.

She laid her head back on the cool, damp ground, thinking for a moment of what might be crawling around her, then struggled to sit up.

Trevor helped her to sit against the wall but crowded her so she couldn't move. "Sit still."

She did as she was told. "Savannah?"

"I'm here. Are you all right?"

"I think so. Are you?"

"Yes. But this is so not what I had in mind for a vacation."

A car door slammed in the distance, followed by the sound of an engine starting.

Trevor started toward the gate in a crouch, then looked over his shoulder at them, cursed, and ducked back behind the wall.

She had no clue what was happening. Fear clawed at her. To top matters off, the sting in her arm was getting worse, the pain starting to radiate up and down her arm. She needed light.

She felt around the ground for Savannah's phone, squinting in the darkness to make sure she didn't put her hand on anything disgusting... or poisonous. She'd had the phone in her hand before Trevor came out, but it was no longer in her hand, and she couldn't remember dropping it. It had to be nearby somewhere. Maybe Trevor had knocked it out of her hand when he'd knocked her down.

"What are you doing?" Savannah grabbed her arm, right on the sore spot.

"Oww!" Gia yanked her arm away and cradled it close against her body.

"Ah, jeez, Gia, are you hurt?" Savannah shifted closer. "Let me see."

"What's wrong?" Trevor said over his shoulder.

"I hurt my arm, and I was looking for Savannah's phone so I could see what's wrong."

"No."

Sirens wailed in the distance.

"What do you mean no?"

"You can't turn on a light. We'll be sitting ducks. Just sit tight until the police get here."

"Trevor, what is going on?" Savannah asked. "Why was someone shooting at your house?"

"They weren't shooting at my house; they were shooting at me. And I don't know what's going on, but I have a feeling it's connected to Ron Parker's murder."

Hunt's jeep tore into the driveway, cutting off anything further Trevor might have said. He stopped just short of the gate, putting the jeep between the gate and the shooter, and hopped out, keeping his head low. "Trevor?"

"Yeah."

"Just hold on. Is anyone hurt?"

"Gia is. I don't know how bad."

"All right. Don't move."

Gia dropped her head back against the wall, cradling her arm close, and closed her eyes. She wasn't going anywhere.

Savannah crouched beside her, arm draped protectively over her shoulders.

Police cruisers filled the cul-de-sac, their flashing lights casting a dizzying blue-and-red strobe effect over her closed lids. Radio chatter cut through the peaceful silence of the night. The gate creaked open.

"Gia?" Hunt squatted at her side, shining a flashlight at her. "Are you all right?"

"My arm hurts." She held it out to him, seeing the nasty gash for the first time. Blood trickled down over her wrist and fingers.

"It's just grazed."

"Grazed?" She lurched away from the wall, and the world started to spin.

"Hold on. Sit back." Hunt eased her back against the wall and waved an EMT over.

"Grazed, as in shot? I've been shot?" Darkness encroached on her peripheral vision, spots of light swirling amidst the black.

Savannah's soft cries gave her something to focus on, and she held the darkness at bay. Barely.

"Gia, stay with me." Hunt cupped her cheek. "You're fine."

"But I was shot?" She couldn't wrap her head around it. Not that the wound hurt any more or less, but the idea of being shot was too incredible to fathom.

"It's just a scratch, Gia."

"It's a bullet wound."

Hunt laughed. *Laughed!* The nerve. "Don't worry, the EMTs will fix you up. I'm pretty sure they have Band-Aids."

"Band—?" She huffed out an indignant breath. How dare he make light of her injury? Who did he think he was? She scooted up a little straighter. "I'll have you know…"

One look at his expression stopped her from continuing. Whatever he said—maybe what he thought would keep her conscious—the fear and concern darkening his eyes kept a lid on her temper. "It would have to be a pretty big Band-Aid."

He worked his clenched jaw back and forth.

"I'm sorry, Hunt. It's not what it looks like."

"We'll talk about it later." He held up a hand and moved aside for the EMT to get a better look at her, then aimed a scowl at Savannah. "Besides, I'm sure your sidekick can fill me in."

Savannah looked down and nodded. Now that the night was lit up like Grand Central Station, she could see the makeup running down Savannah's face due to her tears.

Guilt gripped her chest and squeezed. "I'm sorry, Savannah."

"I know, honey. Don't worry about it. Everything's okay now."

She'd been so lost in her own confusion, she'd never stopped to think how terrified Savannah must have been. First the dog, then a gunman. *Ah jeez, what was I thinking?*

Chapter 15

Gia sulked as she held the door to the All-Day Breakfast Café open for Savannah on Tuesday morning.

"No sense pouting, Gia." Savannah shot her a glare on the way past. "It won't change anything."

"I said I was sorry." About a hundred times—especially for the grilling Savannah had endured by Hunt. She'd apologized all day long while Savannah sat beside her in the hospital, waiting while the doctor cleaned and patched up the gouge in her arm. Then again when Savannah had driven her home and dropped her off to go to sleep, and again when she picked her up this morning and driven her into the café. "I really am sorry."

"Yeah, I know."

Willow looked up from the register. "What are you two doing here? Weren't you supposed to leave for the Keys yesterday morning?"

Earl swung around on his stool.

Gia hadn't eaten all day at the hospital, and by the time she'd reached the house last night, all she'd cared about was sleeping, and Joey still had Thor, so she'd fallen face-first on the bed and passed out as soon as she walked through the door.

"We *were* going to the Keys." Savannah hooked her thumb toward Gia. "Until she got shot."

"Shot!" Earl's bushy gray eyebrows shot up almost to his receding hairline. "Are you all right?"

Willow rushed to her, eyeing the bandage on her arm. "What happened?"

Gia's cheeks heated. "It's nothing, just grazed."

"Here, sit." Willow led her to a stool, then poured a mug of coffee and set it in front of her.

The aroma rose with the steam, and Gia sighed, near tears with gratitude. "Thank you."

"Of course." She set a mug in front of Savannah, who'd sat next to Gia. "Now, what happened?"

Earl slid onto the stool next to hers and rested his hand on her uninjured arm. "Are you sure you're okay?"

"Positive, thank you." She patted his hand.

Hunt had given her a severe warning about discussing what happened. She wouldn't have said anything about it if Savannah hadn't opened her mouth.

Savannah just smirked and blew on her coffee.

Traitor. Not that Gia blamed her. In the past twenty-four hours, she'd screwed up her vacation plans, scared the daylights out of her, gotten her shot at, and gotten her in trouble with Hunt. Oh, and lost her phone. She was going to have to do some serious groveling for forgiveness.

Savannah tapped her long, tangerine nails against the countertop, a steady *rat-a-tat-tat* that pounded through Gia's head.

Gia resisted the urge to slap a hand over hers and still the rhythm.

"Gia?" Willow stared at her. "Are you all right?"

"I'm sorry. I guess I zoned out for a minute." She shook off the haze of fatigue, and probably shock, and tried to focus on what Willow had asked and how much she could say. "It just grazed me, and I'm okay, but I'm not supposed to talk about how it happened while the police are investigating."

"No worries, as long as you're okay." Willow grabbed the order pad from beside the register. "Do you want something to eat?"

Earl reached down the counter for his breakfast and slid it in front of him. The scent of bacon wafted up to her.

Her stomach growled. She was surprised to realize how hungry she was. Apparently, getting shot boosted the appetite. Go figure. "I'm starved, but I don't know what I feel like having."

"Well, I want a meat lover's omelet with cheese and home fries," Savannah said. "And rye toast with extra butter. Oh, and a fruit cup."

"Okay, that sounds good. I'll have the same."

Willow's eyes widened, but she didn't comment as she headed back to put the order up.

Earl snatched the last of the bacon from his plate, and stood. "If you're sure you're okay, and you're not going to dish about what happened, I have to run. I'm picking up my little Emily to take her to the doctor."

"Oh, no. Is she okay?"

"Oh, yeah, fine. She needs a checkup and shots, and she puts up an awful fuss, wails like a banshee. I'm the only one who can deal with her." He laughed. "I just pull out my secret weapon."

"What's that?"

"Good old-fashioned bribery. She gets the shot, and I take her to the toy store and let her pick out whatever she wants."

Gia laughed.

He kissed her cheek. "You feel better."

"Thanks, Earl. Good luck with Emily."

"Thanks, I'm gonna need it." He dropped a few bills beside his plate on his way out. He pitched in often enough when she needed a hand and never accepted money from her. The least she could do was treat him to breakfast, but he insisted on paying.

Savannah rested her elbows on the counter and twisted back and forth on the stool.

Gia sighed. She hated when she and Savannah were off. "Are you ever going to forgive me?"

Savannah sat up straighter. "Oh, stop. You know you're forgiven. It's just…"

"Just what?"

"I can't figure out what's going on and what Trevor has to do with it. I definitely got the impression Hunt knew more about the case than he was saying."

"Did you try Leo?"

"Leo avoided me like the plague last night, after he knew I was okay, of course."

"Hmm…that is suspicious."

"Exactly." She pointed at Gia. "And another thing: Did you notice Hunt didn't treat Trevor like a murder suspect?"

"What do you mean?"

She frowned. "Well, he asked him questions, listened when he spoke, I don't know… I can't explain it, but he seemed to treat him more like a colleague than a suspect."

Gia tried to think about how they'd interacted the day before. She'd been so focused on her arm she hadn't paid much attention, but Savannah could be right. She didn't usually voice an observation unless she was. "So, you don't think he suspects him of killing Ron?"

"No. I don't." Savannah drummed her nails on the counter.

Gia closed her eyes and tried to picture the chart she'd started. Ron Parker, Mitch Anderson. Somehow, they connected to Trevor. "You know, before we left, I started a chart, trying to figure out who might be involved, and the one name that sticks out is Skyla."

"You think she knows something?"

She had acted strange even before Ron Parker had been killed, but her behavior had gotten increasingly odd after she found out. "I do. I'm not sure what, but I have a feeling she knows something."

"Looks like we'll have to talk to Skyla."

"Are you all right?" Cole rushed out from the kitchen, spatula in hand. "Willow just said you got shot."

Willow stood beside the cutout, plates in hand, sheepish smile firmly in place.

"I'm okay, Cole. It was nothing, really." She held up her bandaged arm. "Just a flesh wound."

He let out a low whistle. "Girl, they weren't kidding; you really are a magnet for trouble, aren't you?"

"Who said that?"

He lifted a brow and stared pointedly at her. "Who didn't?"

What could she say? All things considered, the statement seemed fairly accurate.

Willow placed their plates in front of them and whispered, "Sorry."

"Don't worry about it." Gia ground fresh pepper onto her omelet. "How did everything go this morning?"

"Great. Not too big a rush, but a nice steady trickle for a Tuesday morning," Willow answered.

A few customers still sat at tables, eating or drinking coffee.

"Any new gossip?" She took a bite of omelet. Just the right combination of bacon, ham, sausage, eggs, and cheese. She was going to have to take a long walk later. "Mmm...delicious."

"Thank you, ma'am. I aim to please." Cole lowered his head in a mock bow. "As for gossip, don't know. I've been in the kitchen all morning. But they said on the news yesterday morning that Parker was stabbed."

"I heard that." Gia took another bite.

Willow cleared Earl's spot, sticking the dirty dishes in a bin beneath the counter, then lifted the bin and started toward the back. "Oh, a woman came in looking for you this morning. I told her you wouldn't be back until sometime Friday."

Gia finished chewing a bit of toast and swallowed, then followed with a sip of orange juice. "Did she leave her name?"

"Nah, just said she'd come back Friday."

Gia couldn't think of anyone who'd be looking for her. Maybe a solicitor. "What did she look like?"

"Really pretty, long, curly blond hair, green eyes with gold specks in them."

"Donna Mae."

"Who's Donna Mae?" Willow shifted the bin to rest against her hip.

"She's been in a couple of other times in the past few days. She likes oatmeal with blueberries."

"Well, she didn't order breakfast this morning, just asked for you then left when I said you weren't in."

"Thanks, Willow."

"Uh-huh." She headed for the kitchen with the bin.

Gia would have to add a trip to the Boggy Creek Florist to the day's activities. "Would you mind working the rest of the day, Cole?"

"Of course not. I'll work all week if you need me to. Maybe you guys can still get away."

Hunt had told Gia and Savannah both to stick close to home for the time being. Another reason for Savannah to be mad at her.

A group of customers entered, and Willow hurried back out to greet them.

Cole straightened. "I'd better head back. Enjoy your day off, and take care of that arm."

"Thanks, Cole. And breakfast was amazing."

"Anytime, dear."

"You've been unusually quiet," she said to Savannah. "If I really am forgiven, what gives?"

"Just thinking."

"About?"

"Are you going to talk to Skyla?"

Gia ordered her thoughts, able to think more clearly after a good breakfast and a dose of caffeine. "Yes, and then I'll run over to the Boggy Creek Florist to see Donna Mae."

"Do you remember the chart you made?"

"Pretty much. Why?"

"Skyla is more likely to open up if you go alone. Why don't you make me a copy of the chart, and I'll see what I can dig up on whoever's on it."

"Sure thing." She leaned over the counter and grabbed a pen, then smoothed a napkin to write on. She added all the names as close to the order she had them in as she could remember. Trevor, Mitch, and Ron in the center, since things seemed to revolve around them.

She looked around to make sure no one was paying attention, then leaned closer to Savannah. She pointed to Mitch's name with the pen. "Mitch is questionable, only included because he'd apparently been close friends with Ron at one time, before Ron had gone so gung-ho to campaign on his own. So, maybe start with that. See if you can find a connection."

Savannah studied the chart and nodded. "Why do you think Harley and Donna Mae have some involvement?"

"Mostly because Donna Mae's last name is Parker, and she was worried about Harley. Oh, and Harley and Mitch are brothers."

"What?"

"Shh…" Gia looked around to see if anyone was paying attention.

"Sorry, but are you serious? I never would have guessed that."

"Harley and Mitch Anderson are brothers. So, once again, another piece of the puzzle revolves around Mitch."

"Do you think Donna Mae is related to Ron?"

"I don't know it for sure, but I would assume so."

"Hmm… That makes sense."

Gia tapped the pen against the napkin. "Someone on this chart has to know something, at least it seems that way."

"Do you think one of them killed him?" Savannah whispered.

Gia studied the names. Who would have had reason to kill Ron? Mitch was his opponent. He could have wanted to remove Ron from the race. And Harley was related to Mitch. Donna Mae was also afraid they were in danger. She could have been afraid of Ron, but why? And then there was Skyla. Skyla was no killer, of that she was certain. Then again, Trevor wasn't exactly what she'd thought either. But a killer? "I just don't know what to think."

Savannah folded the napkin and tucked it into her purse. "I'll meet up with you later. At your house?"

"I want to swing by your house after I talk to Skyla and Donna Mae and pick up Thor, but I'll need you to drop me off home to get my car first. Do you want to ride out with me later, and I'll drop you back off in the morning?" She was hoping Savannah would say yes, and they could spend the night eating popcorn loaded with butter and watching old movies. At least she could try to make it up to her.

"Sounds good, but don't think you're getting off that easy. I'm still exhausted from yesterday, so I'll accept Xavier's Barbeque and my choice of movie. For tonight. But one night this week, we're going out dancing."

Gia stifled a groan. Not that she didn't enjoy dancing, but Savannah would stay out all night, especially since she'd already taken the week off work.

"And don't give me any of that *I have to get up early for work* nonsense. This is your week off." She swung her purse over her shoulder and strutted out, apparently content Gia would follow, and she'd get her way.

Chapter 16

After Savannah dropped her off home, Gia put on a light jacket to avoid answering questions about her bandaged arm, plugged Boggy Creek Florist into the GPS, then dialed Hunt's number, intent on leaving a message.

"Hey, Gia, is everything okay?" His voice sounded strained.

"Hey, everything's fine. I'm sorry to bother you; I was just planning to leave a message asking if you'd like to come to dinner with Savannah and me tonight. I'm picking up Xavier's."

"I'd love to, but I'm not sure I'll be able to make it."

"Oh." Though she understood, she'd been hoping he'd be able to take an hour off. Seemed their relationship had hit a brick wall lately.

"I'm sorry. I know things have been too busy lately, even before this case. Ever since I took over as acting captain, I've been swamped. I'd understand if you wanted to put us on hold for a while."

Her chest tightened. That was the last thing she wanted. "Is that what you want?"

"Of course not, Gia. I care about you. A lot." He sighed. "But you're not the one who doesn't have time to spend with me right now. And…well, speaking to Trevor and realizing how much time you've been spending with him lately made me also realize how much I've been neglecting you."

"Ah, jeez, Hunt. You're not neglecting me; you're working. And Trevor and I are friends, nothing more."

"Friendships often develop into something more, and that's okay. You deserve to be able to pursue something with someone else if that's what you want."

He'd started off okay, and she'd felt kind of bad for him, but now he was just annoying her. "If that was what I wanted, I'd have told you that.

Trevor and I are friends, just like Savannah and I are friends. I spend a lot of time with Savannah too. But she has Leo, so I hang out with Trevor. It's not like I know a ton of people in town yet, and I enjoy spending time with him. But that's all it is. I am not interested in anything more with him or anyone else, and I'm kind of hurt that you don't trust me."

Especially after she'd put her trust in him, something that didn't come easy. "What's going on with you lately, Hunt?"

"I don't know. I—"

A voice in the background interrupted, but she couldn't make out any of the muffled conversation.

"I'm sorry, Gia. I have to go."

Dang. They needed to finish this conversation. She didn't even know where she stood with him. "That's all right. Call me or come by the house when you have time to talk."

Silence.

"Hunt?" She checked her phone screen. He'd already disconnected. She tossed the phone onto the passenger seat and massaged her temples. Why did he have to be so difficult? Giving up on any hope that the call had dropped and he'd call back, she shifted into gear and headed for the florist.

Gia pulled up in front of the flower shop and parked on the street, then climbed out of the car, locked it, and headed in. Better to visit Donna Mae first, since she actually wanted to talk to Gia. Skyla might require a little convincing to open up.

The overwhelming scent of flowers hit her as soon as she opened the door to the shop.

"Hi. I'll be right with you," Donna Mae called without looking up from whatever she was doing at the counter.

"Sure." Gia looked around as she waited. Flowers adorned every available surface, including large arrangements scattered around the floor and bins of lilies crammed together in the refrigerator. Tall stems with multiple flowers on each filled several more bins.

"Okay, sorry about that, last minute rush order." Donna Mae rounded the counter and approached the refrigerated case where Gia stood contemplating her options. "Now, what can I help you with?"

Gia smiled. "Hi there, Donna Mae."

"Oh, Gia. I'm so sorry, I didn't realize it was you."

"No problem."

"My mind has been a million miles away lately."

"It's okay, I know the feeling. And I'm not sure what you can help me with. Willow told me you came by the café when I was out, so I figured

I'd stop in and see if you wanted anything special and maybe pick up some flowers."

"You didn't have to come all the way over here, but thank you. I'm glad you did." She gestured toward the counter. "Come on and sit down. We'll talk while I'm not busy, then I'll help you pick out something perfect. Would you like a cup of coffee?"

The conversation with Hunt had left her jittery enough. Caffeine was the last thing she needed. "No, thank you."

"Tea?"

"Nothing, thanks, I'm good." She started to follow her, then paused. "What are these tall flowers?"

"Gladioli."

"They're beautiful. You must go through a lot of them, though, to stock so many."

"Actually, that's not even half of what I will have. My mother asked me to provide the flowers for Ron's funeral service, and people have already started ordering arrangements to send to the family."

"Are you and Ron related?"

"Ron was my cousin. He's younger than me, and we weren't ever close, but his death still came as a shock."

"I'm so sorry for your loss."

"Thank you."

"Do you know when the services will be held?"

"The wake will be on Friday and Saturday night, as long as the police release him, which they're expected to. Sunday will be a private viewing for family only, then the funeral mass will take place on Monday morning." Donna Mae flipped up a section of counter and led Gia to a couple of stools at a long worktable behind the counter. She offered Gia a seat, then stood opposite her. "I was hoping to see you. I wanted to talk to you again about Harley."

"What about him? Is he okay?"

"So far. Do you mind if I work while we talk? It's easier for me if I stay busy."

"No, please, go ahead."

She laid out a green sheet of tissue paper on the table and spread lacy, white baby's breath across it. "Even though everything seems to be okay so far, I'm worried about him, and he won't contact me."

"He's close, though, keeping an eye on you. Seems he's just as worried about you."

She nodded and added half a dozen red roses, rolled the tissue paper, then stapled a business card to it, and set the bouquet aside.

"Look, Donna Mae, I'd be happy to help, but there's nothing I can do if I don't know what's going on."

"I know. And I'm sorry for being so secretive. It's just a difficult situation to talk about, something I haven't talked about in a very long time."

"You obviously came to me for a reason."

"Yes. I can't get close to Harley, but you can. He'll listen to you, I think." She took a bowl from beneath the counter, set it on the table, and dropped a foam ball into it. "At least, I hope he will."

"Listen to me about what?"

"He needs to get off the streets. I understand he has a problem going inside buildings, or anything enclosed really, but from what I hear, he did it for you once before."

"That was different."

"But it's not safe for him to be wandering around out in the open. Do you think you could talk to him, maybe talk him into leaving town for a while?"

Although Gia would never want to see Harley in danger, especially after everything he'd done for her, Donna Mae was going to have to be honest with her about what was going on if she wanted her to intervene. "How do you know Harley? He said something about you being his girlfriend."

She started arranging artificial flowers in the foam, jamming the spikes in with more force than seemed necessary. "It was a long time ago. A lifetime, really."

She set the bowl and flowers aside and dropped onto the stool. She smiled, though her eyes held only sadness. "Harley was such a quiet guy when we were in school, stayed to himself mostly, didn't play sports or join clubs or attend school functions. He even cut out of the pep rallies and assemblies. But he was able to go inside buildings back then, and he did attend school."

"Did something happen to change that?"

She nodded and swiped a tear from her cheek. "Yes. But not until after we graduated."

"Did you two date in high school?"

"We started hanging out together toward the end of our senior year, not long before graduation. My boyfriend at the time had broken up with me, said he was going away to college and didn't want to be burdened by a girlfriend back home, and blah, blah, blah…" She waved a hand. "You know how it is when you're seventeen and you get dumped."

Gia smiled. "Pretty much the end of the world."

"Right before prom and graduation parties and all the things we thought were important once upon a time."

Gia hadn't bothered with proms or parties, but she just nodded for her to continue.

"A few nights later, I was sitting alone in the park, crying, and Harley appeared out of nowhere. He sat on the opposite end of the bench from me, didn't say anything, just sat for a while. I wasn't sure what to do, so once I got my emotions under control, I introduced myself and asked if he recognized me from school." She shook her head. "I'll never forget how sweet he was. He nodded and said he recognized me and that I was pretty. He wanted to know why I was crying, so I told him what happened, and he offered to take me to the prom and to the parties if I wanted."

"So, you said yes?"

"I told him I'd like that, but it would just be as friends." She laughed. "He looked so appalled that I might have taken his offer any other way."

Gia could imagine Harley as a boy, doing whatever he could to make a young girl stop feeling sad. He was such a sensitive soul.

"Anyway, we went to all of the senior events together and found we enjoyed each other's company, so while most of our friends went off to college, we spent the summer together. We started dating sometime around Christmas and were together for a few years. He even asked me to marry him." She pulled a thin gold chain from beneath her shirt, and gently cradled the gold ring with the tiny diamond chip that hung from it. "All these years later, I still keep it close to my heart."

"What happened?" Gia forced the words past the lump in her throat, since she already knew this fairy tale wouldn't have a happy ending.

"His brother and his posse."

"Mitch?"

"And my cousin, Ron, and that other kid they used to hang out with."

Gia's heart sank. "Trevor?"

"No, not him. Trevor was always a sweetheart. I'm not sure how he ever ended up hanging out with those three. The other kid…" She snapped her fingers. "Fischetti."

"Bobby?"

"Yeah, that's it." She picked up a broken scrap of stem from the table and started peeling it apart. "The three of them had a party one night. Harley and I were in his room, sitting on the couch watching TV. We couldn't hear anything over the racket they were making, but it didn't matter. It was still nice sitting together, his arm around my shoulder."

She tossed the shredded stem in the garbage pail beside the table. "Then the screaming started."

"Screaming?"

"Horrible screams, like someone was getting killed."

"What happened?"

"Harley told me to wait there, then vaulted over the couch and ran into the other room." She stared past Gia, a faraway look in her eyes, as if reliving what must have been the horror of that night.

"Did you follow him?"

She nodded. "I found him kneeling over a girl who seemed to have been beaten pretty badly. He was trying to revive her when Mitch and his buddies started harassing him, kicking him, hitting him, asking him why he did that to her."

Donna Mae sobbed, and Gia got up and handed her a paper towel from beside the sink. Donna Mae dried her face with the paper towel and blew her nose before she resumed her story.

"It was awful, and when I tried to help, Ron shoved me away. Then the other two dragged me out to the car and drove me home. They dumped me out in front of my house without even stopping all the way and yelled after me to keep my mouth shut if I knew what was good for me."

"And did you?"

"No. I told my parents what happened, and they called the police. By the time they got there, the girl was gone, and so was Harley."

"What happened to her?"

"I have no idea. I never saw her again, and no one ever talked about it. When I did see Harley afterward, he was different, wouldn't even speak to me."

"Did he break up with you?"

"No. He never did, just stopped coming around or calling, disappeared for longer and longer stretches of time. I'm not even sure he ever went home after that. I don't know what they did to him that night, but Harley was never the same."

"So, what happened between the two of you?"

"Nothing. Eventually, when I realized he wasn't coming back to me, I gave up trying to reach him. I dated other men, but never seriously, and I never married, never found that one man who could take Harley's place in my heart."

"I'm so sorry, Donna Mae."

She nodded and wiped her cheeks. "I just want you to understand why I'm so worried about Harley. Whatever those goons did to him that night made something in him snap."

"And Ron? What happened with him?"

"I never spoke to him again after that night. If we ended up at the same function together, I ignored him as if he didn't even exist, until last week."

"You saw him last week?"

She nodded. "And now he turned up dead a few days after I"—she made air quotes with her fingers—"ran into him."

"Ran into whom? Ron?"

"Yeah. He *happened* to be in the parking lot out back when I was leaving last week, asked me if I remembered what happened all those years ago."

"What'd you do?"

"I told him I had no clue what he was talking about and if he didn't leave me alone, I'd call the police."

"Did he leave?"

"Yup. Muttered something under his breath as he walked away, something about keeping it that way. The next time I saw him was on the news the next morning."

"The morning he was found in Storm Scoopers?"

She nodded, sniffed and wiped her eyes.

"Did you tell the police any of this?"

She looked a Gia like she was crazy. "What was there to tell them?"

"He threatened you?"

"Did he? There's no law against running into your long-lost cousin in a parking lot, asking if they remember a night long past, or mumbling as you walk away. And yet, I knew without a doubt it was a threat."

Gia couldn't really argue the point. She was right. He hadn't broken any laws. "What about after he was killed? Did you tell them you saw him the night before?"

"No."

No point in pushing that discussion any further, since she was obviously not going to the police. "Do you remember any of the other kids Mitch hung out with?"

"Not really. I remember Trevor, but only because I know him from the ice cream shop in town. Mitch and Harley weren't close, and I never knew his other friends."

A bell rang, and Gia jumped, startled, as a man walked into the shop.

"Excuse me." Donna Mae hustled over to the front of the shop. "Can I help you, sir?"

"I have to pick up a bouquet for my wife."

"Ah, Mr. Kelly?"

"Yes."

She scooped the roses she'd put together off the table and rang him up, before sending him on his way with a "happy anniversary" and returning to Gia. "Anyway, will you try to talk to Harley?"

"Yes. If I can find him, I'll talk to him."

Her shoulders slumped. "Oh, thank you."

"Don't thank me yet. First, I have to find him, then I have to try to make him listen."

"Believe me, it's a relief to know you're going to try."

Gia nodded and stood, sure their conversation had come to an end.

"Can I help you with anything else? You said you needed flowers; are you looking for anything special?"

"That depends. Do you have anything that says I'm sorry I screwed up your vacation to the Keys?"

Chapter 17

Gia sat in her car in front of Skyla's house. The blinds in every window had been closed. Skyla's was the only car in the driveway, so she was probably home alone, and yet, Gia hesitated.

Skyla had definitely given the impression she didn't want to talk, and she and Gia weren't all that close.

But Gia and Willow were, and Willow was beyond upset about her mom's behavior. Truth be told, Gia was just as concerned, especially after talking to Donna Mae.

Leaving Savannah's huge bouquet of daisies on the passenger seat, she climbed out of the car. Willow would still be at work for a few hours, so now was probably the best time to catch Skyla alone. She locked the car door, walked up the front walkway to the porch, and rang the bell.

A second later, Skyla's quiet voice came through the closed door, so muffled Gia could barely hear her.

"Skyla? It's me, Gia Morelli. Can I come in?"

The door whipped open. "Gia. What happened? Is Willow okay?"

"Willow's fine, Skyla. I'm sorry, I didn't mean to scare you." It hadn't occurred to her what Skyla might think when she found Gia standing on the doorstep. "She is upset, though, and I was wondering if I could talk to you for a few minutes?"

Skyla shoved her hair behind her ear with a shaky hand. "Yes, yes. Of course. Come on in."

"Thank you."

Skyla scanned the street before shutting the door, locking it, throwing the first deadbolt, and then securing a second, shiny, brand-spanking-new-looking deadbolt. When she was done, she finally turned to Gia. "Please, come sit."

Gia followed her through the small living room and into the kitchen, then took a seat at the table.

"Would you like something to drink or anything?"

"No, thank you, Skyla. Why don't you sit down a few minutes, and let's talk?"

She nodded, pulled out a chair, and perched on the edge, as if ready to run with only a moment's notice.

Gia didn't know how to start.

Dark circles ringed Skyla's eyes, and her hair hung in limp, stringy strands.

"Are you okay, Skyla?"

"I'm fine." Even she didn't seem convinced that was true, the statement lacking any conviction.

"You don't seem fine. You seem strung out. And Willow has been upset at work about it."

She clasped and unclasped her hands on the table in front of her. "I'm sorry about Saturday. It was completely my fault Willow didn't show up or call. Please, don't penalize her for it."

"Of course not. Don't be silly. Willow is a wonderful employee, whom I'd hate to lose, but she's also a friend, and she's scared." Gia laid a hand over Skyla's, stilling them and refocusing her attention. "That's why I stopped over. Willow was hoping maybe you'd talk to me."

Skyla rested her elbows on the table and cradled her head between her hands. She remained quiet, staring down. "Please, Gia, I appreciate you coming over, but I don't want to talk."

"Are you sure?"

She swiped the tears from both cheeks with her palms and a bit more force than necessary. "Yeah, thanks."

"Sure." She had to come up with some way to reach her. Or at least stall until she could connect with her. Maybe a more indirect approach would work better. "You know what? I think I'd love a cup of tea, after all."

Skyla bolted from the chair, filled the teakettle, and set it on the burner.

The first time she'd noticed Skyla acting strange had been in the café when they were discussing the election. "So, who do you think will run against Mitch Anderson now?"

Skyla's shoulders relaxed a little. "I heard something about a woman named Moira Banks. I don't know anything about her though."

"Do you think it'll change the outcome of the election?" That was an angle Gia hadn't thought too much about yet. Mitch Anderson was favored to win, but now there was a big shake-up in the opposing campaign. That certainly wouldn't hurt Mitch. Unless, of course, people sympathized over Ron's death, or it turned out someone connected to Mitch Anderson had some involvement in his murder.

"Who knows? I hope not." With the water on the stove to boil, Skyla busied herself filling a plate with cookies.

"Even though Mitch Anderson was in the lead last I heard, it seems others agree with you that he shouldn't become mayor."

She stiffened. Something was there but what? "Oh? Why do you say that?"

"I was talking to the Bailey twins, and they didn't seem to care much for him." Not to mention Donna Mae's feelings about him, but that wasn't her story to share.

"Did they say why?"

Gia shifted in her chair so she could keep an eye on Skyla's expressions as she moved around the kitchen. "They said he was good friends with Ron Parker when they were kids, and they were both sneaks no one expected to amount to much."

Skyla fumbled a cookie but caught it before it could fall and stacked it on the plate with the rest. "What else did they say?"

"That was about it."

She nodded and placed the cookies on the table, then scooped tea into two infusers, dropped them into mugs, and poured water over them.

There had to be some way to figure out what was bothering her, but Gia was at a loss. As much as she wanted to jump in and question her about the two women arguing outside of the café, she first had to think of a way to lead up to it. "Willow said you guys moved here when she was about to start ninth grade. What was that, about four or five years ago?"

"About five years."

"Where'd you live before that?"

"California." Skyla set the mug in front of Gia and finally sat back down.

"Thank you. Is that where you're from?"

"No. I grew up here."

She wasn't sure why that surprised her. For some reason, she'd thought Skyla was new to the area, then she remembered what Gabriella had said about returning to town. "Is that how you know Gabriella Fischetti?"

"Yes, we went to school together." Her mouth tightened to a firm line as she pulled the infuser out of her tea and set it on a plate, then added rock sugar to her cup and passed it to Gia.

Gia backtracked. "When did you leave Boggy Creek?"

She stirred her tea. "Right after high school."

"What made you leave? Did your family move?"

"No." She slapped her spoon onto the table. "Why the interrogation, Gia? What are you hoping to get at?"

"I...uh..." She was obviously not as subtle as she'd thought. At the end of the day, Gia's curiosity didn't matter enough to upset Skyla like this, but Willow's feelings did. "Look, Skyla, I like Willow a lot. She's a great kid, and we've become close, and I don't like seeing her so upset. It's obvious how close the two of you are, and she is beside herself because she can tell something's going on with you, and you won't open up to her. She trusts me. I guess she was hoping you would too."

Gia sipped her tea. She'd done what she could to try to get Skyla to open up, but the rest was up to her. If she chose not to confide in Gia, then so be it. "I'm sorry. I didn't mean to pry."

"No, it's okay. *I'm* sorry. I know you mean well, and I know Willow is worried and upset and probably scared." She laughed, but it held more sadness than humor. "It's not like I haven't been acting crazy lately."

Gia sipped her tea and waited. She'd let Skyla decide how much, if anything, she wanted to share.

After a moment, Skyla started to speak again. "I left town right after I graduated, because I was pregnant with Willow. I came from a very affluent family, powerful in the community at that time. I found out after I came back that my father had since passed away, and my mother moved out of town a few years later with her new husband."

"I'm sorry," Gia said.

Skyla nodded. "Anyway, when I told them what happened, told them I was pregnant, they didn't believe me. My father called me a liar and told me to leave and never come back, while my mother stood by, her expression hard as ice."

"They didn't believe you were pregnant?"

"No..." She cried harder, her shoulders shaking. "They didn't believe it wasn't my choice. Things were different back then. I can't... I was dating someone, a guy from an extremely influential family, a guy who thought nothing of drugging girls and...well..."

Gia rounded the table and wrapped her arms around her. "Ah, jeez, Skyla. I'm sorry."

Skyla leaned into her and cried. Deep sobs racked her body.

Gia just held her and let her cry. She couldn't even imagine how painful that must have been. When the sobs started to die off, she grabbed a stack of napkins and handed them to Skyla.

"I'm sorry," Skyla whispered.

"No, please, it's okay. I understand."

"I've never told anyone else. After my own parents didn't believe me, I kept my mouth shut and moved out." She sniffed and blew her nose, then drank a few sips of tea.

"Did you ever tell him you were pregnant?"

"Yeah," she scoffed. "I packed my bags, went to his house, and found him on the couch with his arm around someone else. When I told him I was pregnant, he laughed and said it wasn't his, so what did I want him to do about it? His new girlfriend laughed right along with him."

Gia's heart ached for the young woman who'd endured so much pain. "He didn't care at all?"

"Let's just say the guy was spoiled and expected to get his way. Always. As far as I know, he always did."

Gia had a feeling Skyla was being kind in her assessment of him. She was tempted to ask his name, but she didn't want to press Skyla too much. Besides, she had her suspicions.

"So, anyway, I left then. I'd been to California a number of times when I was a kid, and I'd always loved it, so I just started driving and ended up there." She shrugged. "I had some money of my own, so I had my baby and made a life for us."

"And you've done an amazing job. I've always envied how close you and Willow are."

She smiled, a genuine, heartfelt smile. "Yes, we are. Willow is my whole world."

The memory of what Willow had told her about her father came back to Gia. The only time she'd ever felt Skyla had avoided answering a question. Now, Gia understood why. "You told Willow her father was dead."

Her eyes widened, maybe surprised Willow had shared that with Gia. "And he was, to me at least."

"You said you only found out about your mother and father when you returned. Didn't you stay friendly with any of your girlfriends when you left?"

"My ex and I ran in the same crowd. All of my friends were also his friends, and they knew. All of them knew, because it wasn't the first time he'd given someone drugs without their knowledge. But no one dared call him on it, because he'd also become violent and erratic."

Something pinged Gia's radar. "Gabriella and Bobby Fischetti were part of that crowd?"

Skyla nodded.

"Who else?"

Skyla waved her off. "It doesn't matter now. It was a long time ago."

Gia had no choice but to let it go. No way she'd pressure her into saying anything she wasn't comfortable with, especially when she seemed so fragile. But with the danger Donna Mae seemed to be in after a run-in with the same crowd, Gia was still concerned. "What made you come back after being away for so long?"

Skyla clenched her jaw and said nothing.

Gia dropped it. She was clearly done answering questions. "Will you ever tell Willow the truth?"

"How can I? I've never lied to her about anything. Except that."

"Why didn't you tell her?" Not that Gia blamed her.

"Because I never wanted her to go looking for him. Men like him… They're charming, and adored, and believed. People get taken in by that, even my own parents. I didn't want that happening to my baby. I didn't want him having any influence over her."

Gia nodded. "I understand. And I bet Willow would too, should you ever decide to tell her. When I first moved here and opened the café, and I was going through such a hard time, Willow came to me one day. She told me the story about you moving her here, how she didn't fit in. She said you taught her that not everyone needed to like her, that those who were important would. She's a good girl, and her priorities are in the right place. She loves you, Skyla, with all of her heart, and I bet she'd understand."

Skyla stayed quiet, twirling her teacup around and around, staring at the swirling contents.

"Are you okay?"

She looked up, and her eyes were dry. "Surprisingly, yes. In all these years, I've never told anyone what happened. It was actually a relief to get it off my chest. Thank you, Gia."

"Of course, and if you ever want to talk more, I'm here."

"You won't say anything to Willow, right?"

"Of course not. I won't ever say anything to anyone."

Gia's phone rang. She silently cursed the timing, quickly checked the caller ID, then silenced the call. She'd call Savannah back when she got in the car.

Skyla contemplated her tea for another minute, then said quietly, "You asked why I came back five years ago."

Gia held her breath.

"Five years ago, I saw a small article online that he was getting ready to run for public office. I had to come back, had to come see for myself if he'd changed or if he was the same spoiled brat he was as a kid, a man who would use his power to get whatever he wanted at anyone else's expense."

"And what happened?"

"He didn't end up running."

"Why not?"

"I don't know. He just decided not to, I guess. Or maybe he couldn't get the support he needed at the time."

"And now?"

"Apparently, now he found the support he needed."

Gia's mind raced, and she knew the answer before she even formed the question. "Who is Willow's father, Skyla?"

She sucked in a deep, shaky breath, then blew it out slowly. "Mitch Anderson."

Chapter 18

After reassuring Skyla again that she wouldn't say anything to Willow, and making sure Skyla knew she could call if she needed someone to talk to, Gia left. As soon as she climbed into the car, she called Savannah back and switched the call to her Bluetooth. She'd have to head back into town to look for Harley, but it didn't matter. She had to pick up Savannah and Thor anyway.

"Hello?" Savannah's voice broke up over the speakers.

Gia hated using the hands-free system, but it was better than risking an accident, as Hunt drilled into her every time she forgot. Her heart ached a bit at the reminder of Hunt. "Hey, Savannah. Where are you?"

"I'm on my way to Tommy's."

"Is everything okay?"

"Everything's fine, but I remembered Tommy was in the same grade as Hunt in school, so I called him and asked if I could borrow his yearbook."

"And?"

"He grumbled about it for a while, then spent an hour digging through the attic until he found it."

Finally, a possible lead about the group Debby had told her about. "Did you find anything?"

"I'm on my way over to pick it up right now. I'll be home in about half an hour."

"Okay, I'm going to stop in the café for a few minutes, then I'll meet you at your house."

"Sounds good."

"Oh, and ask Tommy if he remembers Mitch and Ron from high school."

"I'm a step ahead of you. I'll tell you everything when I see you."

Gia disconnected, pulled the earpiece out and rubbed her ear. She contemplated what she could tell Savannah about her visit with Skyla. Though she usually shared everything with Savannah, she'd never betray a confidence, nor would Savannah ask her to. Unfortunately, not much of what Skyla had told her could be repeated.

Not that she'd fared much better with Donna Mae.

She stuck the earpiece back in, stopped for a red light, and dialed Cybil's number.

She answered on the third ring. "Hello, Gia. And before you ask, no psychic powers, just caller ID."

She laughed. "I'm just checking in to see how Caesar is doing?"

"He's perfect, thank you. And thank you for everything, Gia—for coming with me to pick him out, offering to take him if anything happens to me, oh, and inviting me to breakfast and introducing me to Earl."

"You're welcome. I'm sorry I couldn't sit and chat longer."

"Oh, dear, I understand completely. Besides, Earl seems like a nice man. I enjoyed the company, and I loved hearing stories about his children and grandchildren." She laughed. "Though I will say, I'm not sure I could keep up with all of that."

"Earl is a sweetheart. He brought the whole clan in for breakfast one morning, and while it is a bit overwhelming to have them all in the same place at the same time, I have to admit, I loved every minute of it. He's got a very close, loving family. The kind I've always dreamed of having."

"You don't come from a large family?"

"No. My mother passed away when I was young, and my father raised me until I graduated high school. After that, I was on my own."

"I'm sorry to hear that."

Gia started to shrug it off, as she usually did, then stopped. "It's funny, but it's never bothered me as much as it has recently. I missed growing up with my mother." More than she'd realized.

"What's different lately?"

She didn't really know, but it seemed to have something to do with Boggy Creek. "Maybe it's the small-town, family atmosphere here in Boggy Creek. I look at Savannah and Earl, with their big families, and then at Skyla and Willow, on their own but so close. I guess it just reminds me of what I'm missing."

"You know, family doesn't have to be related by blood. Seems to me, you've gathered quite a family of your own since moving to Florida."

"I guess I have, though I hadn't thought of it that way." She thought of Cybil, living alone, her husband gone, no children, walking around by herself all the time—though at least she now had Caesar. Though Cybil seemed happy enough, Gia couldn't help but wonder if that was her own destiny. "Do you ever get lonely?"

"Often, though I mostly prefer to stay to myself. I do sometimes miss the companionship of a close friend, someone to confide in, to share feelings with, to do things with. Someone like your friend, Savannah, or Trevor."

She'd done her best to avoid thinking about Trevor. She didn't know what to make of him. "Sometimes friends aren't what they seem."

"Oh, I don't know. Friends may not always share everything, but if you spend enough time together, you get to know them—their character, their loyalties, their morals, how they love, the things that make people who they are. Not the circumstances they find themselves in. Circumstances change over time; the heart doesn't."

She wanted so badly to cling to that sentiment. But Hunt had said Trevor had been ordered by the court to attend anger management. That kind of anger went against everything she'd believed about Trevor. And yet, Cybil was right. She didn't know the circumstances surrounding his arrest or his sentence, so who was she to judge. Besides, he was just a kid at the time. Sometimes even people with good hearts handled things badly, especially when they were young. She owed it to Trevor to at least give him the opportunity to explain. Without her getting shot, of course.

"Are you still there, Gia?"

"Oh, yes, I'm sorry, Cybil, just kind of zoned out for a minute."

"The trouble Trevor has found himself in is weighing heavily on you."

"Yes."

"Why? Don't you trust him?"

And there it was. She'd thought she trusted him, but she'd been mistaken, because at the first sign of trouble, she was ready to bolt. After the situation with her ex, she'd become untrusting and jaded. Trust didn't come easy to her, and when it did begin to build, the slightest provocation sent it crashing down. "It's difficult for me to trust anyone."

"Ah, perhaps that's a flaw in your own character rather than your friend's."

"Maybe you're right."

"Usually."

Gia laughed. "It would seem you've hit the nail on the head."

"Give Trevor time, Gia. Your gut will usually tell you the truth about someone."

"Thanks, Cybil. Your advice always seems to put things in perspective."

"You're very welcome. Sometimes it takes being outside of a situation to be able to see it clearly."

If Cybil was right, and family was not about blood relations but the people you felt closest to, then Cybil was certainly becoming a member of Gia's family. "Are you free on Saturday evening?"

"I am."

"I'm trying out a new menu item, steak and eggs, and I'm inviting all of my closest fr—my family to try them out. Would you like to come?"

"I would be delighted, thank you."

"Great, I'll see you then. And thank you again for the advice." She hung up feeling a little better than she had. Whatever was going on with Trevor, he'd tell her about it in his own time. Until then, she'd just have to trust him. And help him if she could—without getting herself into trouble, and more importantly, without earning Hunt's wrath.

She drove slowly through town, searching the sidewalks. No sign of Harley. Depression settled in when she passed Storm Scoopers, the interior dark, Closed sign featured prominently in the window. Nothing she could do about that right now, but maybe she could at least find Harley and warn him.

She headed to the park Harley tended to hang around, but no sign of him there either. With no idea where else to look, she headed to the café, parked out front, then walked through the side alley to the back parking lot, crossed it at a jog, and checked the clearing where Harley often hung out. Nothing.

Giving up for the moment, she returned to the café and strode through the front door. She couldn't deny the weird feeling she got when she walked in and the café was open and running without her being there. Odd how quickly something could become such a huge part of your life.

Willow looked up from the counter. "Hey, Gia. What's going on?"

"I was looking for Harley; have you seen him?"

"Not today. Do you want anything? Coffee? A cold brew, maybe?"

Gia pressed a hand against her stomach to still the churning. She was a little hungry, but they were going to stop at Xavier's as soon as she picked up Savannah. "I'll just grab a muffin."

"Sit, relax, and I'll get it. What kind would you like?"

She hung her bag over the back of a stool at the counter and sat. "What's left?"

"Banana chocolate chip."

"Mmm…my favorite."

"Mine too."

Not too many customers remained, and those who did seemed content. "Why don't you sit a few minutes and have one with me?"

Willow eyed the muffin. "Okay, you talked me into it."

Willow put two muffins on plates, slid one in front of Gia, then sat next to her with the other.

"Was it busy today?"

"Steady, but not too bad."

Although Gia was glad they hadn't been swamped with more than they could handle, steady but not too bad wasn't going to pay the bills forever. She broke off a piece of her muffin and popped it into her mouth, savored the rich flavor for a moment, then swallowed. "I talked to your mom."

Willow halted her hand halfway to her mouth, then lowered her piece of muffin to her plate. "And?"

"She's okay." She was treading on thin ice. How to reassure Willow without telling her anything that should come from Skyla? "She's just got a lot on her mind."

"Did she tell you what?"

"Not really." True enough. Though Skyla had talked about her past, she hadn't said what specifically was bothering her. She was obviously scared of something, but she hadn't confided that in Gia. Gia could only assume it had something to do with whatever had brought Gabriella and Bobby Fischetti back to Boggy Creek and gotten Ron Parker killed. "But give her time. The two of you are very close. I'm sure she'll share whatever's bothering her when she's ready."

Willow ran a finger back and forth across the edge of her plate.

"You okay?"

She nodded. "I guess I just thought she trusted me."

"What do you mean?"

"I don't know." She shoved the plate away and sulked. "Whenever I have something on my mind, I talk to my mom about it. I guess I always hoped she'd trust me the same way."

"Trust is a two-way street, Willow. If you want her to trust you, you have to trust her as well, have to have faith that she'll talk to you when the time is right. Sometimes, people need to work things out in their own minds before they can share their feelings with anyone else."

A man approached the register, and Gia started to get up.

"This is your day off, remember?" Willow stood and gave Gia a quick hug. "You're right. Thanks."

"Anytime."

"Now get out of here before you end up in any more trouble with Savannah."

Chapter 19

As soon as Gia got out of the car at Savannah's, Thor bolted through the front door and headed straight for her.

She backpedaled until her back hit the car, then braced herself. "Easy, boy."

Thankfully, Thor stopped just short of plowing into her.

She petted his head, and once she was sure he'd stay down, she dropped to her knees for a hug. "I missed you too, baby."

"Oh, stop it, Thor." Savannah hefted her overnight bag over her shoulder and strode across the yard toward them. "Don't go acting like Joey didn't spoil you to death."

Gia opened the door, grabbed the big bouquet of daisies, and thrust them toward Savannah.

"For me?" Her hand fluttered to her chest, and she batted her eyes. "Oh, honey, you shouldn't have."

Gia laughed.

Savannah held the flowers close to her nose and inhaled deeply. "But I sure am glad you did."

"Do you want to take them inside and put them in water?"

"Nah, let's take them to your house. I'll probably be there most of the week anyway."

"Uh…" When had they decided that?

"Sorry, hon, but you owe me a vacation. Remember?" She grinned. "But thanks for the flowers; I love daisies."

"Did you look through the yearbook?"

"Not yet. I visited with Tommy and the baby for a while, so I just got home a few minutes ago. I figured we'd stop and get barbeque, then look through it after we eat." She tossed her bag on the floor in the back, then gestured Thor in, before getting in the passenger side with her flowers in her lap. "Now, don't you eat anything, Thor."

Gia slid into the driver's seat, slipped her sunglasses on, and backed out of the driveway.

"So, what happened with Skyla and Donna Mae?"

She wanted so badly to blurt out everything and have Savannah sort through it all with her and try to make sense of how the past connected to the present, but she'd have to make do with sharing what she could. "Donna Mae used to go out with Harley, then apparently something happened to make him change."

"Something?"

"Something to do with Mitch and his buddies, Ron and Bobby."

Savannah's eyes went ice cold, and she balled her hands into fists. No easy feat with her dagger nails. "You mean those three did something to him?"

The memory of Donna Mae's story came crashing back, and Gia rubbed the ache in her chest. Even if she could repeat that without betraying a confidence, she wouldn't. No reason Savannah should suffer with the knowledge of how Harley's brother had treated him. "Let's just say I won't be voting for Mitch Anderson, and neither will you."

"And to think, I actually liked that man."

"I think a lot of people were fooled by him." The man was a liar, a sneak, and a con artist, among other, less favorable things. "It seems Mitch Anderson is not what he pretends to be, but do you think he could be a killer?"

Savannah gasped. "You think Mitch could have killed Ron Parker?"

"I know it sounds far-fetched." Mitch was in a good position, poised to be mayor, especially now that Ron was out of the picture. "But with Ron gone, Mitch has a pretty clear path to becoming mayor."

"He was favored to win anyway, so what's really different now?"

"What if he didn't kill Ron to eliminate the competition? What if Ron had something on him, something he could have used at the last minute to discredit him?"

Savannah stared out the side window as acre after acre of forest passed by.

Perhaps Gia was letting her intense dislike for him interfere with her thought process. But who else had motive to kill him?

"It doesn't make sense," Savannah said after a few minutes.

"What doesn't?"

"Mitch as the killer. Why kill Ron when, according to pretty much everyone, the two of them were good friends?"

"And yet Ron was running against him," Gia pointed out.

"So, our pool of suspects includes Mitch Anderson, Trevor—"

"Hey, I never said—"

"You have to consider him—"

"I'm trying to rule Trevor out."

"Whether you want to or not."

"Ugh… You don't get it."

"I get it, Gia, but you can't just exclude him from the list because you don't want him to be the killer. You have to either prove he didn't do it or prove someone else did."

"That's it!"

"What's it?"

"We have no clue who did kill Ron, but maybe that doesn't matter. All we really have to prove is that Trevor didn't do it. Then it'll be up to the police to figure out who did."

Savannah chuckled.

"Oh, stop. You know what I mean."

"Yeah, I do. And you're right," Savannah agreed. "Now, if we could just figure out what Trevor was doing the night Ron was killed and why he wouldn't answer any of Hunt's questions."

"Which brings us back to the theory that maybe he's protecting someone."

"Yeah, but whom?"

Gia pulled into the gravel parking lot at Xavier's.

Savannah gestured toward the cluster of picnic tables on the side of the building. "Look, there's actually a table free. Do you want to eat here or take it home?"

"Let's take it home, if you don't mind. That way I can take care of Thor before I sit down for the night." Her arm had started to throb, and she needed to take Motrin. "I can leave him in the car with the AC running and the windows cracked if we go to the take-out window."

"Sounds good. Let's get enough for Hunt and Leo, just in case."

Fat chance Hunt would be showing up, but whatever. "Sure."

"Be a good boy, Thor." She left the car running, since it would only be a few feet away, propped her sunglasses on top of her head, and started toward the take-out window.

"Hey." Savannah grabbed her arm. "Don't look."

"Okay." Gia kept her gaze focused on the menu above the window, despite the intense desire to look around and see what Savannah didn't want her to look at.

"When you can do it discreetly, check out the last table in the far corner. Isn't that the woman who freaked Skyla out in the café?"

"Gabriella Fischetti?" Gia whispered.

"Yes."

She waited for Savannah to move ahead of her into the line, then slid her glasses back on and looked around—discreetly, she hoped. "Yeah, that's her."

Gabriella sat in the farthest corner of the courtyard, a full cardboard carryout container in front of her. She made no attempt to eat, just looked around and bounced her leg up and down, faster and faster the more she scanned the area.

"What do you think she's doing?" Savannah stared pointedly ahead of her.

"Looks like she's waiting for someone." Gabriella might hold the answers Gia was looking for. If nothing else, she'd know who the blond woman who confronted her outside the café was. "Do you think I should try to talk to her?"

"Why don't you stand back while I order?" Savannah suggested. "Keep an eye on her, and if she starts to leave, stop her."

"Why not just talk to her now?"

"Because it's obvious she's waiting for someone, and I'm curious to know who it is."

"Hmm…" Gia hung back, lowering her head to seem as if she was searching through her bag but keeping a close eye on Gabriella from beneath her lashes.

Gabriella fidgeted with the full food tray in front of her on the table. She ripped off a piece of cardboard and tapped it up and down against the table, then folded it. She looked down the road one way, then the other, then went back to tapping the folded cardboard.

Gia was running out of ways to appear discreet. How discreet was it to stand there digging through your purse for an hour? She moved back to the car, rested her elbows on the roof, and leaned forward.

Thor mashed his face against the semi-open window, stuck his tongue through the crack, and licked her chin.

"Ugh…" She jerked upright, wiped slobber off her chin, and laughed. "Thor."

Gabriella looked straight at her, then returned to scanning the parking lot and street. Maybe she didn't recognize Gia. No reason she should, really, since she'd only seen her a couple of times, both of them under awkward circumstances.

A black Mercedes pulled into the parking lot, crunched over the gravel until it reached the farthest corner, then stopped. A woman emerged, her straight pencil skirt, stiletto heels, diamonds, and the confidence with which she carried herself screaming opulence. She turned heads as she sauntered through the picnic area toward Gabriella.

If Gabriella's goal had been discretion, she'd failed miserably.

Savannah popped up behind Gia, bags in hand, and gestured toward the newcomer. "You know who that is?"

"No idea."

"Seriously, Gia? Come on." She nudged her with her elbow. "That's Felicity Anderson."

Still didn't ring a bell, though the name Anderson certainly caught her attention. "Who's that?"

"Oh, please, don't you ever pay attention to what's on TV?"

"Not really, unless it's an old movie."

She rolled her eyes. "It's Mitch Anderson's wife."

"What in the world is she doing at a barbeque place in the middle of pretty much nowhere, meeting up with Gabriella Fischetti?"

Savannah shrugged. "You got me, but she sure doesn't seem too worried about drawing attention."

"That's for sure."

"And Gabriella sure doesn't seem happy."

Gia jerked her gaze back to the two women.

Gabriella's posture had stiffened, and she sat rigid while Felicity stood over her, hands pressed against the table, voice pitched way too low for Gia to hear, though in all fairness, she'd have to be yelling for Gia to overhear anything from where she was standing. She took a few steps forward.

Savannah stepped in front of her. With her hands full of bags, she couldn't very well grab her.

Good thing, too, because Gia had no intention of stopping and every intention of finding out what the two women were talking about.

She sidestepped Savannah and inched closer. When she reached the seating area, she joined the small group of customers waiting for seats and pretending not to pay attention to Felicity Anderson. No easy task considering what an imposing figure she made.

Before Gia could make out any of the conversation, Felicity spun on her nude, leather Christian Louboutins and strolled back to her car as if she didn't have a care in the world. The woman didn't even miss a step as she crossed the gravel in those ridiculous—but gorgeous—shoes.

Gabriella kept her head down, her hair falling over her face.

Gia couldn't blame her. There's no way she didn't know the spectacle Felicity had caused.

Felicity's tires spun as she pulled out of the parking lot, shooting gravel up behind them.

When all eyes turned to the Mercedes rocketing down the rural road, Gia approached Gabriella. Savannah wouldn't leave Thor alone, so it was a pretty safe bet she'd have at least a few uninterrupted minutes with Gabriella. Whether or not she could make them count for anything remained to be seen.

"Excuse me?"

Gabriella looked up, her face beet red. "Yes?"

"I'm sorry to bother you, but I was wondering if I could sit for a few minutes while I'm waiting for my friend to get our dinner? My feet are killing me, and there are no other benches free." Gia breathed a silent thank you that Xavier's was always so crowded.

She looked around as if unsure Gia was speaking to her, then shrugged. "Whatever."

"Oh, thanks." Gia plopped onto the bench across the table from Gabriella. She glanced down at her sensible Keds. "I'll tell you what, I have no idea how that woman walks around in those shoes. Never mind the pain they'd cause in my feet and lower back, I'd feel like I was walking on stilts, trying to balance up there, you know?"

A small smile appeared for just a second, or it could have been a twitch.

"You look familiar. Have you ever been in the All-Day Breakfast Café in town?" Gia prodded.

"Once."

Gia narrowed her eyes and studied her, then snapped her fingers and hoped she wasn't overdoing it. "I remember now. You were in with your husband the other day. Skyla's friend."

She perked up at the mention of Skyla's name, studying Gia with a little more interest. "You know Skyla?"

"Of course, her daughter works for me. I own the café." She extended a hand across the table. "Gia Morelli."

"Gabriella Fischetti." She took Gia's hand tentatively. "Nice to meet you."

"Nice to meet you too."

Gia gestured over her shoulder in the direction Felicity had gone. "She's a bit much, huh?"

Gabriella stared after her, though the car had disappeared already. "That she is."

"I don't mean to be nosy, but what was her problem?"

Gabriella studied her closer.

Uh-oh, she may have pushed it too far.

"She's just a witch."

Gia laughed.

"It was nice talking to you, but I have to go." Gabriella stood and dropped her uneaten food into a garbage pail as she walked away.

Darn. She'd been hoping to get at least something. Giving up, she headed back to the car where Savannah stood waiting, keeping one eye on Gia and one eye on the bags of barbeque on the front seat of the car and Thor pacing the seat just behind it.

"So what was that all about?" Savannah asked.

"Nothing she'll share."

"Odd, but every time we run into that woman, she's arguing with someone."

"I wouldn't exactly say arguing, but she does always seem to be on the receiving end of someone's anger."

Chapter 20

Once they were back at Gia's house and Thor was taken care of, Gia and Savannah piled plates high with barbeque and settled on the couch with Tommy's yearbook spread open on the coffee table between their plates.

Savannah flipped to a page in the middle and pointed out Hunt's senior portrait. Even in the same suit and tie everyone else wore, his defiance stood out. His long, shaggy hair barely covered the earring he wore in his left ear, giving him an eighties rocker look that had gone out of style more than a decade before. "Other than the earring, and with the hair a bit shorter, he still looks the same."

"I know. Go figure, he got the good genes."

"Oh, stop, Savannah. Your whole family got the good genes." Savannah still looked the same as she had the day they'd met.

She laughed.

Gia stuck a forkful of pulled pork into her mouth, savored the tangy flavor, then swallowed. "Okay, how do you want to start? With the seniors, or just flip through from the beginning?"

Savannah sipped her Diet Coke, then closed the book before answering. "Since we don't know for sure all of the players were in the same grade, why don't we look through from the beginning?"

"Makes sense, and make sure to stop and check anyone with long blond hair."

"She could have dyed it, you know."

"I hadn't thought of that." Gia tried to remember what the woman from the front of the café looked like, but although her long blond hair stood out, her features didn't. "I don't know if I could pick her out with dark hair. Probably not."

Savannah took another bite and flipped open the yearbook. A senior group picture spelled out the graduation year on the opening pages. "Do you recognize anyone?"

Gia squinted and leaned closer, whacking her head against Savannah's. "Ouch."

Savannah rubbed her temple. "Watch what you're doing. You've got a hard head."

"Skip this. It's too small to make out people I don't know that well, but I did spot Hunt." He stood toward the back, wearing jeans, a T-shirt, and work boots. Gia's stomach flipped over, and she put her fork down. She hadn't had much time to think since they'd last spoken, or more likely she'd just been avoiding thinking about him.

"Hey, you there?" Savannah waved a hand in front of her eyes.

"Oh, yeah, sorry." She dragged her focus back to whatever Savannah was pointing out. "Who's that?"

"I'm pretty sure it's Mitch Anderson, but it's hard to tell from this picture. I'm used to seeing him in a suit and tie, and here he's wearing board shorts and a T-shirt, and he's a lot younger."

Gia tried to imagine the boy in the picture with close-cut salt-and-pepper hair and a suit and tie, but she couldn't be sure. The surfer dude look threw her. "It's hard to tell for sure. Let's keep going."

They skimmed through the staff pages while they ate, then started on the seniors. Mitch Anderson stared out at her from the first page, his politician smile firmly in place, his "Time to Climb" quote beneath the picture in bold print.

Gia pointed the quote out to Savannah. "What do you think that means?"

Savannah shrugged. "I'd take it as time to move up to bigger and better things."

"That's about what I figured too. Do you think he had political aspirations even back then?"

"It would make sense. He comes from a powerful family in the community."

The look in his eyes reminded her of a shark—cold, predatory—but that could be her own opinion of him coloring her perception.

"Do you want to tell me any more about what Skyla told you?"

She thought about it for a fraction of a second, mostly because she thought Savannah's input might help Skyla with whatever she was going through, then dismissed the idea. "I can't, Savannah. I wish I could, believe me, but I can't betray a confidence."

"Can you at least tell me if she's in trouble?"

"I just don't know. She seems scared, and I don't think she told me everything. Everyone involved might be in danger at this point."

"From whom?"

"Isn't that the question of the day?" *And if we could answer it, I bet we'd clear Trevor.*

Gia turned the page, and a younger Gabriella Antonini stared back at her. "I don't know what it is about her, but she looks so timid. Of course, every time I've seen her someone's been yelling at her or confrontational in some way, so maybe I'm just feeling for her, but even in this picture, she just looks...I don't know, meek."

"Let me see." Savannah leaned over the book, careful to avoid Gia's head this time. "Her smile looks fake, and if you look in her eyes, they look empty."

Skyla had mentioned Mitch giving people drugs. "Does it look like she's on drugs to you?"

Savannah considered Gabriella's picture. "Not really, more like she's just jaded or something, or kind of blasé. Even in the picture from when she was a kid, she's got a world-weary look about her."

"I guess." But something about the young girl tugged at Gia.

Savannah flipped through the pages, both of them scanning the pages for a blonde. She stopped and pointed. "Here's Trevor."

The same photo Gia had seen on the website stared back at her.

Gia frowned. "He looks so serious."

"Yeah, like something was on his mind."

"I wonder if this was around the time he was arrested?"

"Arrested?" Savannah blurted and jerked back to stare at Gia.

"Uh..." *Uh-oh.* Keeping secrets from Savannah was unnatural. How could Hunt get mad at her for slipping up? Everyone should realize she shared everything with Savannah. Hunt most of all. If he didn't want Savannah to know something, he shouldn't have told Gia.

"Gia." Her tone held a note of warning.

Gia cringed. "I'm not supposed to tell anyone."

Savannah flopped against the back of the couch and folded her arms over her chest, sulking. "Seems there's an awful lot of that going around lately."

"Savannah—"

"Nope." She held up a hand to stop her. "I wouldn't want you to tell me something you're not supposed to."

"Please, Savannah, I—"

"So, who shared this juicy nugget you're not allowed to tell me about? Skyla? Donna Mae?"

"Uhh…"

"What?" She lifted a brow. "Not even allowed to tell me that much?"

Gia caved. Not like she hadn't already let the cat out of the bag anyway. "He was arrested when he was a juvenile. His record was sealed on the condition he completed an anger management program."

"Hunt made you keep this from me? Really?"

"Come on, Savannah. In all fairness, it's not like that. He didn't even want to tell me, but I wouldn't agree to stay away from Trevor unless he gave me a good reason."

"Was that before or after you dragged me to his house and got shot?"

Touché. "Ugh… Don't be this way, Savannah, please." An argument with Savannah was the last thing she needed.

"Don't be what way?" She slid forward and perched on the edge of her seat. "Any time you've ever needed me, I've stood by your side. I've broken into houses, hotels, yards with big—really big—dogs, even been shot at. And all I've ever asked of you is that you be honest."

"I know. And you're right."

"Am I? Because I don't see a whole lot of honesty going on lately." She shoved to her feet and stormed toward the kitchen. "I need some air."

Thor scrambled to his feet and followed her.

The back door opened, then closed, the two people—well, one person and one dog—that meant more to her than anything else leaving her alone with her thoughts. And then there was Hunt. As if he wasn't already aggravated enough with her, now he was going to be in trouble with Savannah too. Ah, man. She'd really messed up. And for what?

Gia sagged into the couch, weaved her fingers into her hair, and squeezed. At the end of the day, why was everyone mad at her?

Because she believed in a friend and was willing to stand by him no matter what.

She stood and went after Savannah. She found her leaning on the back deck railing, looking over the vast forest surrounding the yard.

As soon as Gia walked out, Thor trotted to her.

She reached down to pet his head, cherishing the moment he spent cuddling against her. At least things with him were good. He took off too quickly, running into the fenced area to stretch his legs.

"I always feel so small when I stand out here." Gia moved to her side and leaned her elbows on the railing, watching as Thor rolled onto his back and squirmed back and forth in the grass.

"Here feels more natural to me. I always felt small when I lived in New York, insignificant, as if I didn't matter," Savannah said quietly.

"You always mattered to me." Savannah had been like a sister to her almost since they'd met. The first family she'd ever truly had. "I'm sorry, Savannah. You're right. I shouldn't have kept things from you."

"No. I'm not right, but thank you for apologizing." She turned to Gia and smiled. "One of the things I love most about you is your loyalty. I would trust you with anything, because I know you'd never betray that trust."

"I didn't want to keep things from you."

"I know. Believe me, I understand. I'm just stressed, on edge with all of this going on, worried someone is going to get hurt, scared you'll get in over your head."

"When have you ever known me to get in over my head?"

Savannah stared hard and lifted a brow.

"All right, but every time I do, you're always there to bail me out."

"I know, but lately I feel like I'm trying to do that with one hand tied behind my back. You've never been secretive—"

"I already told you, I'm not being secretive, it's just—"

"I know, Gia. I understand. But look at it from my point of view. You've barely known Trevor for six months. Granted, he's a local business owner and by all accounts is a really nice guy, but how much do you actually know about him?"

Not as much as she'd thought, obviously.

"You have trust issues with everyone else, but for some reason with Trevor trust comes easily and blindly."

"That's not true." But the argument held no real conviction.

Savannah didn't bother to argue the point. They both knew she was right.

"You don't have to betray any confidences, but could you at least tell me why it is you believe so strongly in him?"

Gia watched a tall, gray bird with red on its head land on the back lawn, followed by another.

Thor lurched to his feet, his attention firmly focused on the newcomers.

"I don't know. I can't explain it, but I do trust him."

"Do you have a thing for him?"

She tried to rein in her patience. What was it with everyone thinking she and Trevor had more than just a friendship? Realization dawned. "Actually, no. I think the reason I trust him so much is that we're just friends. There's no further expectation, so my trust issues don't really factor in."

"I'll help you, Gia, as I always have, but you have to understand I don't share your same faith in him. I'll do everything I can to help prove his innocence, but only if you can agree to at least consider the possibility of his guilt."

The birds flew off, one after the other. "I'll agree to look at all the facts we find."

"Even if they point toward Trevor as the killer?"

She shifted, uncomfortable with the thought, but ultimately agreed. Savannah was right. If she didn't consider the possibility of his guilt, and it turned out he was guilty, she could end up hurt. "I'll keep an open mind."

"Fair enough," Savannah agreed.

"Now, let's go see what we can figure out. Since I'm already going to earn Hunt's wrath for slipping, and even worse getting him into trouble with you, we may as well try to figure it out."

"He'll only get mad at you if I tell him I know."

Hope surged. "You won't tell him?"

She offered a sly smile. "Other people know how to keep secrets too, you know."

"What secrets are you keeping?"

Savannah laughed and called Thor into the house with her.

Gia followed, and they settled back down on the couch.

Thor jumped up between them and lay with his head resting in Gia's lap.

She stroked his soft fur as they resumed where they'd left off with the yearbook. Not wanting to deal with any further discussion about Trevor's guilt, Gia flipped the page. Skyla's picture came next. "Wow, Willow looks exactly like her."

"No kidding. It could be Willow's picture, except her face is a little rounder."

"Yeah." Probably because she was already pregnant with Willow when the picture was taken.

"And her quote is great. 'Why live in the past when the future holds so much promise?' Such a great outlook."

"Yes, it is." Especially considering what's she'd been through.

"Do you notice something, though?"

"What?"

"None of them really look happy."

Gia hadn't considered that, but Savannah was right. "Even in the pictures where someone is smiling, the smiles don't seem genuine."

"Maybe things were no better back then than they are now," Savannah said.

"If what's going on today has anything to do with the past, that would make sense."

"Well, what makes you think it does?"

Gia tried to look at the situation logically, with no emotion clouding her judgment. "Well, first Gabriella and Bobby show up after being away for however long, and also just happen to show up in the café Skyla's daughter works at. Coincidence? Maybe. But who knows? Nothing about either of them particularly stands out, other than the fact that they knew Skyla. If not for that, I could pass them ten times and not recognize them, especially considering how much time I spend in the kitchen."

"You think they came in before that day, hoping to run across her?"

Phrased like that, it didn't seem likely. "Maybe, or maybe they followed Skyla until they figured out a way to arrange a *chance* meeting."

"Possible," Savannah conceded.

"Then Trevor comes in and says he found a man dead in his freezer, a man who turns out to be another member of the high school crew, a man who's running against another man who also hung with that crowd. First, a mysterious blond woman, and then the wife of one of the men, are both seen yelling at a woman who was also part of that group. In public, no less. It's hard to believe the past is not somehow intertwined in the present."

"Yes. It definitely is." Savannah stared at the book as if it would jump up and offer answers. "So, you think one of them is the killer?"

"Or the next victim."

Chapter 21

"Victim?" Savannah turned to face her fully. "What makes you say that?"

"Well, think about it. Ron was killed, then someone went after Trevor—"

"Wait." She gestured toward the bandage around Gia's bicep. "You think whoever shot you was aiming for Trevor?"

"It obviously wasn't a random drive-by. Someone there was the target, and I can't imagine why anyone would have targeted you or me, so yes, I think Trevor was the target. And so does Hunt, obviously, since he doesn't have bodyguards plastered to our sides."

"Leo said pretty much the same thing."

"Wait, what? When did you talk to Leo about it?"

A blush crept up her cheeks. "He might have mentioned it the other night. But he wasn't supposed to talk to me about it, and he made me promise I wouldn't tell anyone, even you since you're so close to Hu...uhhh..."

Gia plastered on her best self-satisfied smile.

"Oh, knock it off. Smug doesn't suit you."

She laughed out loud.

"Getting back to what we were talking about..." Savannah turned her attention back to the book.

"Oh, right. Well, assuming Trevor was the target, that's two of the group. Add in Skyla's being scared enough to take off with Willow..." Though Gia also knew she could simply be afraid of the past being dredged up and Willow's paternity being questioned.

"And don't forget Donna Mae's frantic pleas to look out for Harley," Savannah added.

"Makes you wonder, doesn't it?"

"Yeah. It does."

Gia flipped the pages, skimming through each picture until she came to Robert Fischetti. The quote beneath his picture read, "Bobby the Bully," and the cocky grin he wore drove the sentiment home.

Savannah leaned closer. "That sure is an ugly smile; makes him look like he's fixin' to steal candy from a baby."

Gia tried to imagine the man she'd seen in the café wearing such a nasty grin. "Funny, I don't remember getting that impression when I saw him in the café."

"No?"

"He seemed pleasant enough. An act? Or do you think he just moved away and grew up over the years?"

They searched the rest of the senior portrait pages. Ron Parker's picture didn't come as a surprise, since Gia had already found it online. "Weird, isn't it? He's the only one that looks genuinely happy."

"I almost expected to find Felicity Anderson's picture in here," Savannah said. "Of course, it wouldn't have been Anderson then."

"No. I was looking for a Felicity, but I didn't see one."

"Unless she changed her name." Savannah stood and lifted both glasses. "I'm going to get a refill, want some more?"

"I think I've had enough caffeine for the day. I'd love a cup of tea, though, if you don't mind. There's peach or mint in the canisters." Gia picked up the yearbook and sat back.

Thor scooted farther onto her lap.

"I know you think you're a lap dog, Thor, but this is getting ridiculous." She laughed and sat back to make more room for him, then skimmed the underclassmen photos and the team and club photos. The chess club photo stopped her short. Trevor stood with the rest of the kids but slightly off to the side, there, but not quite included.

By the time she'd finished, Savannah was back with two cups of tea. She set them on coasters on the coffee table and sat back down. She laid a hand on Thor's side. "Anything?"

"Nah. I was kind of expecting to find at least Mitch and maybe Ron in some of the club photos, maybe debate team or one of the political clubs or something like that."

"Nothing?"

"Not that I can find. Just this." She held the book out to Savannah, opened to the chess club picture.

"Hmm... What do you make of that?"

"No idea, but he doesn't look too happy to be there." She leaned over Thor to put the open book back on the coffee table. "Here, help me look through the candid shots; they're harder to search."

Apparently tired of her moving around, and realizing it wasn't yet quiet time, Thor jumped off the couch and settled at her feet with a stuffed chew toy.

Gia started skimming through the photos. By the fifth page, her eyes were going blurry. She closed them for a minute, then opened them and sipped her tea. "None of them seemed particularly popular in high school. That seems odd to me, for a group of kids from affluent families, with ties to the community."

"Yeah, you'd expect them to be taking leadership roles in school." Savannah picked up the book and continued to look. "You said Debby said they stayed to themselves."

"To the exclusion of everyone else, according to her."

"Seems she was right."

Gia settled back and sipped her tea. Peach, her favorite.

"Bingo." Savannah sat up straighter, held out the book, and pointed to a photo in the bottom right corner. "Look."

A group of teens sat in what looked like a park.

"It's all of them, plus a girl named Felicity Meyers and another named Allison Monroe." She pointed both girls out. "And they're all paired up like couples."

Felicity sat on a picnic bench leaning back against Ron Parker, who sat on the table with his arms draped casually over her shoulders.

Gia looked closer. "You think Ron was dating Mitch's wife?"

"It seems that way." Savannah handed her the book. "Look at the others."

"There's Gabriella and Bobby, but we already knew they were a couple, even back then."

Bobby sat with his back against the tree, his legs straddled, while Gabriella sat between them, her back against his chest.

"And there's Trevor lying in the grass next to Allison Monroe. Can you tell if it's the same woman you saw at the café?"

Gia squinted. "No, I can only see the side of her face, because she's looking at Trevor, but it's the same long, blond hair. It could be her. Why didn't we find her in the portraits?"

"Read the caption. Next to Allison and Felicity it says junior in parentheses."

"I'll have to look through the underclassmen photos again. They must have been in eleventh grade. No wonder we didn't find them in the senior portraits."

"They should be easy enough to find now that you have their names and grades."

Gia started to turn the page.

Savannah held out a hand. "Did you see Mitch and Skyla?"

"Yeah."

Skyla sat on the grass, legs folded, elbows resting on her knees, with Mitch next to her, scowling at something in the distance. Not the most flattering picture of him.

"Even though they're not sitting as close, I still get the impression they're a coup..." Savannah's mouth fell open, and her gaze shot to Gia. "Oh, no."

Technically, she hadn't told. But it wasn't hard to figure out. Given Willow's age, the timing was right.

"Ah, jeez. No wonder Skyla's such a mess. Does Willow know?"

"No. Skyla is terrified she'll find out. You can't say anything to anyone, please."

"Of course, I won't. You know me better than that."

"Yes, I do. But Skyla is scared, Savannah. Really scared. She doesn't want Willow anywhere near any of this."

"I don't blame her. Does Mitch know?"

"She told him before she left town, but who knows if he paid enough attention to realize Willow's his daughter?"

"I guess he wasn't interested in being a daddy, since she left alone." Savannah gazed sadly at the picture of a young Skyla.

"The circumstances were less than ideal. According to Skyla, that aspect of the relationship was not exactly consensual."

"Oh, no." Savannah closed her eyes tight and lowered her head. "What a creep."

"Yeah, but he's managed to convince enough people that don't know him that he should be mayor."

"No wonder she freaked out the way she did when she saw him on TV. If it was me, I'd have wanted to put my foot right through the screen."

"No kidding."

"What about Gabriella? Does she know?" Savannah asked.

"Skyla seemed to think everyone did. Why?"

"That might explain why Skyla got so weird running into Gabriella that day. Maybe she was afraid she'd say something in front of Willow."

"True. There's definitely no mistaking Willow is Skyla's daughter. They look too much alike not to be related."

Thor jumped up and barked, then trotted toward the front door just as it opened and Hunt and Leo walked in.

Hunt offered a sheepish smile. "Hey, there."

Gia resisted the urge to stuff the yearbook under a couch cushion. Secrets had caused enough trouble already. But she would still protect Skyla's, so she closed the book before laying it on the coffee table. Hunt and Leo would draw the same conclusion as easily as Savannah had if they studied the picture. "Hey, yourself."

He gestured toward their empty plates. "Got any more of that barbeque I smell laying around?"

"I don't know. I guess that depends on how much you grovel."

He shot her a grin. "I'd be willing to grovel a lot for a piece of Xavier's chicken."

Gia laughed and shook her head. She couldn't stay mad at him. Besides, Savannah had wondered the same thing about her and Trevor, so maybe it was partly her fault. As Savannah had pointed out, she'd found it easy to trust Trevor, while Hunt had kept from moving too fast to give her time to learn to trust him.

Leo sat on the couch with Savannah curled against him.

"Come on." Gia reached for Hunt's hand. "Let's get you and Leo something to eat and give these two lovebirds a little privacy."

Hunt weaved his fingers through hers and held her hand loosely while they walked to the kitchen, then he opened the door and led her out onto the deck. He faced her, clasping both her hands in his. "I'm sorry, Gia."

"Me too."

He frowned. "What are you sorry for?"

"I think trusting Trevor came easier to me than trusting you, because I don't have feelings for him like I do you. He's a friend. Nothing more. And Savannah has already given me a ton of experience trusting a friend."

His already dark eyes darkened even more, twin pools of melted chocolate.

"You mean a lot to me, Hunt, more than I sometimes care to admit, even to myself. When I came here, I was a mess. Frightened, insecure, jumpy, and you were there for me. I was vulnerable, but you didn't take advantage of that like you could have. Instead, you protected me." She took a deep breath. She'd never admitted it before, not even to herself, but there was no denying it. "It's one of the reasons I fell in love with you."

Hunt cradled her cheek and brushed a tear away with his thumb. "I love you too, Gia, and I'm sorry I hurt you. I do trust you, and I do know you'd never betray that trust. I was never really upset with you. I was upset with myself because I didn't pay enough attention, didn't show you how I felt, and because of that, I risked losing you to someone else."

"You're not losing me, Hunt. I'm not needy that way. I love what I do, and it takes up a huge part of my time. And I understand you love what you do, and you shoulder a tremendous amount of responsibility. All I ask from you is to be honest with me and spend time together when we can."

"That I can do." His lips brushed hers, gently at first, then growing more insistent.

The back door opened, and they jerked apart.

"A man could starve in here while you two are out there messing around." Leo grinned.

Gia looked for something to throw at him, but there was nothing around, so she settled for glaring.

He laughed but sobered quickly. "Seriously, though, Hunt, I just got a call. We have to go."

"Now?"

"Right now. Savannah is throwing some food together for us to take with us. Sorry, but it's going to be cold."

Hunt kissed Gia's head. "Sorry."

"No problem. Be careful."

"Always." He turned and left with Leo.

Gia stayed where she was, watching Thor run in his fenced section of the yard. She picked up a ball from the deck, scanned the immediate area for snakes and other creepy-crawlies, then went down the stairs and threw the ball for him. He didn't bring it back to her, though, simply lay down on the ground and started chewing.

When the door opened behind her, she knew it would be Savannah.

She closed the door softly, walked over, and stood beside her. "Are you okay?"

"Yes. I'm good, actually." And she was. Hunt had told her he loved her. Something she'd never thought she'd believe again from a man. But she did believe him.

"Oh, good. You guys looked so serious out here, we hated to interrupt."

Gia turned toward her. "Did Leo say why they had to leave?"

"No, but I was sitting next to him on the couch when the call came in from the dispatcher."

"What did they say?"

"They needed Hunt and Leo at a crime scene, a murder victim they thought might be connected to their case."

"The Ron Parker case?"

"They didn't specify, but I'm assuming so, since there aren't that many murders in Boggy Creek."

"So you keep saying."

Chapter 22

Gia mopped up the coffee she'd spilled while filling Earl's mug. "Sorry, Earl. I don't know why I'm so clumsy this morning."

"Maybe you need a vacation." He winked at Savannah, who sat one stool over from him.

"Ha ha." Gia tossed the dirty rag into a bin beneath the counter.

The keys Gia had left dangling from the locked door jiggled as Cole let himself in.

"Mornin', all. Well, isn't this a surprise? Didn't expect to see you two here this morning."

"Neither did I." Savannah shot Gia a scowl.

"I can't help it. I couldn't sleep, and I wanted to come in and check on everything." She'd actually wanted to come in and check on Willow. Though she had no reason to believe anything threatened her, she'd been terrified when Savannah had told her about the second murder and hadn't slept a wink all night.

Cole laughed. "No worries. Everything here is under control."

"I know. I just…"

"Don't know what to do with yourself when you're not working?" Cole finished for her.

"Something like that." She shrugged him off. He'd hit too close to home.

"Know what you need?" Earl asked.

"No, what?"

"A trip to Disney World."

Savannah perked up. "That's a great idea, Earl. What park do you like best, Gia? I love walking around the worlds at Epcot, but I'd do whatever park you'd like, really. Too bad we can't do the Food and Wine Festival; it's amazing. We'll have to go again in the fall. You'll love it."

"Actually, I've never been to Disney World."

All three of them went still and stared at her.

Gia squirmed. "What?"

Savannah was the first to recover her senses. "What do you mean, you've never been to Disney? Since you moved here?"

"No, I've never been there at all. My father didn't do vacations, and Bradley hated Florida." She shrugged. "So, I've never gone."

"Oh, we are about to change that," Savannah said. "Who's in?"

Ah jeez. What had she gotten herself into now? "Wait, isn't Disney for kids?"

Savannah just laughed at her apparent ignorance.

"I'm game." Earl raised his hand as if in school. "I go all the time with my kids and grandkids. I love it."

"Why don't you see if any of them want to come? We'll plan it for Monday, when the café's closed, so we can all go." Excitement lit Savannah's eyes. "Are you in, Cole?"

"Wouldn't miss it."

"Great. We'll ask Hunt and Leo, and maybe Skyla and Willow would want to come."

Gia couldn't help but laugh at her enthusiasm.

"I'll tell you what…" Earl pulled out his phone. "My youngest works in reservations over there. How about I give her a call and see if she'll book us a few rooms for Sunday night? We can meet up right after the café closes."

Savannah clapped her hands together. "That'd be great, Earl, thank you."

"Wait, I—" Gia started.

Earl ignored her. "What hotel do you like best?"

Savannah grinned. "Hmm…probably Caribbean Beach if it's available. If not, I love Port Orleans Riverside."

"You got it." He stepped away from the excitement to make the call.

"Savannah, I'm not sure—"

"I'm so excited. A mini family vacation. This definitely makes up for not going to the Keys."

Ugh…when she put it like that. "Looks like we're going to Disney."

"Yes." Savannah pumped her fist in the air.

Cole frowned. "How about Universal? Have you been there?"

"Nope."

"Never seen the Harry Potter section?"

"No, and I do love Harry Potter, the books and the movies."

"We'll do that next Monday." Savannah pressed her phone to her ear. Yikes, what had she started?

Willow walked in and locked the door behind her. "What's all the excitement?"

"Looks like we're going to Disney World on Monday," Earl answered. "Would you and your mom like to come?"

"Sure. I love Disney."

"What? Am I the only one who's never been to Disney?"

A chorus of yeses answered her.

She laughed and unlocked the door. No mad rush waited outside, but experience had taught her the busiest time didn't start until about an hour after they'd opened. She twirled the key ring on her finger, turned, and started back toward the counter. A breaking news alert on the TV stopped her short. She gestured toward the TV playing silently in the corner. "Hey, turn that up."

Savannah disconnected her call, grabbed the remote, and turned up the volume.

The reporter stood in front of a small stucco house on a quiet residential street. "...found dead yesterday in what's believed to be his rental home. The police have not issued a statement as of yet, but it's believed to be the body of Robert Fischetti, a local man who's lived in Georgia for the past two decades and only recently returned home. We have no details on how he was killed, other than that his death is considered to have occurred under suspicious circumstances."

Gia's gut cramped. Her gaze shot to Savannah.

"What?" Earl paused with his mug halfway to his mouth. "Who's Robert Fischetti?"

"Remember the woman who came in and made Skyla uncomfortable?" Gia glanced at Willow, who stood staring at the TV.

"Vaguely. Someone she knew when they were kids, right?"

"Yes. Bobby Fischetti was her husband."

"Hmm..." Earl blew on his coffee and took a sip. "What a shame."

She couldn't blame Earl for not understanding the significance of another member of the same group of old friends turning up dead.

Thoughts whirled through Gia's mind, a chaotic mess she had no hope of sorting out. "What do you think happened?"

Savannah sat staring at the TV, her brows drawn together. She shook her head. "I have no clue."

"Do you think that's the call Hunt and Leo got last night?" No sense worrying about keeping anything a secret now.

"I assume so."

When a commercial started playing, Gia muted the volume.

Cole rounded the counter and filled everyone's coffee mugs, then sat and grabbed a muffin from a covered cake dish on the counter. "What's going on?"

Gia tried to sort through the information in her mind and pick out what she was and wasn't allowed to say, taking great care to be careful in front of Willow. "Turns out Ron Parker and Trevor ran in the same crowd when they were kids."

Savannah gestured with her mug toward the TV. "Bobby Fischetti was also a member of their little group."

"I remember those kids. Some of them, anyway." Cole took a big bite of his chocolate peanut butter muffin. "Mmm…"

"I remember Mitch well enough," Earl said.

Cole swallowed. "Sneaky little thing he was."

"I take it you're not a fan?" At this point, Gia couldn't believe anyone would vote for that snake.

"Nah."

"I can't even believe that man ever got to be a candidate." Savannah picked out a blueberry muffin and sat next to Cole.

Earl held up a finger. "Just a minute. Aren't you the one who sat here a few days ago singin' his praises?"

"Yeah, well, it's a woman's prerogative to change her mind."

He spread his hands wide. "Whatever you say, dear. Just sayin'."

She mumbled something under her breath, broke off a piece of muffin, and stuffed it into her mouth. Probably to make sure she didn't blurt anything inappropriate.

Willow finished filling salt and pepper shakers and headed into the back room.

Gia followed. "You're awfully quiet this morning. Is everything okay?"

Keeping her back to Gia, she nodded.

"Willow? What's wrong?"

She turned and flung herself into Gia's arms, crying softly, reminding Gia how young she really was, even though she'd always seemed so much more mature than her years.

Gia rubbed her back. "What happened, Willow? Is your mom okay?"

She nodded against Gia's chest.

"Are you all right?"

She sniffed and nodded again, then stepped back. "I'm sorry."

Gia grabbed both of her arms. "Sorry for what? You haven't done anything."

"I didn't mean to blubber all over you."

"Don't be ridiculous, Willow. I'm here for you anytime you need a shoulder to cry on. Now, what's wrong?" She led her into the office and closed the door behind them. Savannah would cover for her until she pulled herself together.

"I talked to my mom last night. She told me you came to see her, said you told her she should be honest with me about everything."

Uh-oh.

She wiped her eyes. "Thank you for that."

Gia nodded, unsure what to say since she didn't yet know how the conversation had gone. Since Willow was there crying her eyes out, it was possible it hadn't gone well. "What did your mom say?"

"She told me everything."

Gia didn't know what to ask. It seemed stupid to ask if she was okay when she clearly wasn't. And how could she be, under the circumstances?

"My mother is a strong woman, and it breaks my heart she had to go through that alone."

Gia yanked a few tissues from the box on her desk and handed them to Willow.

"Thank you." She wiped her eyes again and blew her nose. "It also makes me realize how lucky I am. My mom would always stand by me, no matter what. I could tell her anything, no matter how far-fetched or unbelievable, and she'd believe me. And even if I was wrong, she'd still have my back."

"Yes, she would." Gia had no doubt about that. Skyla would protect her child with her last breath.

"I don't understand how her parents could have turned their backs on her. And how she could have raised me with so much love after they did."

Skyla was everything to her child that her parents hadn't been to her. A flare of hope surfaced in Gia. She'd always been afraid she wouldn't be a good mother because of the way she'd been raised. But maybe it was just the opposite. "I think sometimes, when our parents hurt us very badly, we go out of our way to make sure we don't repeat their mistakes with our own children."

Willow nodded. "I guess that makes sense."

"Your mother loves you very much."

"Yes, she does, but I don't understand why she took so long to tell me everything." She lowered her voice to a whisper. "Or why she lied about my father. Why didn't she trust me?"

"Did she explain that situation to you?"

"What he did to her?" Shaking her head, she tossed the tissue in the garbage and grabbed another. "Yes, she did."

"I honestly don't think it was a matter of not trusting you. I think she just didn't want you to be hurt." Gia stared into her eyes, trying to gauge how she felt.

"I would never believe a word that man says."

Relief rushed through her. "Now, you wouldn't, after knowing the truth about him. I don't think your mother wanted to keep secrets from you or lie to you. I think she wanted to protect you, to shelter you from knowledge that would hurt you. She's a good mother, Willow, and she did what she thought was best for you, even though I'm sure she would have liked someone she trusted to confide in."

"I hadn't thought of it that way."

"Sometimes, keeping something from the people we love is harder than sharing the burden would be."

Willow sniffed. "I saw the news when I was getting ready for work this morning, the same story that was on out front. Another of her friends was killed yesterday."

"Did Skyla see it?"

"Yes."

"How did she react?"

"Are you kidding me? She freaked out. Totally blew a gasket and started packing our bags."

"Then what are you doing here?"

"I'm not running away. This is the home my mother chose for us, and this is where we'll stay. My mom is a good person, and there's no reason for anyone to hurt her."

While altruistic, it was also naïve. "If your mother doesn't think the two of you are safe here, maybe you should listen to her and take off for a while."

"We'll see what happens. By the time I'd left, she'd calmed down and seemed to be thinking more rationally."

"Did she tell you why she thought you were in danger?"

"No. But she did mumble something about everyone knowing what happened. I don't know if she was talking about what happened with her and Anderson or something else."

It seemed to Gia that Skyla was still keeping secrets.

"You are welcome to stay and work, if you want to, but if you feel threatened or scared at any time, you don't leave alone. Understand? Tell someone and we'll get Hunt or Leo over here to help."

Willow swallowed hard and nodded.

"I've been thinking of hiring a new waitress, anyway."

Willow's eyes went wide. "I thought you said it was okay for me to stay?"

"Oh, no, I didn't mean to replace you. I was thinking of hiring someone part-time to help you out when it gets crazy busy."

She pressed a hand against her chest. "For a minute I thought you were going to fire me."

"Never, Willow. You're my best employee. But don't tell Cole. Or Earl. Or Savannah. Definitely don't tell Savannah."

Willow laughed a little but sobered quickly.

It hurt to see her so sad, to see so much responsibility weighing on her. She was beginning to understand why Skyla had made the choice she'd made.

"Do you really think my mom could be in trouble?"

"I honestly don't know what's going on, but I'm going to try to find out."

"Thank you, Gia."

"If you and your mom don't want to stay home, you're welcome to use the upstairs apartment or stay with me at my house."

"Thank you. I'll call her and let her know."

Gia hugged her. "Are you okay now?"

"Yes. I'm good. Thanks."

"Good. Now get back to work." Gia grinned.

"Yes, ma'am." Willow saluted, then spun and headed for the door. She opened it and started through, then looked back over her shoulder. "You know, I'm not only lucky to have my mom. I'm lucky to have you too. And Savannah, and Earl, and Cole. My mom's friends abandoned her when she needed them most. Mine will rally together to help."

Gia swallowed the lump in her throat and nodded, remembering very well how it felt to be on the receiving end of a loyal friend's help.

Chapter 23

Gia enjoyed the rare pleasure of being able to do whatever she wanted while at work. With Cole manning the kitchen and Earl pitching in when it got busy, and Willow running the dining room with Savannah to lend a hand when needed, Gia felt almost unnecessary.

But it did give her time to play around with more cold brew recipes, so she couldn't complain. With Trevor's shop shut down, she'd ended up stuck with all of the coffee, and it wasn't selling like she'd hoped. She was going to have to start advertising it more. She should have done that in the first place, but she'd hoped word of mouth would be enough. Advertising cost money.

When the door opened, and Scott and Meredith Harper walked in, Gia waved Willow off, grabbed two menus, and greeted them with hugs. "How's my favorite snake wrangler doing?"

Scott laughed. "Haven't had many calls lately. I guess you're settling in?"

"Either that or the snakes are too scared to show up at my house now." There was a time, not very long ago, that she'd never have believed she'd one day be joking about snakes. She shivered. "Come on, and I'll treat you two to breakfast."

"Oh, you don't have to do that."

"I know, but I want to." She grinned. "That's the beauty of being the owner. I can do whatever I'd like."

She showed them to a table against the side wall, chatted for a minute about the new access road under construction at the back of their development, then left them to look over their menus.

She stuck her head into the kitchen. "How's everything going back here?"

"Couldn't be better." Cole flipped three pancakes, poured warm syrup in a small bowl and set it on a plate, then piled the pancakes next to it and stuck the plate on the cutout for Willow.

"How's things out there?"

Gia checked that everything was stocked in the warming trays. It was. "Under control."

Cole turned his back to her, but not before she caught his grin.

"What's so funny?"

"You wanted a chance to be out from in front of the grill. Now you have it, and where are you?"

"Ha ha." She opened the refrigerator. Diced ham bin, full. Tomatoes, full. Onions and peppers, both full.

"Earl came back a little while ago and diced everything up to make sure we'd have enough to get through lunch."

She closed the refrigerator and sighed.

"Why don't you go get a pad and pen, and we'll do up the menu for Saturday?"

"You don't have to coddle me."

"Yes, I do, or you're going to drive me crazy lurking around doing nothing."

"Fine." She ran to her office and grabbed a legal pad and a pen. She considered writing up the ad for a waitress, then dismissed the idea. Willow hadn't seemed all that eager to share her position. Besides, it seemed the staff she had was enough to keep things running smoothly. Why rock the boat?

She returned to the kitchen and pulled a stool up to the counter. "Ready."

"First off, who's coming?" Cole flipped two eggs, then cut open four rolls and set them on plates. He scanned the order tickets, then squirted ketchup onto one roll, slid two eggs and a pile of bacon on top of the ketchup, and piled a western omelet on the next roll. He dropped three breakfast sausages onto the third roll and bacon onto the fourth and added scrambled eggs to both and a slice of cheese to the bacon. He slapped the tops back on all four rolls, cut them, and stuck the plates on the cutout.

The man made working the grill into an art form. No wasted moves, every minute used to its fullest advantage.

Gia realized she could learn a lot from him.

"Did you hear me?" Cole asked.

"Uh, yeah, sorry. My mind wandered."

"Oh, yeah, where to?"

"I was just thinking how lucky I am to have you and how much I enjoy watching you work."

He laughed. "Well, thank you. I enjoy working for you. Very much. I'm glad you offered me a job."

"Seriously? You were retired, living the peaceful life, until I mucked it all up on you. Do you ever miss it?"

"You know how you've been feeling for the past few hours? Wandering around aimlessly, no pressing business to attend to, nowhere special to be, that feeling of not being needed?"

She nodded. He'd nailed it perfectly.

"That's pretty much how I felt ninety percent of the time. Sure, it was fun when I occasionally hung out with a friend or something, but most of my time was spent alone. So, thank you. You really are a great friend, and you have given me exactly what I needed."

"Someone pointed out recently that family doesn't have to be related by blood." She got up and kissed his cheek.

He blushed clear up to his hairline.

"Now, let's figure out who's coming Saturday."

Cole recovered, though his cheeks still remained flushed. Could be the heat from the grill. "Since you're obviously not going to the Keys this week, do you want to switch it to Friday instead?"

"Nah. Let's leave it Saturday. I was thinking of going to Ron Parker's wake on Friday night after we close."

"Oh, yeah? What for?"

She didn't really know. Maybe to see who else was there. "I just figured I'd go pay my respects."

"Gia…" It seemed Cole was starting to know her as well as Savannah did.

"Oh, all right. I'm curious to see who shows up."

"Fine, then. We'll do steak and eggs Saturday and the wake on Friday."

"You're coming with me?"

"Well, I'm certainly not letting you go alone."

"Thanks, Cole."

"Anytime." He gestured toward the pad with the spatula. "Now let's get that list done before it's too late to send you out shopping."

"Me?"

"Yeah, you. I'm busy working the grill." He shot her a cocky grin and lowered his voice to a stage whisper. "Don't tell anyone, but my boss is a slave driver."

"Yeah, right." She laughed.

"You'll want Earl and Savannah."

Gia jotted the names onto the pad. "Hunt and Leo. And I'll ask Willow if she and Skyla would like to come."

"Don't forget to count you and me."

"Right." She scribbled their names, just to be sure she got the count right. "Oh, and Cybil."

"Is that it?"

She thought of inviting Donna Mae but decided against it. Though she liked her, she didn't really know her all that well, and until she knew what was going on, she'd hold off on getting any closer. And Trevor was, of course, out of the question at the moment. "Yup."

"You can always ask Trevor at the last minute after you see how things play out," Cole said gently.

It was her turn to blush, and she simply nodded.

"And how many dishes would you like to try?"

"I don't know. I was thinking maybe three or four. What do you think?"

"That should work. I'll do an omelet, a pan-seared steak with eggs on top, a country-fried steak, and eggs with gravy and biscuits. That should be a good variety, then I'll do a vegetable scramble and home fries with scrambled eggs as sides."

"That sounds perfect."

"We'll do it buffet style. Each person can taste a bit of each and give you feedback. Just remind everyone this is a dinner item, not breakfast. You want it to be a little more substantial."

"Got it." Gia ripped off the page and folded it in half. "I'm really excited about this, Cole. Thank you."

"Anytime. I'm hoping it will pull in the dinner crowd you're hoping to get."

"Me too." She crossed her fingers and held them up.

"Now, go make yourself useful."

She left him to cook and headed out front.

The dining room was in full swing, most tables full. Willow and Savannah rushed around taking orders, filling drinks, and ringing up customers.

Gia headed for the register. If she rang, Willow and Savannah would be free to spend more time on serving customers.

"Hi." She smiled at a gentleman in a business suit. "Did you enjoy your breakfast?"

"Very much. Thank you, ma'am."

"You're welcome." She took his check and money, rang him up, and handed him his change. "Be sure to come again."

"I will, thank you." He met up with a woman who was waiting by the door and left.

An undercurrent buzzed through the café, and a number of customers shifted their attention to the muted TV.

"Excuse me," a woman sitting at the counter said, "could you turn that up for a minute, please?"

Gia turned to see what was going on, grabbed the remote, and turned the volume up enough to be heard but not enough to annoy those who might not be interested. She probably need not have worried, since almost all eyes turned to the TV where Gabriella Fischetti was being led toward a police cruiser, flanked by Hunt and Leo.

"...a new twist as the victim's wife, Gabriella Fischetti, is taken in for questioning."

The camera zoomed closer to Gabriella, giving the world a bird's-eye view of her being led away by the police with blood—presumably her husband's—covering the front of the same shirt she'd been wearing at Xavier's the evening before.

"Holy cow! Are you kidding me?" Savannah stood, tray filled with food balanced precariously, staring wide-eyed at the television. Her gaze shot to Gia. "No way."

"I can't even believe it." Never in a million years would she have pegged Gabriella for a killer. "Do you think it's possible?"

Savannah recovered her senses and strode toward the table full of customers waiting for their breakfast. "Anything is possible."

"I guess." But Gia still had a hard time wrapping her head around Gabriella as a killer. Especially after she'd seen her and her husband together. Even after being together since high school, Gabriella had still looked at Bobby as if she adored him. She waited for Savannah to finish what she was doing.

Gia had told Savannah numerous times she didn't have to pitch in while she was supposed to be on vacation, but Savannah blew her off every time. She enjoyed hanging out in the café, mingling with the customers, catching up on the latest gossip, and Savannah came from a home where you stirred the pot when you walked by, so there was no way she'd sit around doing nothing.

Gia grabbed her on her way back to the kitchen with the empty tray. "Would you be okay here for a little while?"

"Sure. Why?"

"I just need some air, and I want to talk to Zoe about taking Thor overnight when we go to Disney."

"That's a great idea. I have to be honest, I was expecting you to try to find a way to worm your way out of going, and I figured Thor would be the perfect excuse, so I already checked into boarding him down by Disney."

Gia laughed. Leave it to Savannah to think of everything. "I'm not going to back out. Actually, I'm really looking forward to it. But I would rather leave Thor with someone he knows if Zoe can take him."

"I don't blame you. I didn't realize she did overnight visits."

"Me neither, until she mentioned keeping Brandy overnight for Trevor." Savannah frowned. "When was that?"

Gia's mouth went dry. "The same night Ron Parker was killed."

Savannah grabbed her arm and pulled her through the swinging door to the back room. "Are you kidding me, Gia? Did you tell Hunt that?"

Gia bristled. "No, why would I?"

"Seriously? You don't see that as one heck of a coincidence?"

"I don't know. I hadn't thought about it."

"Where was he?"

"I have no idea. I haven't spoken to him, remember?"

"You need to tell Hunt about this."

"Oh, fine. I'll mention it when I see him."

Savannah lowered her chin and raised a brow.

Gia huffed out a breath, annoyed with Savannah's constant suspicions about Trevor. "All right, already. Jeez, I'll call him after I talk to Zoe."

"Thank you."

"Whatever."

"And while you're at it, let him know about Disney on Sunday. I left Leo a message, but he hasn't called or texted me back yet."

"Yeah, okay. Oh, and Cole is doing steak and eggs Saturday night if you and Leo want to come."

"Of course, I'll come, and I'm sure Leo will if he can get away."

"Great."

Savannah wrapped her arms around Gia. "You know I only worry about you because I love you, right?"

Gia hugged her back. "Of course, I do. Sometimes you're just a little overprotective."

"Well, get used to it, 'cuz that's what family does."

Gia smiled and stepped back. As irritating as it could sometimes be, she definitely wanted to get used to it. "Thanks, Savannah."

"No problem. Now get out of here and go talk to Zoe."

Gia tried to order her thoughts as she walked down the sidewalk toward the doggie day care center. No matter how she tried, she just couldn't see

Gabriella as a killer any more than she could see Trevor in that role. Of everyone in the group of kids that had hung out together in high school, she'd have pegged Gabriella, Trevor, Harley, and Donna Mae as the least likely to commit murder. Ron Parker, Bobby Fischetti, and Mitch Anderson would have topped the list. And yet, two of the three of them were now dead. Murdered. And Gia couldn't shake the feeling it had something to do with that group.

She walked past Storm Scoopers on the opposite side of the road. Though she tried to see in the windows, only the reflection of Main Street stared back at her. At least all the crime scene tape had been removed, and the street out front cleared of the litter that had been dropped while hordes of reporters and concerned citizens had stood out front chomping at the bit for information.

She kept walking until she reached the doggie day care.

A petite woman with gray hair she'd never seen before sat at the reception desk when she walked in. "Hi. How are you?"

Gia looked around but didn't see Zoe or any of the regular staff. "I'm doing well, thank you. How are you?"

"Very well, thank you. I'm Layla, Zoe's mother. Just filling in for Janet today, since she's at her daughter's wedding."

"Hi, Layla. It's nice to meet you." Gia extended a hand. "I'm Gia Morelli. I own the café down the street."

"Oh, yes." Layla shook her hand. "Zoe and I have gone to breakfast there many times. I just love your vegetable omelets."

"Thank you."

"What can I help you with today?"

"I was looking for Zoe. I wanted to talk to her about keeping Thor for an overnight visit."

The woman's face twisted up as if she'd sucked a lemon. "I can get her for you, and you can ask, but I'm not sure she'll agree after the last overnight she agreed to."

"Why, what happened?"

"The man never showed up for his dog."

She couldn't possibly be talking about Trevor. "You mean Brandy?"

"Yes. You know her owner?"

"I do."

"Well, if you see him, tell him Zoe still has his dog. Not for nothing, but that's not right."

"No," Gia admitted quietly. "But I can't really judge since I don't know why he never came back."

"Or called."

"Right." What could she say? Though she found Layla's gossiping about Trevor to a woman she'd never even met in poor taste, she could understand her frustration. And she couldn't even begin to imagine why Trevor wouldn't have come for Brandy, or even called, when he'd been released days ago.

"If you'll excuse me for a minute, I'll get Zoe." Layla pushed her chair back and stood. "It was nice meeting you."

"You too, thanks."

Gia stared at the book sitting open on the desk, the book Zoe always jotted down notes regarding Thor's care in, then glanced toward the closed door to the back rooms. She could just take one quick peek through it and see what notes Zoe had made about Brandy on Trevor's page. She plopped onto a chair in the waiting area, then stuck her hands beneath her legs for good measure. She wouldn't want someone walking into the café and invading her privacy.

Zoe saved her from arguing with herself any further when she walked in. "Hey, Gia."

"Hi, Zoe, how's everything?"

"Great." She gestured toward the bandage on Gia's arm. "What happened?"

"Oh, it's nothing. Just a scratch." Scratch, gunshot wound, whatever. It didn't really hurt much anymore, but it had begun to itch in earnest.

Zoe glanced up at the clock on the wall. "Taking off early today?"

"Oh, no. I'm not here to pick Thor up yet, but I did want to ask you about keeping him over Sunday night."

"Oh, uh…"

"Your mom was telling me Trevor never came back for Brandy?"

Her jaw clenched. "I'm sorry about that. As much as I appreciate my mom helping out when I need it, she never has learned a thing about confidentiality."

"No problem. But I am worried about Trevor. Has he called?"

"No, I haven't heard a word from him. Have you?"

She couldn't tell her about the night of the shooting, because Hunt had asked her to keep that quiet.

"He hasn't called me either." True enough. "But I did hear he was released, so hopefully he'll be in touch soon about Brandy."

"I hope so. Now, about Thor…"

"I'm hoping to go to Disney World with Savannah and some friends on Sunday night and stay over until early Tuesday morning." At least, that's what Savannah was hoping. She insisted it would be better to just stay over and sleep for a few hours, then make the forty-five minute drive back to the café early Tuesday morning. Gia had her reservations. But after screwing up her last vacation, Gia didn't want to throw a wrench in this one too. "I'd pick Thor up after work on Tuesday."

Zoe hesitated.

"If it's a problem, I can board him down by Disney. I just preferred to have him with someone he knows and I trust."

She smiled. "Of course, I'll keep him. I'm sorry. I just never expected that from Trevor, you know?"

"Yeah, I do."

They chatted a few more minutes, then Gia played with Thor for a little while before heading back to the café. The time spent relaxing with Thor had stilled her mind, giving her a much-needed reprieve from the situation with Trevor. But walking past Storm Scoopers brought it all crashing back.

On impulse, she looked both ways, jogged across Main Street, and looked in the front window of Storm Scoopers.

Something moved inside, toward the back of the shop.

She squinted against the glare, cupped her hands around her eyes, and leaned closer to the glass. A shadow crossed the doorway to the back room. Definitely someone moving around in there.

She looked up and down Main Street. Plenty of people were milling around, in and out of shops, strolling along, enjoying the warm spring afternoon.

Gia pulled on the door handle, and it eased open, despite the Closed sign hanging smack in the middle of the door. She poked her head inside. "Hello?"

Chapter 24

"We're closed," a familiar voice yelled from the back room.

"Trevor? Is that you?"

Trevor appeared in the doorway to the back room. "What are you doing here, Gia?"

"What am I doing here?" Good question, actually. Not that she had any intention of answering, since she had no clue. "What are you doing here? And why haven't you called Zoe about Brandy?"

He shoved a hand through his already disheveled hair, and it flopped right back into his face. "Is Brandy all right?"

His concern tugged at her heart a little, and she softened her tone. "She's fine, but Zoe's worried sick about you."

"I know, and I'm sorry."

Gia moved farther into the shop, then leaned against the table by the booth closest to him. "Trevor, what is going on? Please, talk to me."

"I can't, Gia. You have to let it go."

"Don't you get it? I can't. You're my friend. And I trusted you, something that doesn't come easy for me."

"I know, and I'm sorry."

"Stop saying that. I don't care if you're sorry. Sorry for what? And what don't you know? Talk to me."

He slumped against the doorway and folded his arms across his chest. "I think I might have screwed up."

"Ya think?"

"No need to be sarcastic."

"You're right." She was trying to get him to confide in her, not alienate him. "I'm sorry. I've just been frustrated."

"Trust me, I feel your pain. I've pretty much cornered the market on frustrated."

"Why don't you come sit down?" Gia gestured toward the booth behind her.

Trevor hesitated for another moment, then gave in and crossed the room. He rubbed a hand along the back of the booth seat. "This was my dream, you know?"

"What? Storm Scoopers?"

"Yeah." He dropped onto the booth bench, rested his forearms on the table, and hung his head. "I always wanted an old-fashioned ice cream parlor. The kind where families go to celebrate special occasions and kids came to hang out after school."

"How long have you been open?" Funny, she'd never thought to ask that.

"Almost ten years."

"That's a long time."

"Yeah." He traced a heart someone had carved into the table, ran his finger around and around the outline. "Some of the kids in my class couldn't wait to escape the small-town life the minute they graduated, but not me. I embraced it. I loved it. I never wanted to leave and go anywhere else."

She already knew he'd been out of high school for eighteen years. "What did you do when you graduated, before you opened the shop?"

"A little of this, a little of that, mostly nothing but feel sorry for myself and the mess I'd made."

Her interest piqued. She couldn't help but wonder if the mess he was talking about had anything to do with what was happening now. "What do you mean? What mess?"

He sighed and slumped against the back of the seat, dropping his hands into his lap beneath the table. Where she couldn't see them.

A small jolt of fear shot through her, then she scolded herself. This was Trevor. He wasn't going to do anything to her. He was her friend. "Tell me, Trevor. I want to help. Who knows? Maybe I can."

He shook his head and looked down. "You can't. No one can."

"What do you mean? Did you try talking to Hunt, answering his questions? I don't understand why you wouldn't talk to him. He's a friend, Trevor." She lowered her voice, even though there was no one around to hear her. "He helped me when I was in trouble."

"There's one big difference, though."

"Oh?" She sat back, frustrated with his attitude. "What's that?"

He leaned toward her, folding his arms on the table. "You weren't guilty."

She gasped and jerked back as if he'd slapped her. Her chest tightened, sweat popped out on her brow, and she sucked in a breath to scream, then remembered no one was close enough to hear her. It wouldn't have mattered anyway. Turned out all she could manage was a wheeze. "Guilty?"

He held his hands up in front of him. "Ah, jeez, Gia. I don't mean I killed Ron."

She struggled to regain control of her breathing.

Trevor jumped up and ran to the refrigerator case by the front door, grabbed a water bottle, then came back and handed it to her.

She uncapped it and sucked down a big gulp, then recapped the bottle and set it on the table and glared at him. "You're going to want to be careful how you phrase that."

"Ugh... You're right. I'm so sorry." He shook his head. "But the fact that you could even have thought that says a lot, doesn't it?"

"Yeah, it says you've been acting strange lately. I try to call you, and you don't answer or return any of my calls. You don't bother to pick up your dog, or even call to see how she is. I come to your house to see if I can talk to you, and it turns out to be a fortress, complete with concrete wall and guard dogs, and then, as if that's not enough, someone shoots me. So, what do you think, Trevor? Do you think it should shock me when you sit there and confess your guilt?"

"I guess not."

"Well, it did."

His gaze shot to hers.

"Because I never once, through all of that, never once thought you were guilty."

"Ah, Gia." He clasped her hands in his. "I'm so sorry. It's not that I don't trust you. It's just that I care about you, and I didn't want to get you involved. And as for Brandy, I love her so much, and I didn't want to take a chance of her getting hurt, so I left her where I thought she'd be safe."

"You're my friend, Trevor, a very good friend. How could you think I wouldn't get involved if you needed help?"

A small smile played at the corner of his mouth. "I guess I should have known better."

She laughed. "You got that right."

He lowered his head to rest on their joined hands, and she accepted he was going to keep his secrets bottled up tight. He released her hands and sat back. "How's your arm?"

She looked down at the bandage. "It's fine."

"I'm sorry you got hurt. I never wanted that. I never wanted anyone to get hurt."

"I know. It's okay. That wasn't your fault; it was my own."

"If I had answered your calls, you wouldn't have felt the need to scale my gate in the middle of the night, and you wouldn't have gotten shot."

What could she say? He was right. "Technically, it was morning. Just very early morning. And, for the record, we went over the wall, not the gate."

"I guess I'll have to rethink my security set up."

"You're going to need a bigger wall."

He laughed, then sighed and rolled his shoulders. "Ah, Gia. I really screwed up."

She stayed quiet. No sense offering to hear him out or help again. She'd offered enough times. If and when he wanted to talk, he would. Until then, she'd just sit there with him and be his friend.

As Savannah had done for her when she'd needed it. Sometimes you didn't need a friend to interfere; sometimes you needed them to stand by while you made a mess of your life, then jump in and help pick up the pieces.

"All through school, I hung out with one group of kids. The rich kids. The ones who came from powerful families. The ones with high ambitions. The kids who would one day rule the world. Mitch swore he'd be president one day. And Ron was going to be right there with him, his vice president, his right-hand man, as he'd been all through school."

"Then how did Ron end up running against him?"

He spread his hands wide. "I have no idea. I kind of figured they had some sort of disagreement. It's just the only thing that makes sense."

Gia had to agree. "What about Bobby Fischetti?"

"Bobby didn't have political aspirations, but he was next in line to run his old man's oil company, as powerful a position as any."

"Did he end up running the company?"

"No, actually. He took off, and his younger brother inherited the throne, so to speak. It was quite a scandal at the time."

"What about Gabriella Fischetti?"

"All of the girls in our group had high hopes of becoming important and influential figures. Except for Gabriella. All she ever wanted was to get married and have a houseful of kids."

Gia realized she didn't know if Gabriella had ever fulfilled that dream. She'd never seen any kids with them or heard any mention of them, but it was just as possible they'd chosen to keep them far away from this mess.

"And I wanted to open an ice cream parlor."

Gia smiled at the young, goofy kid she imagined him to be.

"The point is, I didn't fit in with them. Not really. Not even back then. They were mean and ruthless in a way I could never be. They were willing to climb over anyone to make it to the top."

"What about Skyla? She doesn't strike me that way."

"Skyla was always kind of quiet, but her family held a lot of power. They'd have expected her to enter the political arena, for sure."

"But she didn't."

"No." Trevor squirmed in his seat. "She left town."

Gia let it drop. She'd already heard the story from Skyla, but she couldn't help asking the question that nagged at her. "If you were so different, then why did you hang out with them?"

"Who knows? Because I was expected to, I guess. From the time I could walk, my parents dressed me up and hauled me off to every one of their birthday parties, holiday gatherings, and social events. As I got older, I just continued to go. The other kids didn't really bother with any of us, so even when I did try to do something else, I ended up alone."

Her heart ached as she remembered the picture she'd found in the yearbook, him with the chess club, standing slightly apart from everyone else. The only picture she'd found of any of his group with anyone but each other.

"By twelfth grade, all of the other kids in our group had paired off, leaving me and Allison Monroe untethered. She latched on, and we ended up together through the rest of that year. Not really a relationship, more like what I had with my parents. She told me where to be, and I got dressed and showed up. It was more for appearances than anything else."

"Were you happy with that?"

He shrugged. "Not really, but it didn't matter. It was the life I was used to, doing what I was told, when I was told, and on and on and on."

Gia could understand following along and doing the things you were supposed to do, the things society expected of you. She'd done it often enough while married to Bradley, attending function after function to keep up appearances, even after his victims had started coming forward.

"Allison was never faithful to me. We didn't have that kind of relationship, and I was fine with it, accepted it for what it was. We were basically friends, nothing more." He went back to tracing the carved heart with his finger. "Then one day, I walked in on her and Mitch. I'd had enough, and I told her we were done."

"I'm sorry."

"I should have realized...did realize that she didn't seem right when I caught them together. She seemed out of it, like she wasn't even really aware of my presence or its implications."

Skyla's story rocketed to the front of her mind. "Oh, no, Trevor."

"She sought me out after, apologized, though there was really no need. She told me what he'd done. She thought he'd slipped some kind of drug into her drink." He balled his hands and bounced the sides of his fists up and down on the table. "And I didn't believe her. She'd never lied to me before. And Allison never drank or used drugs. She was too into herself, too into taking care of her body to damage it with alcohol or drugs. I knew that, and still, I didn't believe her."

"So, what happened?"

"There was a party. Mitch's party a few weeks later. I hadn't seen Allison at all in between, but when I saw her that night, she was wrecked. Not acting herself, unkempt, not at all the girl I knew. I caught Mitch in private and asked him what was going on."

"And he denied it?"

"No, quite the contrary. He bragged about it, said he was slipping drugs into her drinks, making her do things with him that she'd refused to do before." He weaved his hands into his hair and squeezed so hard she thought he would pull it out. "And I lost it. I went ballistic, beat him so badly they had to call an ambulance to come take him away."

He stared hard into Gia's eyes. "Honestly, Gia, if Ron and Bobby hadn't pulled me off and beat me to within an inch of my life, I think I might have killed him."

"Oh, Trevor."

"Anyway, before the ambulance even left, Allison passed out and stopped breathing. I don't know what he was giving her, but whatever it was, he gave her too much. Had the ambulance not already been there, she probably wouldn't have made it."

"Did Mitch get arrested?"

Trevor laughed, but it held only anger. "No. Mitch had political aspirations, goals his father shared. His father came to me while I was still in the hospital recuperating. He offered me a large sum of money to keep my mouth shut."

"And?"

"I told him what he could do with his money. But then Allison came to see me, and she begged me to keep quiet. She didn't want to go through court, have to tell what he'd done to her, what she'd done with him. So, I kept my mouth shut."

"You respected her, Trevor. There's nothing wrong with that."

"No? It wasn't the first time, Gia. It wasn't the first time Mitch had done something to a girl. There had been an incident with another girl a few weeks before. If Harley hadn't intervened then, I don't know what would have happened to her. As it was, she was never the same after. And neither was Harley. How many women do you think Mitch has done that to? Women who might not have suffered if I'd opened my mouth. How many lives do you think that man has wrecked?"

"Then why didn't you say something?"

"Because I had no proof. Allison refused to testify, the other girl disappeared, Harley wouldn't talk to me, I never saw any drugs. It was my word against his, and I couldn't prove a thing."

"I'm sorry, Trevor."

"Yeah. Me too."

Gia took a deep breath and tried to digest everything he'd told her. "Did Mitch press charges against you for hitting him?"

"Yeah," he scoffed. "Just to prove he could make my life miserable if I told. But I didn't care. My father had some power of his own, and he believed me. He spoke to the judge, and arranged a plea bargain. He spoke to him privately about the situation with Mitch too. Unfortunately, there was nothing that could be done."

"Then you did try."

"For all the good it did."

Gia squeezed his hand. There wasn't much she could say to alleviate his guilt. "I don't understand why you wouldn't answer Hunt's questions. Why not just tell him all of this if you think it relates to Ron Parker's murder?"

"Because the night Ron was killed, Allison called me. She said she was back in town and wanted to get together. I left Brandy with Zoe and met Allison at her hotel. We had a drink and some appetizers at the hotel bar, and then I started to feel sick. She said she wasn't feeling well either, so we went back to her room to sit down and hope it passed. The next thing I remember, it was morning. I was lying on one of the hotel room beds, and Allison was on the other. She said she didn't remember anything that happened. My wallet and the keys to my car and house were on the nightstand, where I have no memory of putting them, but the key to Storm Scoopers was gone."

"Did you find it?"

"No. I went home and got the spare before I came in the next day."

Realization dawned. "You think Allison killed them."

"I'm not sure." He ran his hand through his hair. "But I'm afraid she might have."

Gia shoved to her feet. "Jeez, Trevor, why wouldn't you tell Hunt that?"

"Because I'm not sure. I can't be sure. I was obviously set up to take the fall for Ron's murder. What if we were both drugged and set up? How can I put her through that?"

"Ah, man." She paced back and forth beside the booth. "Have you talked to her?"

"No. Not since that morning, before I found him."

"You think she—or someone—set you up to take the blame for Ron's murder?"

"Well, let's see. Whoever did it used my key to enter my shop and either lured him there and killed him or dragged him there after they killed him. Either way. What do you think?"

Chapter 25

Gia strode through the All-Day Breakfast café door early Friday morning ready to get back into the swing of things. While she'd sort of enjoyed the few days of not having to be responsible, she couldn't help the thrill she got from things returning to normal.

It had taken the better part of two hours and a promise from Hunt that he'd treat the information confidential and try to look into it discreetly, without involving Allison unless absolutely necessary, for Gia to talk Trevor into confiding in Hunt. Once Hunt had arrived at Storm Scoopers, Gia had left. She hadn't heard from either of them since.

She'd spent Thursday shopping with Savannah, who had insisted they needed new clothes for their upcoming Disney trip, despite Gia's argument that they'd only be gone for a day. She'd even allowed herself to be talked into a mani-pedi, which she had to admit had felt kind of good. She didn't often treat herself. Then she'd picked up everything Cole would need for their steak and egg dinner Saturday night and dropped it off at the café.

But her break was over. She locked the door behind her and busied herself with the familiar routine of getting ready to open. She restocked the refrigerator, which was easy since Earl and Cole had prepped everything the night before, turned on the grill to warm up, set out and filled warming trays with bacon, sausage, home fries, grits, and gravy, and refilled the shelves with breads and English muffins. Once the kitchen was ready, and the aromas of breakfast meats and potatoes filled the air, Gia headed out front to start all the coffee pots and fill the cake dishes with breakfast pies and assorted muffins. She wrote "Now Serving Cold Brew Coffee" on the big chalkboard she used for the daily specials and dragged it out onto the sidewalk.

By the time she was finished, the fresh Kaiser rolls had been delivered, and she hoisted the bag up and brought it to the kitchen.

A knock sounded on the front door.

"Coming," she yelled, though Earl probably couldn't hear her from the back room. She hurried out to unlock the door, then held it open for Earl and Cole. "Good morning, guys."

They both took their usual seats at the counter.

"I didn't expect to see you this morning, Cole. I figured you probably had enough the past few days." She set out three mugs and poured coffee for all of them.

"I got used to getting up early, so I figured I'd come in and meet Earl for breakfast."

"Well, I'm glad you did, and thank you again for running things all week."

"Anytime, dear. I had a blast." Cole leaned over the counter and grabbed the remote. He turned on the TV and turned up the volume.

Gia looked up at the TV, but there was a commercial playing. "Is something going on?"

"They're supposed to be having a press conference about the deaths of Ron Parker and Bobby Fischetti," Cole said.

"I saw that on the news before I left," Earl chimed in. "Said it was supposed to be coming up soon."

The commercial ended, and they switched to a live shot of a podium set up in front of the courthouse. Reporters jostled for positions as a team of investigators, Hunt noticeably absent, approached the podium.

A heavyset man with gray hair held his hands up for quiet, then introduced himself as the medical examiner and began his update. He didn't really say anything new, except to offer his opinion that both victims had been killed with the same weapon, an ice pick, which still hadn't been recovered.

All of the investigators to take the stand rattled the same line, ongoing investigation, still pursuing active leads, and blah, blah, blah… The one new bit of information they offered was that they believed the first killing may not have been premeditated, while they believed the second one was.

"How could they say that wasn't premeditated?" Cole pointed at the TV.

"Maybe he was stabbed during an argument that got out of hand," Earl said.

"I guess, but then what were they doing in Trevor's shop when it was closed?"

Gia tried to conjure an image of Allison as the killer. When Gia had seen her, she'd been angry, nasty, but a killer? Maybe. She could see that before she could see Trevor killing anyone. Still. Why would she have killed him? The more Gia thought about it, the more it seemed he had to have been killed over something that had gone on in the past. She just couldn't come up with anyone with a motive to have killed him now.

"They had to have been in his shop for a reason and..." Earl shot Gia an apologetic look. "Sorry, Gia, but I can't imagine Trevor wouldn't know they were there."

"No, it's okay." She'd accepted the fact that Trevor did appear guilty, or at the very least, an accessory in some way, and she couldn't defend him without admitting she'd spoken to him, so she just kept her mouth shut.

Willow unlocked the door and came in, saving her from having to get any further involved in Earl and Cole's conversation.

"Good morning, Willow."

"Hey, Gia." She held the door open for Skyla. "My mom wanted to have breakfast and hang out for a while this morning. Is that okay?"

"Of course." She set two more mugs on the counter and filled them.

Skyla took a seat, but Willow set right to work readying the dining room, filling salt and pepper shakers, wiping down the menus, making sure the chairs were at the right tables, and changing any dirty slip covers on the cushions. Every once in a while, stopping to sip her coffee.

"Cole and Skyla, do you know what you want for breakfast?" Gia asked.

Cole hooked a thumb toward Earl. "I'll have what he's having."

Skyla didn't bother looking at the menu. "I'll have a vegetable omelet and a glass of orange juice, please."

"I'll get the juice." Willow slid behind Gia and opened the small refrigerator beneath the counter. She poured three glasses of juice, then returned the pitcher and refilled the coffee pot they'd already drained.

With everything in the dining room under control, Gia pulled on an apron and got to work in the kitchen. She lined bacon and sausage to heat, then scrambled six eggs and poured them onto the grill. She grabbed the pre-cut vegetables from the refrigerator—spinach, squash, zucchini, mushrooms, and tomato—and sprinkled them on the grill to warm, then scrambled three more eggs.

She broke up Earl and Cole's eggs and stirred them, dropped a couple of warm biscuits onto each of their plates, ladled out two small bowls of gravy, two orders of home fries, and two orders of grits, put them all on a plate, and stuck them on the cutout. She dropped two slices of the multigrain bread Skyla liked in the toaster, flipped Skyla's eggs, spread the vegetable mixture on one half of the circle, flipped the other half over it and added a sprinkling of cheese to the top, put the scrambled eggs, bacon, and sausage on Earl and Cole's plates, then slid Skyla's omelet onto hers and buttered her toast. She set all of the plates on the cutout and peeked through into the dining room.

Though Willow had already seated two tables, their orders hadn't come back yet.

She ran into the back and grabbed another carton of eggs. When she returned, the plates were gone and two order slips hung above the grill.

Two slices of breakfast pie. Easy enough. She popped two slices of white bread and two of rye into the toasters, then ladled pancake batter onto the grill for the next order, lined sausage up next to it, and put one slice of western and one slice of meat lover's pie onto plates. When the toast popped, she buttered it, added a small side bowl of jelly to each and put the plates on the cutout. She flipped the pancakes, filled two bowls with butter and two carafes with warm syrup, put the sausage on the plates, and stacked the pancakes next to them.

With both orders done, she started washing the dishes she'd left in the sink.

"Knock, knock." Savannah stuck her head in the kitchen.

"Hey, I thought you were going back to work today?"

"Nah, I took the day off." She grabbed a plate and put a slice of western pie on it, then forked open an English muffin and dropped it into the toaster. "No sense going back when I'm just going to take off Monday anyway."

"Your boss didn't mind?"

"Nope. I never take time off, and I always cover when someone else wants to, so he was fine with it. Besides, I work on commission, remember?"

Her English muffin popped up, and she slathered it with butter, put it on her plate, put the plate on the counter, and pulled up a stool. "I talked to Leo."

Gia fumbled the stainless-steel bin she was in the middle of washing and it clattered into the sink. "And?"

Savannah took a bite of pie. "Mmm...delicious."

"Thanks."

She swallowed, then got up and poured a glass of orange juice from the fridge. "He said Trevor came in and talked to Hunt. He agreed to having Leo present, since he's Hunt's partner."

She shut the water off and turned toward Savannah. "Did he tell them everything?"

"Leo didn't say specifically what he told him, but he did say he answered their questions this time. He also said he understood why he was afraid to the first time they questioned him."

"Do they still think he had anything to do with Ron's murder?" She held her breath.

"No. Trevor has pretty much been cleared of all charges, as long as nothing new comes up."

Gia sighed in relief.

"He also said to tell you Hunt said thank you and he's sorry, and he'll call you when he can."

She nodded. "Thanks, Savannah."

She cut a piece of her pie with her fork, then pushed it around her dish. "I'm sorry, Gia."

"For what?"

She looked up at Gia. "I should have trusted you when you were so sure Trevor didn't do it."

"Don't be silly. Trevor didn't handle everything the best either. If he'd have just answered their questions in the first place, he wouldn't have looked so guilty."

"I'm sure he had his reasons."

"Yeah." And they were good reasons, which she understood, but it didn't change anything.

Cole poked his head in the kitchen. "I'm taking off, but thank you for breakfast."

"You're very welcome. I hope you enjoyed it."

"Delicious, as always." He waved to Savannah. "I'll see you ladies later."

"Later?" Savannah asked.

He paused. "Are we still attending Ron Parker's wake?"

Savannah looked at Gia.

She'd forgotten all about that. "Sure. I'll meet you there at seven."

"Sounds good. See ya then."

"What's that all about? I didn't know you were going to the wake."

"I mentioned wanting to go before Trevor went in to talk to Hunt, and Cole said he'd go with me. May as well pay my respects to the family."

"I'll tell you what. I'll pick Thor up and bring him to Joey, then I'll come back and pick you up, and we'll go together."

"That works, but I'm picking Thor up right after and going home. I haven't gotten to spend enough time with him lately, and I miss him."

"No problem." Savannah bit into her English muffin, chewed, and swallowed. "I'm very curious to see who shows up."

"Yeah, me too."

Willow ran in and tacked up three orders. "We're starting to get busy now."

Leaving the rest of the dishes, Gia washed her hands, pulled on her gloves, and started the orders.

Chapter 26

The cloying scent of flowers hung thick in the air, threatening to choke Gia when she walked into the funeral home. "Looks like half the town sent flowers."

"Do you think Donna Mae did them all?" Savannah looked at one of the cards attached to a beautiful spray of the gladioli Donna Mae had pointed out in the shop.

"I don't know, but she said she already had a lot of orders when I was in there at the beginning of the week."

Savannah admired another arrangement. "She does good work. This wreath is beautiful."

"Yes, it is."

"Do you want to go up and pay our respects?" Savannah gestured toward the front of the room where a closed casket sat covered in a blanket of blue roses.

"Why don't we just stand in back for a few minutes?" Gia was beginning to regret attending. Despite the incredible number of people lined up to pay their respects, she still felt out of place.

"Sure." Savannah squeezed between two people on line and melded into the crowd in the back corner.

Gia stayed as close as she could. When they reached the corner, and Gia felt less conspicuous, she searched the room for Cole, then leaned close to Savannah and whispered, "Watch for Cole. He should be here any minute."

"Sure."

A lot of the faces entering the room were familiar from the café or around town. Her gaze skipped right over Gabriella seated in the back row, then shot back when she realized who she was. "What do you think she's doing here?"

"Who?"

Gia gestured toward the back row. "Gabriella Fischetti."

"Huh…no idea. I didn't even realize they'd released her."

"Me neither, but I never heard she was arrested, just taken in for questioning."

Savannah frowned. "I'm surprised she's out at such a public event so soon after her husband's death."

"Me too. But maybe she wanted to pay her respects."

Gabriella sat staring at the door. Waiting for someone perhaps?

Savannah nudged Gia with her elbow and pointed toward the doorway. "There's Cole. And is that Skyla with him?"

"Looks like it." Gia lifted a hand to get Cole's attention, then waved him over. "Ah, jeez. Is that Hunt and Leo behind him?"

"Yup." Savannah leaned back against the wall between a chair and a small table, obviously trying to make herself invisible. "Maybe they won't notice us."

Cole reached her and kissed her cheek, then Savannah's. "Look who I found outside."

"Hi, Skyla." Gia hugged her. "I didn't expect to see you here."

Skyla dropped her gaze to her clasped hands. "It seemed like the right thing to do."

"I know what you mean." Gia leaned close to her and lowered her voice. "Willow said you talked to her. Did everything go okay?"

"Yes, it did. I should have realized the need to tell her on my own, but I'm grateful to you for pointing it out when I didn't."

"No problem. That's what friends are for." As Savannah so often reminded her.

When Trevor walked in and slid into a seat in the back row, a low hum started through the room, many people staring what they seemed to think was discreetly and whispering to their companions.

Trevor held his head high and stared straight ahead.

Gia started toward him.

"Gia?" Donna Mae called quietly. She left the arrangement she was setting up and crossed the small space to Gia, then hugged her and stepped back. "I only have a minute. I still have more flowers to bring in, but I wanted to say thank you."

"For what?"

"For looking out for Harley." A smile lit her eyes, brightening the gold flecks. "I spoke to him. He finally approached me outside the shop, and he talked to me."

"Oh, Donna Mae, that's fantastic."

Joy radiated from her. "Yes, it is. It's been such a long time, but he's still every bit the sweetheart he always was."

"Yes, he is."

"Our time may have passed, but it comforts me to know the Harley I remember is still in there. And who knows, maybe we can work on being friends of sorts. At least I feel like we've taken the first step in that direction. And I have you to thank for it, so again, thank you."

"You're very welcome. I hope things work out."

She nodded and Gia watched her go back to work. It couldn't be easy for her, but Gia was relieved she had at least found some peace.

A strong arm wrapped around her waist, and Hunt kissed her temple. "I'm not even going to ask. Just stay out of trouble."

"Don't I always?"

He laughed out loud, earning more than one dirty look.

"Shh…" Gia hushed him.

He lowered his voice. "Sorry."

"Did you get my message about dinner tomorrow night?"

"Yes. If I can be there, I will."

She leaned into him for just a minute, enjoying the feel of his arm holding her close, the woodsy scent of his aftershave embracing her.

"Gotta go." He kissed her cheek, then he and Leo left the room together.

Gia turned to Savannah. "Did Leo say where they were going?"

"No, how about Hunt?"

Gia scoffed. "Seriously?"

"I don't believe it."

"I don't see why not. Hunt never says where he's going."

"No, not that. That." Savannah nodded toward the front of the room, where Felicity Anderson had just stood from kneeling beside the casket and turned toward them. "Boy, the whole gang's here tonight, huh?"

"Not yet." Mitch and Allison had yet to show up.

"Hi, Gia." Trevor stood in front of her, hands in his pants pockets.

"Hey, Trevor. How's everything going?"

"It's okay, I guess. Hey, Savannah."

"Hi, Trevor."

He looked around the room. "Funny, isn't it? How the news that I was arrested traveled like wildfire, yet when I'm cleared? Nothing. It's like no one's heard a thing."

"Don't worry about it. I'll make sure the news hits the rumor mill before the night is over." Seemingly happy to have a mission, Savannah started working the room.

Gia rubbed a hand up and down his arm. "Don't worry about it. When Savannah sets her mind to something, you'd be surprised at the results."

Trevor's gaze fell on something toward the front of the room, and he stilled.

Gia followed his gaze.

A woman wearing a black veil disappeared through a door at the front corner of the room.

"Excuse me." Trevor weaved his way between mourners, heading in the same direction the woman had gone.

Cole and Skyla were both involved in conversations.

With a quick glance around, Gia followed Trevor.

When she reached the door, which turned out to be a fire exit, she pushed through and found herself in the back parking lot.

"Allison, wait. I just want to talk to you." Trevor chased after the woman in black.

Undecided whether to go after Trevor or go look for Hunt, Gia froze just outside the door.

Allison, if it even was Allison, kept going, never even slowing down. She started across the street behind the funeral parlor at a jog.

Apparently giving up on trying to get her to stop, Trevor threw his arms in the air and watched her go, then stood with his hands on his hips looking after her, before he turned around and headed back toward Gia.

A car accelerated out of nowhere, headed straight toward him.

Gia screamed.

Trevor whirled back around as if in slow motion. He would never get out of the way in time.

Gia ran toward him, but before she'd taken three steps the car plowed into Trevor.

He rolled over the hood and tumbled off the side.

"Trevor!" Gia screamed as she ran toward him.

The car screeched to a stop, then slammed into reverse and rocketed backward out of the lot and onto the street. When the driver stopped to shift into drive, Gia got a good look at her.

"Hey, what's going on out here?" An overweight, balding man in a dark suit climbed out of his car and yelled to her.

"Get help!" Gia yelled and dropped to her knees beside Trevor.

The man turned and ran around the side of the building.

She shook his arm. "Trevor, are you okay?"

He sat up, rested his elbows on his knees, and clasped his hands behind his head. "Yeah, I'm okay. Thank you."

"For what?"

"If you hadn't screamed, he'd have mowed me down for sure. As it was, you gave me just enough warning to roll over the hood."

"She."

"Huh?"

"She'd have mowed you down. Not a man, a woman."

"Gia, is that you?" Hunt squatted beside them. "Why am I not surprised? Are either of you hurt?"

"I'm not, but Trevor got hit by a car."

"Are you all right, Trevor?" Hunt practically vibrated with energy, or maybe nerves that she'd been hurt.

"I'm fine. Just go find whoever hit me."

"All right." Hunt stood and looked around.

Gia pointed down the street in the direction the car had gone.

Hunt directed two men to follow. "I don't suppose you were able to get a license plate, huh, Nancy Drew? How about a description of the car?"

"It was dark-colored, but I don't know the make or model."

"Anything else you can tell me?"

"Yeah, I can tell you the name of the driver. I saw her clear as day when she stopped beneath the light to shift into drive and looked over toward where she'd deliberately hit Trevor."

"She?"

"Yes, Felicity Anderson was driving the car."

"Felicity Anderson? Mitch Anderson's wife?" He raked a hand through his hair, which had been unusually in place until then, probably because he was at a funeral. It definitely couldn't be lack of stress.

"Yes."

"Gia, are you sure?" Hunt swiped a hand over his mouth. "You have to be a hundred percent sure before I can pursue her."

"I'm positive, Hunt. I saw her the other day at Xavier's giving Gabriella Fischetti a hard time about something."

Hunt radioed the patrol car with Felicity's name. "Do you know what they were arguing about?"

"No, I was too far away to hear, but a lot of other people weren't, so someone probably overheard them. Felicity wasn't exactly subtle."

Hunt helped Trevor to his feet. "Are you sure you're all right? Do you want an ambulance?"

"No, thank you. I'm fine. Thanks to Gia yelling when she did."

Hunt gave her a look somewhere between *Good job* and *When are you going to learn to mind your own business?*

"You're welcome," she said to Hunt.

He ignored her and lowered his gaze, but not before she caught the telltale twitch that turned up the corners of his mouth. "Why don't you go in and get cleaned up?"

She looked down at her black slacks, the knees of which were covered in dirt from the parking lot, including what looked like a piece of chewed gum. "Are you coming in?"

"No, I'm going to see what I can find out about Felicity Anderson." He hugged her quickly and dropped a kiss on top of her head. "Go ahead. I want to make sure you get in before I go."

"I'll walk her in," Trevor offered.

Hunt nodded. "Thanks."

Since the fire exit door was locked and couldn't be opened from the outside, they had to walk around the front. When she walked into the lobby, more than one head turned her way.

She looked down at the mess on her pants and noticed the bandage on her arm was soaked in blood.

"Jeez, Gia. You opened that up again." Trevor took her arm. "That's the second time you've been injured on my behalf. The same injury, actually."

She must have banged it against something in her haste to reach Trevor and hadn't even noticed. She laid her hand over his. "It's all right, Trevor. I'll go into the bathroom and clean it up."

"Are you sure? I could take you to the hospital."

"No, no. Thank you. I'm fine." But she desperately wanted out of that lobby where more and more people were taking notice of her condition. "I'll meet you inside in a few minutes."

"Sure." He walked her to the restroom door.

"I'm fine, Trevor. I promise. Now go sit down." She left him standing there, completely positive he'd be waiting in the exact same spot when she came out.

She approached the sink and looked in the mirror. Her hair and what little makeup she wore were mostly okay, but she wet a piece of paper towel and wiped a bit of eyeliner that had smudged beneath her eye. When she was done, she tossed it in the trash and wet a bigger wad, then looked around for somewhere to put it down.

Gabriella Fischetti walked in, her eyes swollen and red from crying, and spotted her. She started to back away, then noticed Gia's arm. "Oh, my. Do you need help?"

Her first instinct was to refuse, then she thought better of the idea. Why not take advantage of having her alone for a few minutes? Maybe this time, she wouldn't blow it. "Sure, thanks."

"What can I do?"

"Would you mind holding this?" Gia held out the wad of wet paper towels. "I have to unwind my bandage, but I don't want to put it down anywhere."

"Sure." She took the paper towels.

Gia unwound the bandage wrapped around her arm and threw it in the garbage, then lifted the gauze. A thin line of blood trickled down her arm.

"That looks nasty." Gabriella handed her the paper towels.

Gia pressed them against her arm, then slid her purse off her shoulder. "Would you mind getting the gauze and bandages out for me?"

"Of course." Gabriella took her bag and rummaged through for what she needed. She pulled out the gauze and opened the paper wrapper, then handed a thick piece to Gia. "Is one enough?"

"It should be, thank you."

"Do you mind if I ask what happened?"

"Noth...uh..." Something stopped her from issuing her usual *it's nothing* reply. Since Gabriella seemed to be smack in the middle of this mess, why not be honest? "I was shot."

She gasped. "Shot? How?"

Now it got a little dicey. "I was at my friend's house, and someone took a shot, presumably at him, and missed."

"Sounds like a friend you should stay away from."

She watched for her reaction in the mirror—discreetly, she hoped. "Nah, Trevor's a really nice guy. It wasn't his fault."

"Trevor?" Her eyes widened with recognition. Bingo. She knew exactly who Gia was talking about.

"Yes, Trevor Barnes. Do you know him?"

Gabriella backed up, and Gia was afraid she was about to bolt.

She held the gauze tight against her arm. "Would you unroll some of the bandage for me?"

Gabriella shook off whatever fear had gripped her and nodded. She unwound a length of bandage. "Will this be long enough?"

"Perfect, thanks." She ripped it off, and Gia wound it around her arm, careful to keep pressure on her wound. "I'm sorry about your husband."

Gabriella's lower lip quivered, and she nodded.

"You two seemed very close when I saw you in the café the other day."

"We were." She sucked in a shaky breath.

"I can't imagine being with someone since high school."

"Bobby was the love of my life." Tears poured down her cheeks. She grabbed a tissue and wiped her nose, then hiccupped. "It wasn't supposed to be this way. We came here to do the right thing, and now he's gone."

Gia taped the bandage around her arm and led Gabriella to a row of chairs in a small alcove. "What happened, Gabriella?"

She shook her head as she sat.

Gia sat down next to her. "Look, Gabriella, whether I like it or not, I'm smack in the middle of this mess. I already know a lot of what's gone on in the past, including Mitch Anderson's track record with women."

Gabriella's eyes went wide but she said nothing.

"The other day, I was shot, and a few minutes ago, I watched—" Gia caught herself just in time to keep from blurting Felicity Anderson's name. "I watched someone run over my friend."

"Oh, no. Trevor?"

"Yes."

"Is he all right?"

"He'll be okay. He was able to roll over the hood at the last minute."

Gabriella sagged back in the chair. "I can't even believe this."

"Please, Gabriella, let me help you. Tell me what's going on."

She picked at a chip in her maroon nail polish. "I tried to tell Bobby to let it go, but he wouldn't listen. He felt responsible." She shook her head. "I told him what he did when he was a kid was over, it was past, and he should just let it go, but he couldn't."

Gia held her breath, waiting to see if she'd continue.

"When Bobby realized Mitch was going to win the election, he said there was no way he could be mayor, no way he should be afforded the opportunity to one day climb even higher than that." She looked at Gia, her eyes filled with a plea for understanding. "My Bobby wasn't a good kid, but once we left here, he grew into an amazing man."

Gia nodded, understanding her need for people to know her husband had tried to do the right thing.

"Anyway, since Ron was running against Mitch, Bobby figured maybe he'd changed too. Turned out Ron was trying desperately to keep Mitch from becoming mayor, but without involving anyone from the past. Apparently, he was worried about his cousin being involved, said he'd already caused her enough grief. But he finally agreed to work with us, as long as Donna

Mae was kept out of it. We found more than one woman willing to testify, but the one we wanted most refused."

The pieces fell into place. "Allison Monroe."

If she was surprised that Gia knew, it didn't show. "Yes. No matter how many times we reached out, she wouldn't cross him. Honestly, I didn't blame her. She was terrified. As it turns out, rightfully so."

Gabriella sat up straighter, anger starting to replace some of the sadness. "It also turned out Mitch had a mole in Ron's campaign. When it got back to Mitch that there was a string of women willing to testify against him, as well as evidence of some of the crimes he'd committed, he knew Ron had betrayed him, and he went ballistic."

"How'd you find that out?"

She stared pointedly at Gia. "Mitch wasn't the only one with spies."

Gia nodded. It made sense Ron would have put someone in place to keep an eye on things.

"But Felicity was the one who really freaked out. She'd put up with Mitch's abuse and infidelity for years, all for the promise of one day being first lady, and her aspirations were about to come crashing down in the worst possible way. Bobby and I came to town at Ron's request, when he was ready to go public with his findings. Next thing we knew, Ron was gone."

"Do you know who killed him?"

"No, but I have my suspicions."

Gia tried to tread gently. "Do you know what happened to Bobby?"

She shook her head. "When I came home and found him that way, I was terrified. I took off, driving aimlessly, praying whoever did it wouldn't find me. After a while, I gave up. What difference did it make anyway? Bobby was gone, and I needed to finish what he started, so I came back. Then the police took me in for questioning."

"Did you tell them everything?"

"No, not yet, but I'm going to. When I leave here, I'm going straight to the police station with my lawyer, and I'm going to tell them everything."

Gia's heart broke for her. "Rest in the knowledge that Bobby did what was right, and let the police handle the rest."

Chapter 27

"Are Skyla and Willow coming?" Cole set several trays of food along the counter, buffet style.

"No. They're out of town." Gia smiled. When Willow had first called that morning and asked for the weekend off, Gia had been concerned. Then she told her Skyla had contacted her mother, Willow's grandmother. She'd been so excited to hear from Skyla, she'd insisted on flying them up to Virginia to visit right away. She said after her husband's death, she'd wanted to reach out but hadn't known where to find them and feared they'd reject her. "They'll meet up with us at Disney Monday morning."

"Disney?" Trevor came up beside her. "Who's going to Disney?"

"All of us. Want to come?"

"I'd love to, thank you." He wrapped an arm around her shoulders and squeezed. "And thank you for everything, Gia. It means a lot to me that you never lost faith in me."

She kissed his cheek. "You're welcome."

Twin red patches flared on his cheeks as he stepped back. "Do you mind if I bring a friend?"

"Of course not. Anyone I know?"

"I was thinking of asking Zoe. She took such good care of Brandy for me, and she was very understanding when I explained why I couldn't come for her right away."

"That would be great." Gia hoped things would work out between them. Zoe was a kind woman, someone who'd be good for Trevor. Of course, that meant she'd have to ask Joey to watch Thor. She started to turn away, then remembered what she'd been playing around with in her spare time. "Oh, and I have something for you to try after dinner."

"What's that?"

"Well, I was playing around with cold brew recipes, looking for something that would be more dessert-like for Storm Scoopers..." She held her breath. Trevor hadn't said he was going to reopen, but she really hoped he would. When he simply nodded, she took it for encouragement and continued. "I found a s'mores recipe. Cold brew coffee with toasted marshmallow and chocolate, then topped with whipped cream and crushed graham crackers sprinkled over the top."

"That sounds delicious."

"Then you'll really love the one with chocolate and mint ice cream."

"Okay, folks." Cole slid one last tray onto the counter and rubbed his hands together. "Dinner's ready."

Cybil inhaled deeply. "Everything smells delicious."

"Why, thank you, Cybil." Cole kissed the back of her hand.

She blushed and shooed him away.

Hunt piled his plate with a variety of steak and egg dishes. "It does look amazing."

Gia hugged his arm. "I'm just glad you could make it."

He leaned over and kissed her head. "Me too. I wasn't sure I would, but Mitch and Felicity clammed up when we brought them in, right after they asked for their lawyer."

Savannah frowned. "Are you worried they'll get away with it?"

Hunt put his dish on the table and poured a mug of coffee. "No. Ron's mole was willing to work with us, and we were able to get some pretty incriminating evidence on tape. Mitch stopped short of confessing to murder, but we found the murder weapon in his safe, and traffic cameras put his car parked on Main Street at the time of Ron's murder. It seems he figured he could get rid of Ron and pin it on Trevor, given their history of bad blood. Then he figured he'd take out Trevor as well, so he couldn't point the finger elsewhere. At least, that's our theory. There's no other reason for Mitch to have held onto the murder weapon."

"How did Ron get someone in there who Mitch would open up to?"

Hunt's jaw clenched. "Ron was no dummy. Putting a young, attractive woman in his campaign was pretty smart."

"And pretty dangerous," Leo chimed in.

"Very true," Hunt agreed. "I read Gabriella Fischetti the riot act about that and about not coming to us in the first place."

"Is she heading back to Georgia?" Savannah put her plate on the table and sat.

"No, she's decided not to. She said without Bobby there's nothing left for her there. She'll start fresh somewhere new." Leo sat next to Savannah and squeezed her hand.

Cybil sat between Earl and Cole. "She won't stay in Boggy Creek?"

Hunt shrugged. "She blamed herself for Bobby's murder. That's part of the reason she ran afterward."

"It wasn't Gabriella's fault he was killed," Savannah said.

"No, but she felt like they should have handled things better, that if they had, Ron and Bobby might not have been killed."

No one said anything. There was really no need.

After filling her plate with a little of each dish, Gia sat next to Hunt. She started with a bite of pan-seared steak. A burst of flavor shot into her mouth. "Oh, my gosh, Cole, this is amazing."

"I told you it would be," he said and winked at her. "It's my own special blend of seasonings, which I wrote down for you and stuck in your recipe box."

"That's perfect, thank you." She took another bite.

"So, are you guys coming to Disney with us tomorrow night?" Savannah bit into a piece of steak and moaned, "This is the most tender steak I've ever eaten."

Cole grinned. "Why, thank you, ma'am."

"Yes, we should be able to make it," Leo said.

"Awesome." Excitement lit Savannah's eyes. "And don't forget, we're going to the Keys this fall."

A niggle of guilt crept in, and Gia resisted the urge to apologize for ruining their trip. Again. "Oh, come on, Savannah, I don't want to leave Thor again too soon, but we don't have to wait *that* long."

She pursed her lips and stared at Gia. "Honey, I love you, but it's become obvious you and I were not meant to go to the Keys together."

"So, who are you going with, and why wait until fall?"

She gazed at Leo and smiled. "We're going on our honeymoon."

Cheers erupted.

"It's about time you two finally set a date." Hunt hugged Savannah, then clapped Leo on the back. "You'd better be good to her, man."

"You know I'll treat her like gold." Leo gazed at Savannah with all the love he'd carried since he was a child.

Gia jumped up and hugged each of them. "Congratulations! I am so happy for both of you."

Savannah pulled her aside and whispered in her ear. "I'm hoping you'll be my maid of honor."

Tears filled her eyes. "I'd love to, Savannah. Thank you."

"I wouldn't have anyone else." She hugged her tight.

"I'm sorry I screwed up our trip to the Keys."

"Don't worry about it. Some things happen for a reason. Besides, we're going to have a great time at Disney." She raised her voice. "And this time, I'm not taking any chances on you getting sidetracked."

"What do you mean?"

She pointed a finger at her. "You're driving with Hunt."

They all laughed.

A knock on the front door brought Gia up short, and she turned to find Harley peeking in. "I'll be right back."

She unlocked the door and opened it. "Hey, Harley. Do you want to come in?"

"No, thank you."

Gia stepped outside and let the door fall shut. "Is everything okay?"

Harley twisted a red baseball cap in his hands. "Yes, I just wanted to say thank you."

"For what?"

"For everything, but mostly for looking out for Donna Mae."

"You're welcome, Harley."

He nodded once, fitted the cap over his head, and limped off.

Gia watched him slip away into the darkness, truly hoping he'd find happiness now that his nightmare had been resolved. She then turned to go back to dinner with her friends—her chosen family.

If you enjoyed *A Cold Brew Killing*, **be sure not to miss the rest of Lena Gregory's All-Day Breakfast Café Mystery series, including**

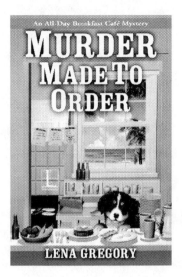

To save her cozy Florida diner, Gia Morelli must choke down a heaping helping of murder...

New York native Gia Morelli is just getting used to life in Florida when she gets word that the town government wants to shut down her pride and joy: the charming little diner known as the All-Day Breakfast Café. A forgotten zoning regulation means that the café was opened illegally, and hardboiled council president Marcia Steers refuses to budge. Gia is considering hanging up her apron and going back to New York, but before she gives up on her dream, she discovers something shocking in the local swamp: Marcia Steers, dead in the water. There's a secret buried in the books at town hall, and someone killed to keep it hidden. To save her café and bring a killer to justice, Gia and her friends will have to figure out a killer's recipe for murder...

A Lyrical Underground e-book on sale now.

Keep reading for a special look!

Chapter 1

"Fools!"

Savannah Mills swiveled back and forth on a stool at the All-Day Breakfast Café counter and tapped a steady rhythm against the butcher-block countertop with her long, powder blue nails. "Every last one of them."

Gia Morelli scrubbed the already spotless counter one more time for good measure, then flung the dishcloth into a bin beneath the counter, the steady *rat-a-tat-tat* of Savannah's rhythmic drumming making it almost impossible to think straight. "What I don't get is how they think they can get away with this?"

Earl snorted. The elderly man, who'd been the All-Day Breakfast Café's first customer, and had since become a friend, had made a habit of arriving at the café before they opened and lingering over coffee until Gia officially unlocked the door and started cooking. "The council members are so used to doing whatever they want with no opposition they're like a pack of spoiled brats."

"Yeah, well, not this time." Gia checked the clock—just about time to open. She rounded the counter and headed for the door. "No way I'm giving up everything I've worked for because that bunch found some antiquated zoning mistake."

"How are you going to get around it, though?" Earl asked.

"I have no idea. Yet." Gia unlocked the door, then dragged the chalkboard with the day's specials out onto the sidewalk and set it up. She looked up and down Main Street. Winter in Boggy Creek was certainly milder than the harsh bite of winter in New York, and yet there was something inside her, a small niggle of homesickness, that missed the change of seasons. Still… If she was going to give everything up and go back to New York, it would be on her terms, not because she was forced out. She strode back into the café more determined than ever to fight the council's rulings. "Did your brother get back to you yet, Savannah?"

She shook her head. "He still hasn't heard back from his lawyer friend. Of course, you did only get the letter last night."

Gia resisted the urge to argue. Savannah was right. She hadn't gotten the mail until after closing yesterday, and it was barely six o'clock in the morning now. Savannah's brother, Tommy, who also sat on the town council, would call as soon as he heard something. Until then…

Willow, the young woman who served as hostess, waitress, and cashier, breezed through the door, her usual smile firmly in place. "Good morning."

"Morning." Earl nodded.

Willow slowed, taking in the three of them. "Is something wrong?"

Gia sighed. Not like she wasn't going to find out anyway. Heck, half of Boggy Creek had probably already heard, and the remainder of the residents would know everything within an hour of the shops on Main Street opening. "I received a letter from the town council. They're closing the café."

Willow's mouth fell open.

Savannah spun her stool toward Gia. "Oh, stop being dramatic, Gia. They're not closing the café, exactly, they're just…"

Gia lifted a brow and waited.

"Oh, all right. So they're *trying* to close the café, but they aren't going to get away with it."

"No, they're not. But I need to know why they're trying before I can figure out how to fight them." And that was the problem. The letter only asked her to willingly close the café, said it had been brought to their attention that the historic building that housed the café and the small apartment above it had never been zoned commercial. Instead, it was the only building on Main Street that was still zoned residential.

"Could be it's a mistake," Savannah offered.

"I guess." Gia shrugged.

Earl sipped his coffee, then lowered his mug to the counter. "Of course, yours is the last shop on the block, and the area of town past it is zoned residential."

Gia just looked at him.

"What?" he said innocently. "I know how to use Google."

Earl had quickly become a close friend. He'd believed in her when a lot of other people hadn't, and she cherished his friendship. "When did you find out about the letter?"

"Last night." His cheeks reddened. "One of my sons might have called."

Well, at least the Boggy Creek rumor mill was still up and running. Truth be told, he'd probably known before she had. Since she was always stuck in the kitchen, it had been late before she'd gotten the mail. Then she'd had to feed and walk Thor before she finally found time to open the letter. "But why did the letter ask me to close? They could have said they wanted to discuss the matter or offered advice on how to change the zoning, anything. Something."

Savannah and Earl glanced at each other, a quick, passing look, but something definitely simmered just beneath the surface.

"Okay, spill it. What don't I know?"

"Weeell…" Savannah looked at Earl once more, then returned her attention to Gia. "Do you know who any of the council members are?"

"No. Well, other than your brother, which I only found out last night. Oh, and the president, Marcia something, is it? Whoever signed the letter." Between running the café, unpacking and putting everything away at the house, and taking care of Thor, she didn't have time to worry about who sat on the town council. "I get a newsletter from them every month, but honestly, I usually just chuck it in the trash."

"Yeah, well, you probably should have paid closer attention," Savannah said.

"Why's that?"

"Maybelle sits on the council."

"Are you kidding me?" Great. Just what she needed, an enemy on the council. "How could someone that lazy—"

The front door opened, and an older couple walked in.

Gia plastered on a smile and went to greet them. She'd have to try to sort everything out later. "Good morning."

"Hello," the man answered and glanced at Earl. "Hey there, Earl."

Earl stood and extended a hand. "Harry. How are you?"

"Good, good." He shook Earl's hand, then stepped back and gestured toward the woman Gia assumed was his wife. "Theresa and I figured we'd check out the breakfast you're always raving about."

"Well, you won't be disappointed." Earl winked at Gia. "This here's Gia, and she makes a mean breakfast."

"Nice to meet you, Gia."

"It's a pleasure to meet both of you." She grabbed two menus. "Can I show you to a table?"

After settling them with coffee and their menus, Gia retreated to the kitchen. She grabbed tongs and moved a few slices of bacon and sausage from the warming trays to the grill, then started scrambling three eggs.

Maybelle Sanford. It figured. That woman was destined to be a thorn in her side. She'd only worked—to use the term loosely—at the café for a day, and yet she kept coming back to haunt her. Since Maybelle had accused Gia of murder last time she'd seen her, it was hard not to jump to the conclusion she had something to do with the zoning fiasco. And yet…

Gia had been ready to fire Maybelle for being so lazy. Useless as a steering wheel on a mule according to Savannah. That being the case, it was hard to believe Maybelle had found the ambition to search for a way to close the café.

Gia dismissed any thought of Maybelle. Nothing she could do about it right now anyway, and all it was doing was aggravating her. She'd have to wait until Tommy called Savannah back. If not for his wife having their first baby last month, he'd have been at the latest council meeting, and she might have had a head's up. As it was, she'd have to wait for him to get caught up.

She drizzled a small amount of oil onto the grill, let it heat until it sizzled, then poured the eggs onto the hot oil. While they cooked, she spooned out a serving of grits and one of home fries, which Earl had added to his usual breakfast after the first time he'd tried hers. She filled a bowl with gravy, dropped two biscuits onto a small plate, and set the dish on the cutout counter between the kitchen and dining room.

Earl ate an unbelievable amount of food for breakfast every day while still managing to stay rail thin. The man was in remarkably good shape for almost eighty years old, despite consuming a week's work of fat each morning.

She'd miss this if she had to give up the café. She enjoyed cooking, and she'd enjoyed making friends in Boggy Creek. In addition to Earl, there was Trevor, who owned the ice cream parlor down the street, Savannah, who'd been a good friend for years, and Hunt, who she held out hope would become more than just a friend. She dismissed the thought. Detective Tall, Dark and Gorgeous was the last thing she needed to concern herself with at the moment.

She'd even gotten used to the solitude of living in her small house at the edge of the Ocala National Forest. Sort of. Thor helped. It was hard to believe Savannah had to talk her into getting the big Bernese Mountain Dog puppy. Now, she had no clue what she'd do without him. He made her life complete.

"Here you go." Willow rushed in, ripped the top page off her order pad, and stuck it above the grill, then frowned. "Are you all right?"

"I'll be okay." She smiled. "As soon as I get past being blindsided and figure out what my options are."

"If I can do anything to help, just let me know."

"Thanks."

She grabbed Earl's breakfast order and headed back to the dining room. Willow was a good kid and a hard worker. She'd also become a friend.

Another plus in the stay-and-fight-for-her-café column.

She started the next order. Unfortunately, she hadn't had much luck finding a cook after Maybelle and her replacement both hadn't worked out—or in Maybelle's case, just hadn't worked—which left Gia stuck in the kitchen all day. As much as she loved cooking, she really wanted to get out from in front of the grill and get to know her customers a little better. If she was going to make this work, she might have to give in and hire a cook. Third time's the charm? She certainly hoped so.

Truth be told, Boggy Creek was growing on her. At least, the people were. The critters, not so much.

The sound of raised voices right outside the kitchen pulled her attention.

Gia set the finished order on the cutout for Willow, pulled off her apron, and draped it over a stool. She strode through the doorway but stopped short when she ran into Savannah and a woman she didn't know in the hallway outside her office door. "Everything okay?"

Savannah peeked into Gia's office, then glanced at the other woman and pulled the door shut. She tucked her hair behind her ear, a nervous habit Gia had become familiar with when they'd lived together in New York. "Gia, this is Marcia Steers."

She only recognized the name because she'd recently received the letter from the council with Marcia Steers's name scrawled across the bottom and her title, Council President, typed in bold print beneath it. Gia eyed the woman standing in front of her, then swallowed her anger and extended a hand. "It's nice to meet you, Ms. Steers."

A hot pink sundress clung to Marcia's ample curves, and bleach blond hair framed her round face in a mane of over-teased frizz. High-heeled, leopard print sandals laced up her calves. She sneered and folded her arms across her chest. "Ms. Morelli."

Okay. Gia lowered her hand. "What can I help you with?"

"I want to discuss something with you." She raked her gaze over Savannah. "In private."

Savannah offered her sweetest smile. "As I already told you, Ms. Morelli is working. She will be happy to meet with you after the café closes."

Marcia ignored her, instead honing in on Gia. "And as I already told Ms. Mills, I need to speak with you."

"Actually, I'd like to speak with you as well." She forced a smile. "I'm hoping we can clear up the zoning mistake so I can keep the café open."

"There's no mistake, Ms. Morelli." Though Marcia's expression remained hard, her gaze darted repeatedly between the closed back door to the parking lot and the swinging door to the dining room. She stood stiff, like a cornered animal. "The café will close. The matter I must discuss with you is of a more personal nature."

Savannah eyed Gia and gave a discreet head shake behind Marcia's back.

Great. Now she had to either irritate Marcia, the woman who quite possibly held Gia's fate in her hands, or go against Savannah, which she couldn't do. She cracked the swinging door to the dining room open and peeked in. Willow had already seated several more tables and was taking an order. "I'm so sorry, Ms. Steers, but I'm the only cook, and I can't leave the kitchen just now. Can we meet later on?"

Marcia eyed her for a moment, then relented. "Fine. I want to look into something anyway. The café is closed on Mondays, right?"

"Yes."

"I'll meet you here tomorrow around noon."

"Sounds good. I—"

Before Gia could finish speaking, Marcia shot Savannah a dirty look, whirled away from Gia, then shoved through the swinging doors into the dining room.

Gia stared after her. "Maybe I should have just talked to her."

Savannah blew out a breath. "And what about your customers? Are you going to make them sit and wait while you two have it out in the middle of the café?"

The fact that she was right did nothing to lessen Gia's apprehension.

"She's clearly agitated about something. A public confrontation is the last thing you need right now." Savannah shook her head, then opened the door and walked into Gia's office. "Besides, I was helping Willow out, pouring coffee while people waited to order their breakfast. When I looked up, I caught sight of someone heading through the doors toward the kitchen. I couldn't tell who it was, so I came back to see what was going on, and I found Marcia coming out of your office."

Savannah shuffled through a small stack of papers on the desk. "You should really go through these and see if anything's missing before you meet with her."

"I guess—"

"Gia?" Willow stuck her head in the doorway. "Is everything all right?" she asked for the third time since arriving.

Gia needed to get her act together. "Umm…yeah."

Willow frowned but let it drop. "I just put three orders up, and one of them is a group of seven."

"Got it." She quickly scanned the papers on the desk. There was nothing of importance that she could see, but she'd have to look more carefully later. "Thanks, Savannah."

"No problem. But I think I'll give my brother another call." She looked up and caught Gia's gaze. "And maybe you'd better think about calling a lawyer."

Meet the Author

Lena Gregory lives in a small town on the south shore of eastern Long Island with her husband and three children. When she was growing up, she spent many lazy afternoons on the beach, in the yard, anywhere she could find to curl up with a good book. She loves reading as much now as she did then, but she now enjoys the added pleasure of creating her own stories. She is also the author of the Bay Island Psychic Mystery series, published by Berkley. Please visit her website at www.lenagregory.com.

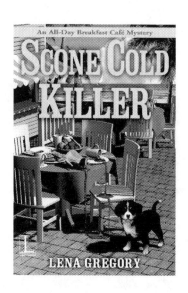

For Florida diner owner Gia Morelli, there's no such thing as too much breakfast—unless it kills you...

When Gia Morelli's marriage falls apart, she knows it's time to get out of New York. Her husband was a scam artist who swindled half the millionaires in town, and she doesn't want to be there when they decide to take revenge. On the spur of the moment, she follows her best friend to a small town in Central Florida, where she braves snakes, bears, and giant spiders to open a cheery little diner called the All-Day Breakfast Café. Owning a restaurant has been her lifelong dream, but it turns into a nightmare the morning she opens her dumpster and finds her ex-husband crammed inside. As the suspect du jour, Gia will have to scramble fast to prove her innocence before a killer orders another cup of murder...

"Hold on to your plates for this fast-paced mystery that will leave you hungering for more!"
—J.C. Eaton, author of the Sophie Kimball Mysteries

Printed in the United States
by Baker & Taylor Publisher Services